Kingston Libraries

This item can be returned
or renewed at a Kingston
Borough Library on or
before the latest date
stamped below. If the item
is not reserved by anoth...
reader it may be ren...
by telephone up...
maximum of...
quoting v...
number. ...issued
for the star... three-week
loan period are renewable.
www.kingston.gov.uk/libraries

Royal
Kingston

T... or Drive Library
...dor Dri...
...n upon Thames
Surrey
KT2 5QH
Tel: 020 8547 6456

New Malden
Tel No: 020 8547 6491

Soo6

Thérèse Raquin

Thérèse Raquin

Translated and with an
Introduction by Leonard Tancock

Émile Zola

THORNDIKE
CHIVERS

This Large Print edition is published by Thorndike Press®, Waterville, Maine USA and by BBC Audiobooks, Ltd, Bath, England.

Published in 2005 in the U.S. by arrangement with Penguin Group Ltd.

Published in 2005 in the U.K. by arrangement with Penguin Books Ltd.

U.S. Hardcover 0-7862-7193-0 (Perennial Bestsellers)
U.K. Hardcover 1-4056-3259-3 (Chivers Large Print)

The text of this Large Print edition is unabridged.
Other aspects of the book may vary from the original edition.

Set in 16 pt. Plantin by Christina S. Huff.

Printed in the United States on permanent paper.

British Library Cataloguing-in-Publication Data available

Library of Congress Cataloging-in-Publication Data

Zola, Émile, 1840–1902
    [Thérèse Raquin. English]
    Therese Raquin / by Emile Zola ; translated and with an introduction by Leonard Tancock. — Large print ed.
        p. (large print) cm.
    ISBN 0-7862-7193-0 (lg. print : hc : alk. paper)
    1. Large type books. I. Tancock, Leonard. II. Title.
PQ2521.T3E5 2005

For K. M. T.

Contents

Introduction

Thérèse Raquin is the earliest of Émile Zola's novels to have maintained a position as a literary work of some intrinsic value and not merely as one of his historically interesting *juvenilia* or worthless pot-boilers. It is the first Zola novel (though M. Henri Guillemin, in his book *Zola, légende ou vérité?*, says this of the still earlier *La Confession de Claude*) with unmistakable marks of the personality and manner of the future creator of the Rougon-Macquart series. It was the first to be greeted by the critics with an outcry about pornography, and this outcry not only gave Zola a welcome publicity boost, as such fusses always do, but forced him to clarify his own position and define the new literary creed of Naturalism in a preface to the second edition, reproduced at the head of this translation.

The novel, inspired by a story he had seen in a newspaper, first appeared as a serial in *L'Artiste* between August and October 1867 under the title: *Un Mariage d'amour*, but when it was issued in book form during the

9

same autumn it was given the much more striking title of the heroine's name, *Thérèse Raquin*. Its success, doubtless partly scandalous, was such that a second edition had to be printed in the spring of 1868, together with the famous preface. Subsequently Zola dramatized his own work, and the concentrated, economical construction of the story and its sustained tension have made it his only really successful play. It has maintained itself in theatrical repertoires to this day. In recent years there have been several revivals of the play in London and a notable French film.

Born in 1840, Zola was a young man of twenty-six or twenty-seven when he was very carefully writing *Thérèse Raquin* in the mornings while dashing off a huge, shapeless, serial thriller, *Les Mystères de Marseille*, in the afternoons. He had been struggling in the literary battle since he was twenty, and his earliest attempts had included much verse (unpublished) and a curious novel of romantic young love in a sordid setting, *La Confession de Claude*, in the manner of a seedy, latter-day Alfred de Musset, and probably largely autobiographical. He had gradually made some headway with hack work, book reviewing, and art criticism, during which his tendency had been increasingly to abandon the cult of poetry and the soulful in favour of the portrayal of real, contemporary life in its most materialistic aspects. This was partly due to his always keen business sense, for 'realism' was the order of the day, and partly because scientific materialism was the prevailing philosophy of the age.

2

Historians of literature and 'thought' sometimes appear to overlook the elementary truth that the character of a literature, at least of a successful and popular literature, depends upon the nature of the reading public. Perhaps at no moment in the history of the world did the nature of the fiction-reading public change so radically in such a short time as in Western Europe during the first half of the nineteenth century. Before then literature, except dramatic, addressed itself to the small minority who could read and write, for the mass of the common people were illiterate. But the concentration of thousands of workers in the new industrial areas, the spread of primary education to give these workers the minimum knowledge of the three Rs necessary to make them efficient factory workers, produced, by the 30s and

11

40s of the nineteenth century, a huge new semiliterate public with an appetite for cheap, easily-read fiction. Now, the hitherto fashionable Romantic genres in France — the historical novel with its conscientious local colour, the novel of morbid self-analysis, the sufferings and suicides of young men with not enough to do — meant little to these people with no cultural background whatever and no interests outside their daily work and grievances, the politics, scandals, or crimes of the moment. We all seek in our literature certain things in proportions varying with our own state of education and awareness; we look for recognizableness, for escape from our own humdrum existence into some new world of wider experience and, whether we admit it or not, for an idealization of ourselves and justification of our points of view and prejudices. And so it was that to cater for the new demands and tastes certain astute newspaper owners in France introduced the popular serial story, *le roman-feuilleton*, the greatest supplier of which was Eugène Sue, with his *Wandering Jew*, *Mysteries of Paris*, and many other interminable tales. The tendency in these novels was to place the action in known, contemporary, recognizable, urban settings (usually Paris), to cater for escapist dreams while fomenting class hatred by having scenes of luxury and splendour like those of modern films, and to flatter the working and lower middle-class readers by having humble or down-trodden heroes and wealthy aristocratic or ecclesiastical villains, and naturally the political flavour was left-wing. Violent social contrasts, melodramatic action, cruel injustices finally righted, and a general absence of any shades of colour except black and white characterized the plots, which could almost be summarized in the well-known lines:

> She was poor, but she was honest,
> Victim of a rich man's whim . . .

Meanwhile the more literary novel was being transformed in the hands of Balzac, whose vast output of linked novels, the *Comédie humaine,* was intended to be a complete picture of contemporary civilization between about 1830 and the year of Balzac's death, 1850. Inspired by the prevailing scientific determinism of the age, he sought to demonstrate the formative influence upon human beings of their material environment. Hence the vital and sometimes tedious role of detailed, technical, realistic description, and the animal nature of so many of his creations, who are dominated by the more elementary passions. But Balzac's personal views in moral, political, and religious matters were much too strong to let him be simply a detached observer of external reality. At every turn he concentrates, magnifies, interprets his own creations, until his novels become, to our great gain, works of art far transcending mere scientific demonstrations or sociological studies.

After Balzac's death, in the early 1850s, a new school sprang up calling itself Realism. Apart from the immense influence of Balzac this school was influenced by the discovery of Stendhal, whose novels of ruthless psychological sincerity, uncovering the real and usually unheroic motives of human conduct, cast in a deliberately plain and almost anti-artistic form, had been relatively unknown during his lifetime. Realism was in the air, and not only in literature but in the painting of such men as Courbet.

These strands were gathered together, as always happens sooner or later in France, into a more or less coherent literary doctrine supported by manifestoes, definitions, and programmes. Two minor writers, Champfleury, whose novel *Les Bourgeois de Molinchart* (1855), a dull account of adultery in a boring provincial setting and thus an immediate predecessor in matter, though not in form, of *Madame Bovary*, had a certain success, and Duranty, his young admirer and trumpeter, who defined in his short-lived periodical *Le Réalisme* the theory of meticulous reproduction of contemporary reality without point of view, personal opinion, or moral bias, were the principal exponents of this genre; it was the very negation of art, for they maintained that any attempt at selection, arrangement, style, and literary effect would be a falsification of scientific truth.

And then this inartistic, limited genre interested one of the most fastidious stylists in French literature, Gustave Flaubert, whose *Madame Bovary* (1857) carried Realism to the summit of artistic achievement; and it also appealed to the brothers Edmond and Jules de Goncourt, whose main preoccupation, however sordid and 'realist' the matter of such a novel as *Germinie Lacerteux* (1864) might be, was a highly-wrought, artificial style calculated to act directly upon the readers' nerves like the glare and din of a modern city.

Underlying the whole movement was, of course, the philosophy of materialism and scientific determinism of the age of Auguste Comte, Darwin, Huxley, and Taine, which tended to eliminate all spiritual interpretations of human behaviour, and therefore attributed paramount importance to the physiological functions and the material environment as the only explanation of man's conduct.

Finally, the vulgarity and philistinism, the social injustices, the cynical immorality and hypocrisy of the empire of Napoleon III forced all those artists and writers not directly committed for personal or religious reasons into the camp of the socialist opposition. A striking example was the evolution, admittedly not uninfluenced by personal grudges (but who is?), of the already almost legendary figure of French literature, Victor Hugo. For years, in the midst of his poetical and other activities, and in the safety of his exile in the Channel Islands, he worked away at a huge novel of the people of Paris, an epic of the poor and underprivileged of this world, and in 1862 he gave mankind, in *Les Misérables*, a new set of mythological characters. This book is in reality another working-class serial in the Eugène Sue tradition, embellished and inflated by Hugo's unique and sometimes uncontrollable gifts of language and imagination.

This mixture of literary, scientific, and so-

cial tendencies, and above all the materialistic cult of the environment, explain why
the subject matter of the Realist novel is almost invariably drab, banal, and mediocre.
It is not so much that in a modern, urban-
ized world there is no room for extravagant,
Romantic, imaginative fiction, as that if you
wish to stress the fatal pressure of environment you will not choose a highly individual, independent, titanic personality but
colourless, weak, mentally or morally un-
stable people, whom the environment can
easily crush or mould. These 'scientists'
chose favourable material to work on.

3

This is the background against which Zola
wrote his novel and the apology for it con-
tained in the preface. The tone of this preface
is bumptious and over-confident, the style
that of the debating-society with its 'brilliant'
undergraduate wit and use of such tricks as
false *naïveté*, feigned astonishment, injured
innocence, crushing sarcasm, heavy irony.
But Zola makes his points, namely that the
Naturalist novelist (one of the earliest times
this term is used) is a scientist on the same
footing as a surgeon or any other experi-
menter upon organic matter, that his charac-

ters are animals motivated solely by the physical processes of their bodies and nervous systems, and therefore that to accuse him of pornography is not only untrue but quite irrelevant, since the scientist must go where his matter leads him and is not subject to moral laws. Although he is hard put to it to reconcile 'remorse' with the purely physical processes, he is quite right, in the case of *Thérèse Raquin*, to refute the charge of pornography, for the hunter after sexual thrills will find little to tickle his appetite in this tale of adultery, which in this respect at least is classical in its omission of all unnecessary detail. But Zola is also a shrewd self-critic, for he admits that he has loaded the dice and taken over-simplified and therefore abnormal cases. Indeed, this preface, read in conjunction with the novel shows up his weaknesses as a 'scientist':

I have chosen [he writes] people completely dominated by their nerves and blood, without free will, drawn to each action of their lives by the inexorable laws of their physical nature. Thérèse and Laurent are human animals, nothing more . . . what I have had to call their remorse really amounts to a simple organic disorder, a revolt of the nervous system when strained to breaking point.

There is a complete absence of soul, I freely admit, since that is how I meant it to be.

This is almost a confession that in order to demonstrate the 'scientific' truth of his own inventions he has so arranged things that it would have been a miracle if anything other than adultery and murder had been the outcome. But worse follows:

... in a word, I had only one desire: given a highly-sexed man and an unsatisfied woman, to uncover the animal side of them and see that alone, then throw them together in a violent drama and note down with scrupulous care the sensations and actions of these creatures. I simply applied to two living bodies the analytical method that surgeons apply to corpses.

That is to say that the scientific demonstration or experiment is a rigged affair. In exactly the same way, in *La Faute de l'abbé Mouret* (1875), Zola will take as data a neurotic young priest, emerging from a nervous breakdown brought on by excessive asceticism, but still suffering from loss of memory, and an 'animal' young girl, put them together, without a care or responsibility in the world, in an environment consisting of a luxuriant Mediterranean garden, and demonstrate with much scientific seriousness natural instinct triumphing over religious superstitions and inhibitions. The formula is to arrange some 'temperaments', add some medical or neurological jargon, deliberately omit the interplay of character and all purely psychological reactions, and call the mixture 'fatality'.

4

If *Thérèse Raquin* were simply what Zola represented it to be, a scientific demonstration, it would be a failure. But it is nothing of the kind, and it is not a failure.

In a study of Proudhon and Courbet published in *Mes Haines* in 1866, Zola had already begged the question by defining art in these terms: *Une oeuvre d'art est un coin de la création vu à travers un tempérament.* Paraphrasing this in English we might say that any work of art is a picture of the world, or a corner of it, distorted, coloured, arranged by the personality of the artist.

Fortunately Zola's practice fits in much better with this sensible definition than do his false analogies between scientific determinism and literature. In a purely material world there could be no place for an author's personal views and tastes, no emotional reactions, no ethical standards. But *Thérèse Raquin* bears upon every page the imprint of its author's personality, fingerprints of the real man, which betray the scientific *persona* he was trying to make us accept. This real man is a sensitive, timid soul, an emotional and even puritanical man haunted by visions of sin, death, and decay, morbidly attracted and repelled by sex, tending to over-compensate in the directions of brutality and the macabre, just as diminutive men tend to be loud and aggressive. Even the moral bias is clear, for Zola shows here, as so often later in the Rougon-Macquart novels, that sexual indulgence leads to the deterioration of a man's character and intellect, brings him down to the level of the beast, and inevitably leads to degradation and physical and moral decay. For the first time explicitly, but by no means the last, Zola dwells upon the danger, in a triangle, that the woman's first lover will return, alive or dead, and plague the second. And conscience, however disguised as physiological processes, drives transgressors to despair and madness. *Thérèse Raquin* is a cautionary tale on the sixth and seventh Commandments, and it is not surprising that one of the English adaptations of Zola's dramatization of his novel, in which Nancy Price scored a great London success as Madame Raquin in 1938, was entitled *Thou shalt not* ...

Equally unscientific and personal are the literary devices and qualities which give *Thérèse Raquin* its haunting power.

Zola the poet, who had recently championed, in his articles on the Salon in 1866, the wonderful treatment of light and atmosphere in the paintings of Manet, exploits emotionally-charged descriptions and atmospheres as strikingly as any Romantic. The initial description of the shop in the dismal arcade, the intoxicating joy of a May morning, above all the hushed expectancy of the river at dusk immediately before the murder, are not easily forgotten. But it is when things themselves take on a kind of life and play a malignant part in the action, when the scar on Laurent's neck becomes the very presence of his victim, relentless as an avenging Hound of Hell, when the portrait of Camille (carefully characterized *before* the murder as looking green and gruesome like a drowned man) takes on ever more hideous shapes and colours, when the rotting corpses in the Morgue begin to move, grin and disintegrate before Laurent's hallucinated eyes, that the self-conscious literary artist bears the would-be scientist far away into realms of imaginative fiction and black, macabre poetry. Even the taut, economical construction, the faultless logic of the first two-thirds of the book, are contrived and simplified. The symbolical appearances of the cat François, the ironies of so many of poor Madame Raquin's amiable remarks, the almost expected but, for Zola, extremely successful comic relief in the form of the boring Thursday evening visits of the impossible Michauds and the pompous Grivet, all these things belong to the novelist's art and give the book its individuality.

5

For no two texts are alike; each sets its peculiar problems to the translator. That is why, within the limits of English syntax, a translator must attempt to reproduce the mannerisms, flavour, virtues and vices of his text. A translator is not an editor; he has no right to manipulate his material in order to 'improve' it by smoothing out what may seem to him to be imperfections. His task, as the etymology of his name says, is to *pass across* the author's work as intact as he can keep it. The peculiar problems of *Thérèse Raquin* are these:

23

Some of its vocabulary is repetitive: whether because of mere poverty of invention or because, like the Goncourt brothers, Zola was anxious to work on the reader's nerves by obsessive hammer-blows, we need not decide. After his death Camille is referred to a hundred times as *le noyé;* all through the text the elder Michaud is *l'ancien commissaire de police;* many times, although we and everybody in the novel know it perfectly well, Madame Raquin is *la vieille mercière.* Clearly 'the drowned man' must be used repeatedly because it is as such that he haunts his murderers, but some variations from 'the old haberdashery lady' and such impossibly clumsy locutions have to be found. Usually a proper name is the simplest.

Much more serious than this is the astonishing vagueness of this young man who claimed to be doing a piece of exact scientific writing. Some irresistible urge seems to force him to use such expressions as *une vague sensation de . . . , une sorte de vague impression de . . . , une espèce de . . . , je ne sais quel . . .* , as though a plain, precise noun or adjective would be inadequate. I have of course rendered such mannerisms as faithfully as I have been able.

The scientific jargon speaks for itself, but

there is one more characteristic very notice-able to a translator, and a serious challenge. Perhaps because he was still young and rela-tively inexperienced, perhaps because his tale of horror carried its author away, Zola fails to graduate his climaxes and so sounds too shrill a note, uses unsurpassable super-latives too early. The book is excellently composed and beautifully graded until the end of Chapter 21, but the last third is *fortis-simo* nearly all the time. Not only are words like *épouvante, terreur, horreur,* used too early, not only does Laurent's face go white and his hair stand on end too often, but we are told a disconcerting number of times that such and such an event finally drove Laurent or Thérèse completely out of his or her mind. Faced with such raw material the translator can only repeat himself and pile superlative upon superlative.

But the would-be reader should not feel discouraged, for the latter part of the book, where this kind of thing occurs, is still a first-rate thriller. *Thérèse Raquin* should not be judged as scientific realism o'erleaping itself, but as a grim tale of sin, murder, and revenge in an enclosed, stifling, nightmarish setting which, by the simplest of means, with only four main characters, one of whom disappears early in the story, four walkers-on, and the absolute minimum of physical action, proceeds as inexorably as a tragedy of Racine, and has kept its power for over a hundred years.

★

The text used for this translation is the standard Bibliothèque Charpentier edition (Fasquelle), in this case dated 1954. The text, however, differs in one or two small details from the more recent Livre de Poche edition (1957) also published by Fasquelle. On each occasion it is quite clear that one of the texts contains a meaningless misprint, and the only reasonable reading has been followed.

The best books in English on Zola are: Angus Wilson, *Émile Zola, An introductory study of his novels* (London, Secker & Warburg, 1952); F. W. J. Hemmings, *Émile Zola* (Oxford, Clarendon Press, revised edition, 1966). The second is one of the best books on the subject in any language.

L. W. T.

Preface
to the Second Edition
(1868)

I was simple enough to suppose that this novel could do without a preface. Being accustomed to express my thoughts quite clearly and to stress even the minutest details of what I write, I hoped to be understood and judged without preliminary explanations. It seems I was mistaken.

The critics greeted this book with a churlish and horrified outcry. Certain virtuous people, in newspapers no less virtuous, made a grimace of disgust as they picked it up with the tongs to throw it into the fire. Even the minor literary reviews, the ones that retail nightly the tittle-tattle from alcoves and private rooms, held their noses and talked of filth and stench. I am not complaining about this reception; on the contrary I am delighted to observe that my colleagues have such maidenly susceptibilities. Obviously my work is the property of my judges and they can find it nauseating without my having any right to object, but what I do complain of is that not one of the modest journalists who blushed when they read *Thérèse Raquin* seems to have understood the novel. If they had, they might perhaps have blushed still more, but at any rate I should at the present moment be enjoying the deep satisfaction of having disgusted them for the right reason. Nothing is more annoying than hearing worthy people shouting about depravity when you know within yourself that they are doing so without any idea what they are shouting about.

So I am obliged to introduce my own work to my judges. I will do so in a few lines, simply to forestall any future misunderstanding.

In *Thérèse Raquin* my aim has been to study temperaments and not characters. That is the whole point of the book. I have chosen people completely dominated by their nerves and blood, without free will, drawn into each action of their lives by the inexorable laws of their physical nature. Thérèse and Laurent are human animals, nothing more. I have endeavoured to follow these animals through the devious working of their passions, the compulsion of their instincts, and the mental unbalance resulting

28

from a nervous crisis. The sexual adventures of my hero and heroine are the satisfaction of a need, the murder they commit a consequence of their adultery, a consequence they accept just as wolves accept the slaughter of sheep. And finally, what I have had to call their remorse really amounts to a simple organic disorder, a revolt of the nervous system when strained to breaking-point. There is a complete absence of soul, I freely admit, since that is how I meant it to be.

I hope that by now it is becoming clear that my object has been first and foremost a scientific one. When my two characters, Thérèse and Laurent, were created, I set myself certain problems and solved them for the interest of the thing. I tried to explain the mysterious attraction that can spring up between two different temperaments, and I demonstrated the deep-seated disturbances of a sanguine nature brought into contact with a nervous one. If the novel is read with care, it will be seen that each chapter is a study of a curious physiological case. In a word, I had only one desire: given a highly-sexed man and an unsatisfied woman, to uncover the animal side of them and see that alone, then throw them together in a violent drama and note down with scrupulous care the sensations and actions of these creatures. I simply applied to two living bodies the analytical method that surgeons apply to corpses.

You must allow that it is hard, on emerging from such a toil, still wholly given over to the serious satisfactions of the search for truth, to hear people accuse one of having had no other object than the painting of obscene pictures. I found myself in the same position as those painters who copy the nude without themselves being touched by the slightest sexual feeling, and are quite astonished when a critic declares that he is scandalized by the lifelike bodies in their work. While I was busy writing *Thérèse Raquin* I forgot the world and devoted myself to copying life exactly and meticulously, giving myself up entirely to precise analysis of the mechanism of the human being, and I assure you that the ferocious sexual relationship of Thérèse and Laurent meant nothing immoral to me, nothing calculated to provoke indulgence in evil passions. The human side of the models ceased to exist, just as it ceases to exist for the eye of the artist who has a naked woman sprawled in front of him but who is solely concerned with getting on to his canvas a true representation of her shape and coloration. How great, therefore, was my surprise when I heard my work referred to as a quagmire of slime and blood, a sewer, garbage, and so forth. I know all about the fun and games of criticism, I have played at it myself, but I confess that the unanimity of the attack disconcerted me a little. What! not one of my colleagues prepared to explain my book, let alone defend it! Amid the concert of voices bawling: 'The author of *Thérèse Raquin* is a hysterical wretch who revels in displays of pornography,' I waited in vain for one voice to reply: 'No, the writer is simply an analyst who may have become engrossed in human corruption, but who has done so as a surgeon might in an operating theatre.'

Note that I am by no means asking for the sympathy of the gentlemen of the press towards a work which offends, we are told, their delicate sensibilities. I am not so ambitious. I am merely astonished that my colleagues have turned me into a kind of literary sewerman, for they are the very people whose expert eyes should recognize a novelist's intentions within ten pages, and I must content myself with humbly begging them to be so good as to see me in future as I am and consider me for what I am.

And yet it should have been easy to understand *Thérèse Raquin*, to take up a position in the realm of observation and analysis and show me my real weaknesses without picking up a handful of mud and flinging it in my face in the name of morality. It needed, of course, a little intelligence and a few general notions about real criticism. In the world of science an accusation of immorality proves nothing whatsoever. I do not know whether my novel is immoral, but I admit that I have never gone out of my way to make it more or less chaste. What I do know is that I never for one moment dreamed of putting in the indecencies that moral people are discovering therein, for I wrote every scene, even the most impassioned, with scientific curiosity alone. I defy my judges to find one really licentious page put in to cater for readers of those little rose-coloured books, those boudoir and back-stage disclosures, which run to ten thousand copies and are warmly welcomed by the very papers that have been nauseated by the truths in *Thérèse Raquin*.

Up to now all I have read about my work is a few insults and a lot of silliness. I say this here quite calmly, as I would to a friend asking me in private what I thought of the attitude of the critics towards me. A very distinguished writer to whom I grumbled about the lack of sympathy I am finding, gave me this profound answer: 'You have a tremendous drawback which will close every door against you; you cannot talk to a fool for two minutes without making him realize he is a fool.' That must be the case; I see the harm I do myself in the eyes of the critics by accusing them of lack of intelligence, and yet I cannot help showing the scorn I feel for their narrow horizon and groping judgements totally devoid of method. I refer, of course, to current criticism, which judges with all the literary prejudices of fools, being incapable of taking up the broadly humane standpoint that a humane work demands if it is to be understood. I have never seen such ineptitude. The few punches aimed at me by petty critics in the matter of *Thérèse Raquin* have as usual missed and hit the air. This criticism is essentially wrong-headed; it applauds the caperings of some painted actress and then raises a cry of immorality about a physiological study, understands nothing, does not want to understand anything, but always hits out straight in front whenever its stupidity takes fright and suggests hitting out. It is exasperating to be chastised for a sin one has not committed. At times I am sorry I have not written obscenities, for I feel I should be happy to re-

33

ceive a well-merited whacking amid this hail of blows falling senselessly on my head like a lot of tiles, without my knowing why.

At the present time there are scarcely more than two or three men who can read, appreciate, and judge a book. From these I am willing to take lessons, because I am satisfied that they will not speak before they have grasped my intentions and appreciated the results of my efforts. They would take good care not to pronounce great big empty words like morality and literary decency, and they would acknowledge my right, in these days of artistic freedom, to choose my subjects where I see fit, and only require conscientious work on my part, knowing that only silliness endangers the dignity of letters. What is certain is that they would not be surprised by the kind of scientific analysis I have attempted in *Thérèse Raquin*, for in it they would recognize the modern method of universal inquiry which is the tool our age is using so enthusiastically to open up the future. Whatever their own conclusions, they would approve of my starting-point, the study of temperament, and of the profound modifications of an organism subjected to the pressure of environments and circumstances. I should be standing before genuine judges, men seeking after truth in good faith, without puerility or false modesty, men who do not think they are obliged to look disgusted at the sight of naked living anatomical specimens. Sincere study, like fire, purifies all things. Of course, in the eyes of the tribunal I am choosing to envisage at the moment, my work would be a very humble affair, and I should invite the critics to exercise all their severity upon it, indeed I should like it to emerge black with corrections. But at any rate I should have had the deep satisfaction of seeing myself criticized for what I have tried to do, and not for what I have not done.

I think I can hear even now the sentence passed by real criticism, I mean the methodical and naturalist criticism that has revived the sciences, history, and literature: '*Thérèse Raquin* is a study of too exceptional a case; the drama of modern life is more flexible and not so hemmed in by horror and madness. Such cases should be relegated to a subsidiary position in a book. The desire not to sacrifice any of his observations has led the author to stress every single detail, and that has given still more tension and harshness to the whole. Moreover the style lacks the simplicity that an analytical novel demands. In short, if the writer is now to write a good novel, he must see society with greater breadth of vision, depict it in its many and varied aspects, and above all use clear and natural language.'

I meant to devote a score of lines to answering attacks that are irritating by the very *naïveté* of their bad faith, and I see that I am embarking on a chat with myself, as always happens to me when I keep a pen in my hand too long. So I desist, knowing that readers do not like that sort of thing. If I had had the leisure and the will to write a manifesto I might have tried to defend what one journalist, referring to *Thérèse Raquin*, has called 'putrid literature'. But what is the point? The group of naturalist writers to which I have the honour of belonging has enough courage and energy to produce powerful works containing their own defence. It takes all the deliberate blindness of a certain kind of criticism to force a novelist to write a preface. Since I have committed the sin of writing one because I am a lover of light, I crave the forgiveness of men of intelligence who do not need me to light a lamp for them in broad daylight to help them see clearly.

Émile Zola

1

At the end of the rue Guénégaud, as you come up from the river, you find the Passage du Pont-Neuf, a sort of narrow, dark corridor connecting rue Mazarine and rue de Seine. This passage is thirty yards long and two in width at the most; it is paved with yellowish flagstones, worn and loose, which always exude a damp, pungent smell, and it is covered with a flat, glazed roofing black with grime.

On fine summer days, when the streets are baking in the oppressive heat, a whitish light does fall through the dingy glass roofing and hang dismally about this arcade, but on nasty winter ones, on foggy mornings, the panes send down nothing but gloom on to the greasy pavement below, and dirty, evil gloom at that.

To the left open out dark, low, shallow shops from which come whiffs of cold, vault-like air. Here there are booksellers, vendors of toys, cardboard dealers, whose window displays are grey with dust and slumber dimly in the shadows; the small window-panes cast strange greenish mottlings on the goods for sale. The murky shops behind are just so many black holes in which weird shapes move and have their being. To the right a wall runs the whole length of the passage and on it the shopkeepers opposite have hung narrow cupboards, where on flimsy shelves painted a horrible brown colour are displayed a lot of nondescript odds and ends that have been mouldering there for the last twenty years. A vendor of artificial jewellery has set out her stock in one of these cupboards, and here fifteen-sou rings are for sale, daintily perched on blue velvet cushions in mahogany boxes.

Above the glass roof rises the black, rough-plastered wall, looking as though it were covered with a leprous rash and slashed with scars.

The Passage du Pont-Neuf is no place to go for a nice stroll. You use it as a short cut and time-saver. Its frequenters are busy people whose one idea is to go straight on quickly: aproned apprentices, seamstresses delivering their work, men and women carrying parcels. But there are also old people picking their slow way through the dismal gloom shed by the glass roofing, and troops of little children just out of school who come running through here to make as much clatter as they can with their sabots on the flagstones. All day long the quick, irregular tap-tap of footsteps on the pavement gets on your nerves; nobody says a word, nobody stands still, everybody gets on with the job, head down, walking rapidly, with never a glance at the shops. When by a miracle passers-by do stop in front of their windows, the shopkeepers eye them anxiously.

At night the arcade is lit by three gas jets in heavy square lanterns. These gas jets hang from the glass roof, on to which they cast up patches of lurid light, while they send down palely luminous circles that dance fitfully and now and again seem to disappear altogether. Then the arcade takes on the sinister look of a real cutthroat alley; great shadows creep along the paving-stones and damp draughts blow in from the street until it seems like an underground gallery dimly lit by three funeral lamps. By way of lighting the shopkeepers make do with the feeble beams that these lanterns send through their windows, and inside the shop they merely light a shaded lamp and stand it on a corner of the counter, and then passers-by can make out what there is inside these burrows where in daytime there is nothing but darkness. The windows of a dealer in cardboard make a blaze of light against the row of dismal shop-fronts, for two shale-oil lamps pierce the gloom with their yellow flames. On the opposite side a candle in a lamp-glass fills the case of artificial jewellery with starry lights. The proprietress sits dozing in her cupboard with her hands under her shawl.

Some years ago, opposite this woman's pitch, was a shop whose bottle-green woodwork exuded damp from every crack. A long, narrow plank which served as a sign bore the word HABERDASHERY in black letters, and across one of the panes in the door a woman's name, THÉRÈSE RAQUIN, was written in red. On each side were deep shop-windows lined with blue paper.

In daylight all you could see was the goods displayed standing out in soft relief.

In one window there were some odd bits of clothing: goffered muslin caps at two or three francs each, muslin collars and cuffs, also knitted goods, stockings, socks, braces. Each item, yellowed and tatty-looking, hung pitifully on a wire hook, and the window was filled from top to bottom with odds and ends of whitish stuff looking mournful in the transparent darkness. The new caps, with their brighter whiteness, stood out crudely against the blue shelf-paper. And some coloured socks, hanging over a rod, added their sombre hues to the vague, neutral pallor of the muslin.

In the other window, which was narrower, were piled large balls of green wool, black buttons on white cards, and boxes of all colours and sizes, hair-nets with steel beads lying on rounds of bluish paper, bundles of knitting-needles, needlework patterns, spools of ribbon, a pile of dull, faded things that might have been lying there for five or six years. All the colours had gone a dirty grey in this cupboard decaying with dust and damp.

In summer, at noonday, when the sun scorched squares and streets with its glaring rays, you could make out, behind the bonnets in the other window, the pale and serious profile of a young woman. This profile stood out dimly from the darkness filling the shop. Her low, clear-cut forehead came down to meet a long, narrow, finely tapering nose, her lips were two thin, pale pink lines, and the small but firm chin reached the neck by way of a supple and well-covered jaw-line. Her body could not be seen, for it was lost in shadow, but only this profile, a flat white shape pierced by one wide-open dark eye, and, as it were, weighed down by a thick mass of dark hair. There it was for hours on end, still and calm between two caps on which the damp rods had left lines of rust.

In the evening, when the lamp was lit, the inside of the shop was revealed. It was wider than it was deep; at one end was a small counter and at the other a spiral staircase leading up to the first-floor rooms. Along the walls there were glass-fronted show-cases, cupboards, and rows of green card-board boxes, and the furnishing was completed by four chairs and a table. It all looked bare and forbidding, for the stock was in parcels packed away in corners, and not lying about the place in a gay clash of colours.

Usually there were two women sitting be-hind the counter — the young one with the dignified profile and an old lady dozing and smiling. She was about sixty, and her plump, placid face showed white in the lamplight. A big tabby cat lay on a corner of the counter, watching her sleep.

Sitting on a chair, at a lower level, there was a man of about thirty reading or talking to the younger woman in an undertone. He looked small, sickly, and languid, and with his colourless fair hair, almost beardless face, and blotchy skin he looked like a deli-cate spoilt child.

Shortly before ten the old lady woke up,

the shop was shut and the whole family went up to bed. The tabby cat purred his way upstairs after his owners, rubbing his head against each banister.

The accommodation upstairs consisted of three rooms. The stairs led straight into a combined dining and living room. To the left was a porcelain stove in a recess, a sideboard opposite, then some chairs along the walls, and a round table, with the flaps up, standing in the middle. At the back behind a glazed partition was a pitch black kitchen, and on each side of the dining-room was a bedroom.

Having kissed her son and daughter-in-law good night, the old lady retired. The cat went to sleep on a chair in the kitchen. The married couple went into their bedroom, which had a second door opening on to a staircase which led to the Passage through a dark and narrow alley.

The husband, who was in a permanent state of feverish shivering, went to bed at once, but the wife would throw open the window so as to close the Venetian shutters, and there she would stay for a minute or two, facing the high, black plastered wall that rises above the arcade. She would gaze vacantly at this wall and then without a word come to bed herself, coldly apathetic.

2

Madame Raquin had formerly had a haberdashery business at Vernon, where she had
lived in the same small shop for nearly twenty-
five years. A few years after her husband's
death, getting tired of it all, she had sold up.
Her savings, added to the proceeds of the sale,
gave her some forty thousand francs in hand,
which when invested, brought her in two
thousand francs a year. This sum was more
than enough for her needs. She led a retired
life, all unaware of the poignant joys and sor-
rows of this world, in fact she had made for
herself an existence of peaceful, quiet bliss.

She took a little house with a garden going
down to the Seine, at a rent of four hundred
francs. A vague atmosphere of the cloister
pervaded the secretive privacy of this house,
which was hidden away among broad
meadows and reached by a narrow path; its
windows looked over the river to the empty
hills on the other side. The good lady, now
past fifty, shut herself away in this lonely
spot, where she enjoyed uneventful days
with her son Camille and her niece Thérèse.

Camille was then twenty, but his mother still coddled him like a little boy. All through his long childhood of illnesses — he had had all the fevers and all the complaints one after the other — she had wrestled with death on his behalf, and now she idolized him. For fifteen years Madame Raquin had waged war against this succession of terrible ills trying to snatch her boy from her. And she beat them all by patience, loving care, and adoration.

Saved from death, Camille had grown up, but was left badly shaken by the repeated assaults of pain his body had sustained. His growth had been retarded and he was now small and weedy. His skinny limbs moved slowly as though they were tired out. This crippling weakness only made his mother love him the more. She gazed triumphantly on his poor pale little face, remembering that she had given him life more than ten times over.

In the rare respites between his illnesses the boy attended classes at a commercial school in Vernon, where he learned spelling and arithmetic. His knowledge stopped at 'the four rules' and the merest smattering of grammar. Later on he had lessons in writing and book-keeping. At any suggestion that he should go off to boarding-school Ma-

45

dame Raquin went all of a tremble: away from her he would die, she was certain, and she always said that books would be the death of him. So Camille remained ignorant, and his ignorance was an additional weakness.

At eighteen, with nothing to do and bored to death by the officious kindness lavished on him by his mother, he got a job as a clerk with a cloth merchant, at a salary of sixty francs a month. His was a restless nature which made idleness unbearable, and he felt calmer and better in health in the grinding toil of this routine job that kept him all day long poring over invoices and huge columns that he totted up patiently figure by figure. By evening, knocked up and without an idea in his head, he would find infinite delight in the profound vacancy of mind into which he sank. He only got into the job at the cloth merchant's by dint of a scene with his mother, who wanted to keep him by her side for ever, wrapped in cotton wool, away from the accidents of life. But the young man showed who was master, and demanded work to do, not in any spirit of duty but as a natural need, as other children demand toys. His mother's doting care had made him fiercely egoistical; he thought he loved those who pitied and caressed him, but in reality he lived apart, wrapped up in himself, caring for nothing but his own well-being and out to multiply his own pleasures by every possible means. When Madame Raquin's doting affection sickened him, he threw himself joyfully into a brainless job because it rescued him from infusions and potions. And in the evening, when he got back from his office, he rushed off to the river banks with his cousin Thérèse.

Thérèse was just on eighteen. One day, sixteen years earlier, while Madame Raquin was still in haberdashery, her brother Captain Degans had brought her a little girl in his arms. He had come from Algeria.

'You are this little girl's aunt,' he said with a smile. 'Her mother is dead . . . I don't know what to do with her. Here you are, you have her.'

She took the child, smiled at her, and kissed her rosy cheeks. Degans stayed at Vernon for a week. His sister scarcely asked him anything about this daughter he was giving her. She vaguely knew that the little dear was born in Oran and that her mother had been a native woman of great beauty. An hour before leaving, the captain gave her a birth certificate in which Thérèse was recognized by him and bore his name. He went away and was never seen again. Some years later he met his death in Africa.

Thérèse grew up sharing Camille's bed and her aunt's tender affection. She had an iron constitution but was coddled like an ailing child, sharing her cousin's medicines, kept in the hothouse atmosphere of the little invalid's room. For hours together she would stay crouching in front of the fire, lost in thought and staring at the flames without flickering an eyelid. This enforced invalidism turned her in upon herself, and she developed the habit of speaking in a whisper, moving without making a sound, sitting silent and motionless on a chair with open but expressionless eyes. But when she raised an arm or put a foot forward it was possible to divine the feline litheness, the taut and powerful muscles, all the stored-up energy, and passion lying dormant in her quiescent body. One day her cousin had collapsed in a fainting fit, and she had deftly picked him up and carried him, and this exertion brought out great patches of red on her cheeks. The cloistered life she led, and the lowering diet inflicted on her, failed to weaken her robust, wiry body, but her face took on a pale and slightly sallow colour, and when the light was not on her she looked almost ugly. From time to time she would go to the window and gaze at the houses opposite, over which the sun spread its cloth of gold.

When Madame Raquin sold her business and retired to the cottage by the river, Thérèse's heart leaped within her, but she did not show it, for her aunt had so often repeated, 'Don't make a noise, keep quiet,' that she kept all the impulsive ardour of her nature carefully hidden. She had supreme self-control, an external tranquillity that concealed terrible bursts of passion. She always thought of herself as being in her cousin's room, at the bedside of a dying child, and she had the restrained movements, the periods of silence and stillness, the faltering words of an old woman. When she saw the garden, the silver river, the spacious green hills sweeping up to the horizon, a wild urge to run about possessed her; she felt her heart knocking fiercely in her breast. But never a muscle of her face moved, and when her aunt asked if this new home was to her liking she merely smiled.

From that moment her life took a turn for the better. She kept her graceful movements, her calm, indifferent expression, she was still the child who shared an invalid's bed, but her inner life was aflame with passion. When she was alone in the grass or at the water's edge she would lie flat on her stomach like an animal, with black, dilated eyes and body coiled ready to spring, and there she would stay for hours, thinking of nothing, but kissed by the sun and happy to dig her fingers into the earth. She dreamed wild dreams, looked defiantly at the murmuring river, imagining that the water was about to leap up and attack her; then she would stiffen and put herself on guard, furiously asking herself how she could overcome the waters.

In the evenings, Thérèse, now soothed and quiet, would sit sewing with her aunt, and her face seemed to be slumbering in the soft light from the shaded lamp. Camille, huddled deep in an armchair, turned his figures over in his mind. Nothing disturbed the quietness of this peaceful domestic scene save an occasional word spoken in an undertone.

Madame Raquin looked on her children with serene goodwill. She had made up her mind to pair them off. She still treated her son as though he were at death's door, and trembled at the thought that some day she would die and leave him alone and ill. And so she relied on Thérèse, telling herself that the girl would make a watchful nurse for

Camille. With her gentle ways and silent devotion, her niece filled her with unlimited confidence. She had watched her in action and meant to give her to her son as a guardian angel. The marriage was the logical end of the story, settled in advance.

For a long time the young people had known that they were to be married some day. They had grown up with the idea, and it had become familiar and natural to them. The union was referred to in the family as something necessary and inevitable. Madame Raquin had said 'We will wait until Thérèse is twenty-one.' And they waited, in patience and with no fuss or embarrassment.

Camille, whose ill-health had impoverished his blood, knew nothing of the fierce desires of adolescence. His attitude towards his cousin was still that of a little boy, and he kissed her as he kissed his mother, mechanically, losing none of his self-centred calm. He saw her as an obliging companion who saved him from getting too bored and upon occasion made his herb tea. When he played with her and held her in his arms she might just as well have been a boy, for his flesh was not disturbed in the least. It had never occurred to him at such times to kiss Thérèse's warm lips as, laughing nervously, she fought and struggled.

And the girl, for her part, seemed to remain cold and indifferent. At times she would turn her big eyes on Camille and study him for several minutes with supremely untroubled attention. Then her lips alone moved almost imperceptibly. This strong face, kept constantly gentle and attentive by sheer will-power, remained quite inscrutable. When her marriage was mentioned Thérèse became thoughtful and merely nodded agreement with whatever Madame Raquin was saying. Camille would drop off to sleep.

On summer evenings the pair would run off to the riverside. His mother's incessant attentions got on Camille's nerves, and he had moments of rebellion when he wanted to run, make himself ill, anything to get away from these endearments that revolted him. And then he would drag Thérèse away, make her wrestle and roll about on the ground. One day he gave her a push and knocked her over: she leaped to her feet like a wild beast, and with face aflame and bloodshot eyes flew at him with both arms raised. Camille managed to slip to the ground. He was afraid.

The months and years went by, and the day fixed for the wedding arrived. Madame Raquin took Thérèse to one side, told her about her father and mother and the circumstances of her birth. Thérèse listened to what her aunt had to say, then kissed her without a word.

That night, instead of going to her bedroom, which was to the left of the stairs, Thérèse went into her cousin's which was to the right. That was all the change there was in her life. Next morning, when the bridal pair came down, Camille was as listless and sickly as ever, wrapped in his sacred egoistical tranquillity. Thérèse was still meek and indifferent, and her face, under perfect control, frighteningly calm.

3

A week after his marriage Camille bluntly informed his mother that he meant to leave Vernon and go to live in Paris. Madame Raquin was up in arms: she had mapped out her existence and did not want to alter a single detail of it. Her son flew into a tantrum and threatened to be ill unless she gave in to his desire.

'I have never gone against any of your ideas,' he said; 'I have married my cousin and swallowed all the medicines you have given me. The least you can do is let me have a will of my own now, and think the same way as I do. . . . We are going at the end of the month.'

Madame Raquin had a sleepless night. Camille's decision turned her whole life upside down, and she desperately cast about for some way of making it liveable again. But gradually she calmed down as she reflected that the young people might have children and that when that happened her limited means would no longer be adequate. Some more money would have to be found, she would have to go back into business and find a profitable occupation for Thérèse. By the next day she was used to the idea of going and had laid plans for a new life.

At lunch she was quite jolly.

'This is what we are going to do,' she told her children. 'Tomorrow I'm off to Paris to look for a little business, and Thérèse and I will go back to selling needles and cotton. It will be something for us to do. As for you, Camille, you can do what you like — either walk about in the sunshine or find a job.'

'I shall find a job,' said the young man.

The truth was that the only thing that had urged Camille to move was an absurd ambition to be an employee in some large concern, and as he visualized himself at the centre of some vast office, wearing shiny artificial cuffs and with a pen behind his ear, he went pink with pleasure.

Thérèse was not consulted. She had always shown such passive obedience that her aunt and husband no longer bothered to ask her opinion. She went where they went, did what they did, without a word of complaint or reproach, without even appearing to notice that she was moving at all.

Madame Raquin went to Paris and made straight for the Passage du Pont-Neuf. An elderly spinster in Vernon had put her in touch with a relation of hers who had a haberdashery business in the Passage and wanted to give it up. She thought the shop rather small and rather dark, but on her way across Paris she had been terrified by the clatter of the streets and the luxury of the shops, and this narrow arcade and these modest windows reminded her of her old shop which had been so peaceful. Here she could fancy herself still in the provinces, and she breathed again, thinking that her dear children would be happy in this remote corner. What decided her was the reasonable price of the goodwill — they would let her have it for two thousand francs. The rent of the shop and the floor above was only twelve hundred. Madame Raquin, who had nearly four thousand saved, worked out that she could pay for the business and pay for the first year's rent without touching her capital. Camille's salary and the profits from the business would be enough, she thought, for day-to-day needs. Thus she would leave her income untouched and let it go to swell the capital for her grandchildren's inheritance.

She came back to Vernon radiant, saying that she had found a treasure, a delectable retreat in the very heart of Paris. Gradually, as the next few days went by, the damp, dark shop in the arcade became in the course of her evening talks a palace, and in her recollections she saw it as comfortable, spacious, quiet, and endowed with a thousand inestimable advantages.

'Oh my dear Thérèse,' she said, 'we are going to be happy there, believe me. . . . Three beautiful rooms upstairs. . . . The arcade is full of people. . . . We shall have lovely window displays. . . . We shan't have a dull moment, I can tell you!'

And so on and so forth. All her dormant shopkeeper's instincts revived; she gave Thérèse advice about buying and selling, about all the tricks of the trade. At length the day came for the family to leave the house by the Seine, and on the same evening they were moving into the Passage du Pont Neuf.

As Thérèse entered the shop that from now on was to be her home, she felt as though she were going down into a newly-dug grave. A sort of nausea seized her in the throat and she shuddered. She looked at the dingy, damp arcade, went over the shop, went upstairs, went round each room, and these bare unfurnished rooms were terrifying in their solitude and decay. She could not move or utter a word, but was chilled through and through. When her aunt and husband had gone downstairs again she sat on a trunk. Her hands were numbed and her breast was bursting with sobs but she could not cry.

Confronted with the reality, Madame Raquin was embarrassed and ashamed of her dreams. She tried to defend her purchase, finding a way out of every difficulty that turned up, explaining away the darkness by saying that the weather was dull, and winding up by declaring that only a good sweeping was needed.

'Who cares?' said Camille, 'it's quite all right. Anyhow we shan't be up here except in the evenings. . . . You two will have each other and get along famously.'

The young man himself would never have agreed to live in such a hole had he not been looking forward to the snug comfort of his office. He said to himself that he would be nice and warm all day long in his grand department, and that he would go to bed early.

For a week or more the shop and flat were in a muddle. From the very first day Thérèse took her seat behind the counter and never stirred from that position again. This passive attitude astonished Madame Raquin, for she had thought that Thérèse would try to cheer up the home, put flowers on the window-sills, want new wallpapers, curtains, carpets. When she suggested some repair or improvement her niece would reply in her quiet voice:

'What's the point? We are quite all right as we are; we don't want luxuries.'

And so it was Madame Raquin who had to arrange the rooms and put the shop to rights. The sight of her constantly fussing about finally got on Thérèse's nerves, and she took on a charwoman and forced her aunt to come and sit with her.

It took Camille a month to find a job. He came into the shop as little as possible, but wandered about all day. He got so bored that he talked of going back to Vernon. But in the end he joined the office staff of the Orleans Railway, where he earned a hundred francs a month. His dream had come true.

He left at eight in the morning, went down the rue Guénégaud as far as the embankment, and then, with his hands in his pockets, sauntered along the Seine from the Institut to the Jardin des Plantes. He never tired of this long walk which he did twice a day. He watched the flow of the current, stopped to look at rafts of timber going downstream, but his mind was a blank. Often he took up his stand opposite Notre-Dame and looked at the scaffolding sur-

rounding the cathedral, which was being repaired at that time, and the huge balks of
timber amused him, though he did not
know why. Then he would give a passing
glance to the Port aux Vins, and count the
cabs coming from the station. In the evening, dead beat and with his head full of
some silly story that had been going round
the office, he would go through the Zoo and,
if he had time, have a look at the bears. He
would stay there half an hour, leaning over
the pit, following the bears with his eyes as
they swayed clumsily from side to side, for
the gait of the huge creatures appealed to
him. He examined them open-mouthed and
goggle-eyed, finding an idiotic delight in
seeing them move. Finally he would make
up his mind to go home, which he did with
dragging steps, looking at passers-by, car-
riages, and shops.

As soon as he got in he ate and then began
reading. He had bought the works of
Buffon, and every evening he set himself
some twenty or thirty pages, bored though
he was by such reading-matter. He also read
the *Histoire du Consulat et de l'Empire* of
Thiers and the *Histoire des Girondins* of
Lamartine, or perhaps works of popular science, all in ten-centime numbers. He
thought he was going on with his education.

Sometimes he forced his wife to listen as he read out certain pages or anecdotes. He was very much surprised that Thérèse could stay pensive and silent throughout a whole evening without being tempted to pick up a book. Really he had to admit that his wife was a bit weak in the intellect.

Thérèse impatiently refused the books. She preferred to do nothing, staring in front of her and letting her thoughts run on. She still remained equable and easy to get on with — indeed she devoted her whole will-power to making herself a passive instrument, completely acquiescent and free from all self-interest.

The business went quietly on, bringing in the same profits regularly each month. The customers were working girls of the neighbourhood. Every five minutes a girl came in for a few sous worth of something. Thérèse served the customers always with the same words and the same set smile on her lips. Madame Raquin was more adaptable and chatty, and it was she, to be sure, who attracted and held the trade.

For three years days followed days, all alike. Camille never once stayed away from his office, his mother and wife seldom left the shop. Living in musty shadows and dismal, oppressive silence, Thérèse could see her whole life stretching out before her totally void, bringing night after night the same cold bed and morning after morning the same empty day.

4

Once a week, on Thursday evenings, the Raquins entertained. A big lamp was lit in the dining-room and a kettle of water was put on the fire for the tea. It was quite a performance. This one evening stood out from all the others, and in the family routine had assumed almost the character of a wild but respectable orgy. Bedtime was eleven o'clock.

In Paris Madame Raquin met one of her old friends again, Police Superintendent Michaud, who had been stationed at Vernon for twenty years and had lived in the same building as herself. They had become close friends, and then when the widow had sold up and gone to live down by the river they had gradually lost touch. Some months later Michaud had left the provinces and gone to live quietly on his fifteen-hundred-franc pension in Paris, in the rue de Seine. One rainy day he met his old friend in the Passage du Pont-Neuf, and that very evening he dined with the Raquins.

This was the origin of the Thursday evenings. The ex-superintendent got into the habit of coming regularly once a week. In due course he brought along his son, Olivier, thirty, tall, lean, and angular, who had married a very small wife, dull and ailing. Olivier had a three-thousand-franc post at the Préfecture of Police, of which Camille was particularly jealous; he was a chief clerk in the Department of Public Order and Safety. From the outset Thérèse loathed this stiff, cold fellow who thought he was honouring the shop in the arcade by parading his own spare, lanky body and the delicate health of his poor little wife.

Camille brought in another guest, an old employee of the Orleans Railway. Grivet had served the company for twenty years, was a chief clerk, and earned two thousand one hundred francs. He it was who allocated the work to the staff of Camille's office, and the latter showed him a certain deference. In his dreams he told himself that Grivet would die some day and that he might take his place in a matter of ten years' time. Grivet was delighted with Madame Raquin's kind welcome and came back every week with unfailing regularity. After six months had gone by, his Thursday visit had become a duty: he went to the Passage du Pont-Neuf as he went to the office every morning, automatically, out of sheer animal instinct.

From then onwards the parties were delightful. At seven o'clock Madame Raquin lit the fire, put the lamp in the middle of the table, flanked by a set of dominoes, and then polished the tea-service on the sideboard. At eight o'clock sharp old Michaud and Grivet met in front of the shop, one coming from the rue de Seine and the other from the rue Mazarine. They came in, and the whole family went upstairs. They sat round the table waiting for Olivier and his wife, who were always late. When the company was complete, Madame Raquin poured the tea, Camille tipped out the dominoes on to the oilcloth table-cover, and each one became engrossed in his own play. Not a sound could now be heard except the clicking of the dominoes. After each game the players had an argument for two or three minutes, and then silence was resumed, a dismal silence broken by the staccato clicks.

Thérèse played with a lack of interest that annoyed Camille. She would lift François on to her lap — he was the big tabby cat Madame Raquin had brought from Vernon — and stroke him with one hand, putting down the dominoes with the other. Thursday evenings were a torture to her, and often she complained of feeling out of sorts, of a bad headache, so that she need not play but could sit idle and half asleep, with one elbow on the table and her cheek in her cupped hand, studying the guests of her aunt and husband, seeing them through a sort of smoky haze from the lamp. All these faces exasperated her. She looked from one to the other with profound distaste and veiled irritation. Old Michaud displayed his pasty face with red blotches, the typical expressionless face of an old man in his dotage. Grivet had the narrow features, round eyes, and thin lips of a cretin, Olivier, whose cheekbones almost came through his skin, solemnly carried a stiff and insignificant head on a ridiculous body, and as for Suzanne, Olivier's wife, she was quite colourless — vague eyes, white lips, flabby face. Thérèse could not find one human being, not one living thing, amongst these grotesque and sinister creatures with whom she was cooped up. Sometimes she was seized with hallucinations and thought she was buried in some vault together with a lot of puppet-like corpses which nodded their heads and moved their legs and arms when you pulled the strings. The heavy air in the dining-room stifled her, and the eerie silence, the yellow glimmer of the lamp, filled her with vague terror and inexpressible anguish.

Down in the shop a bell had been put on the door to tinkle a warning when customers came in. Thérèse listened hard, and when the bell rang she hurried down, happy and relieved to get out of the dining-room. She took her time over serving the customer, and when she was left alone she sat behind the counter and stayed there as long as possible, afraid to go up again and finding positive enjoyment in not having Grivet and Olivier in front of her eyes. The damp shop air seemed to cool her burning hands, and she relapsed into her usual quiet seriousness.

But she could not stay like that for long. Camille would take offence at her absence, not understanding how anybody could prefer the shop to the dining-room on Thursday evenings, and he would hang over the banisters and look for his wife.

'What's the matter?' he would shout. 'What are you doing down there? Why don't you come up? Grivet's got the devil's own luck, he's won again!'

She would reluctantly get to her feet and come and take her place again opposite old Michaud, whose loose lips leered in a sickening manner. And there she would stay huddled on her chair until eleven, keeping her eye on François, whom she held in her arms so as not to see the cardboard dolls grinning all round her.

5

One Thursday Camille brought back with him from the office a tall, square-shouldered fellow whom he pushed into the shop with a friendly shove.

'Mother, do you recognize this gentleman?' he asked, pointing at him.

The old lady looked at the tall young man, hunted about in her memory, but found no answer. Thérèse looked placidly on at the scene.

'What!' Camille went on, 'don't you recognize Laurent, young Laurent, son of old Laurent who had such lovely cornfields over Jeufosse way? Don't you remember? I went to school with him and he used to call for me in the mornings, on his way from his uncle's who lived near us, and you used to give him bread and jam.'

Madame Raquin suddenly did remember young Laurent, whom she found extraordinarily grown-up now. It was a good twenty years since she had seen him, and now she was anxious to make him forget her failure to place him, pouring out a flood of recollections and motherly endearments. Laurent had taken a seat and was smiling blissfully, answering in a clear voice, and looking about him in a quiet and self-assured manner.

'Just fancy!' said Camille, 'this character has been an employee in the Orleans Station for eighteen months, and we only met and recognized each other this evening. It shows how big and important our concern is.'

As the young man made this remark he opened his eyes wide and pursed his lips, as proud as anything to be a humble cog in a vast machine.

Wagging his head, he went on:

'Oh, he's doing very well; he has studied, he already gets fifteen hundred francs. . . . His father sent him to college, he has studied law and learned how to paint. Haven't you, Laurent? . . . You'll stay to dinner?'

'I don't mind if I do,' Laurent answered, making no bones about it.

He put his hat down and made himself at home in the shop. Madame Raquin ran to look at her pots and pans. Thérèse, who had not yet uttered a word, continued to look at the newcomer. She had never seen a real man before. Laurent, with his height and breadth and healthy colour, amazed her. It was with a kind of wonder that she took in

70

his low forehead surmounted by a thick mop of black hair, full cheeks, red lips, and regular features — a handsome man in a full-blooded way. Her glance paused for a moment at his neck; it was broad and short, thick and powerful. Then she let her attention rest on his big hands, which he held open over his knees; the fingers were square and his clenched fist could easily have felled an ox. Laurent was of genuine peasant stock, a little ponderous and stooping, with slow, precise movements, calm and stubborn-looking. You could sense the hard, well-developed muscles beneath his clothes, the whole organism built of solid, firm flesh. And Thérèse examined him with some curiosity, going from his fists to his face, and feeling a little thrill when her eyes rested on his bull neck.

Camille displayed his volumes of Buffon and the ten-centime parts, to show his friend that he studied too. Then, as though answering a question he had been asking himself for some time:

'But surely you know my wife?' he said to Laurent. 'Don't you remember the little cousin who used to play with us at Vernon?'

'Of course. I recognized her at once,' answered Laurent, looking hard at Thérèse.

This direct stare, which seemed to look

right through her, had something disconcerting about it to the young woman. She
forced a smile, exchanged a few words with
Laurent and her husband, and hastened off
to join her aunt. She felt uneasy.

They sat down to dinner. As soon as they
had started on the soup Camille thought he
ought to entertain his friend.

'How is your father getting on?' he asked.

'I've no idea,' Laurent answered; 'we have
fallen out and haven't written to each other
for five years.'

'Well I never!' exclaimed the clerk, appalled at such horrors.

'Oh yes, the dear man has his own
ideas. . . . As he is for ever having the law on
his neighbours, he sent me to college with
visions of using me later on as a lawyer to
win all his cases for him. . . . Oh, I can tell
you, Daddy Laurent only goes in for useful
ambitions. Even his follies have to be made
to pay.'

'And you didn't want to be a lawyer?' said
Camille, more and more astonished.

'Good Lord, no,' laughed his friend. 'For
two years I pretended to attend lectures so
as to get the twelve-hundred-franc allowance father forked out. I lived with one of
my school friends who is an artist, as I had
begun to do some painting too. It appealed

to me — it is an amusing job, and not tiring. We smoked and chatted all day long.'

The Raquin family goggled.

'Unfortunately,' went on Laurent, 'it couldn't go on like that for ever. Dad found out I was telling fibs; he cut off my hundred francs a month there and then and invited me to come and till the soil with him. So then I tried my hand at devotional pictures — no money in it. As I could clearly see death by starvation looming ahead, I chucked art to the devil and looked for a job. The old man is bound to die one of these days, and I'm waiting for that so as to live without doing anything.'

Laurent spoke in a matter-of-fact voice. In a few words he had told a typical story that characterized him perfectly. A lazy man at bottom, he had animal appetites, very clear-cut desires for easy and lasting pleasures. All his great powerful body wanted was to do nothing, to wallow in never-ending idleness and self-indulgence. He would have liked to eat well, sleep well, satisfy his passions liberally, without stirring from one spot or risking the misfortune of a bit of fatigue.

The legal profession appalled him, and he shuddered at the ideal of tilling the soil. He had thrown himself into art in the hope of finding a lazy man's job, for the brush seemed a nice light tool to wield and he thought success was easy. He dreamed of a life of cheap pleasures, a fine life full of women, of lolling on divans, blow-outs, and boozings. The dream lasted as long as Laurent senior sent the cash. But when the young man, who was already thirty, saw starvation on the horizon, he began to do some thinking; he felt his courage fail in the face of privations, and would not have put up with a day without food for the greater glory of art. So, as he said, he chucked painting to the devil as soon as he saw that it would never satisfy his large appetites. His first attempts never even rose to mediocrity; his peasant eye saw nature clumsily and messily, and his muddy, badly composed, grimacing canvases defied all criticism. Not that he seemed particularly vain as an artist, and he was not unduly depressed when he threw down his brushes. All he really missed was his old school-friend's vast studio in which he had lazed so delectably for four or five years. And he also missed the women who came and posed there, and whose favours were within the reach of his purse. The brutish enjoyments of these circles had left him with imperative sensual needs. And yet he was quite at home as an employee;

this humdrum life suited him perfectly, and he liked a day-to-day task which was not tiring and saved him from having to think. There were only two annoying things: the lack of women, and the food in the eighteen-sou restaurants that did not appease his ravenous stomach.

Camille listened, gazing at him with guileless astonishment. This feeble young man, whose soft, limp body had never felt a single tremor of desire, had childish visions of the studio life his friend was telling him about. He thought of the women, displaying their bare flesh, and he interrogated Laurent:

'So you mean that there have really been women who have taken their clothes off in front of you?'

'Why not?' Laurent grinned and looked at Thérèse, who turned very pale.

'That must make you feel ever so funny,' went on Camille, giggling. 'I should feel awful. . . . The first time it happened you couldn't have known where to look.'

Laurent had opened one of his big hands and was examining the palm attentively. His fingers trembled slightly and a flush came to his cheeks.

'The first time,' he went on, as though talking to himself, 'I think I found it quite natural. . . . It's great fun, this art racket, only it doesn't bring in a sou. I had a lovely red-head as a model — firm white flesh, gorgeous bust, hips as wide as . . .'

He looked up and saw Thérèse sitting in front of him silent and motionless, looking at him with burning intensity. Her dull black eyes looked like two bottomless pits and through her parted lips could be seen the pink flesh of her mouth, caught by the light. She seemed crushed, withdrawn into herself, but she was listening.

Laurent's eyes travelled from Camille to Thérèse, and he repressed a smile. He finished his sentence with a gesture, a sweeping, voluptuous gesture which she followed with her eyes. They had got as far as dessert, and Madame Raquin had gone down to serve a customer.

When the table was cleared Laurent, who had been thoughtful for some moments, suddenly said to Camille:

'You know, I must paint your portrait.'

The idea delighted Madame Raquin and her son. Thérèse said nothing.

'It is summer now,' Laurent went on, 'and as we leave the office at four I can come here and get you to sit for two hours in the evening. It will be done in a week.'

'That would be fine!' said Camille, pink with joy; 'and you can have dinner with us. . . . I'll get my hair curled and put on my long black coat.'

It struck eight, and Grivet and Michaud made their entrance. Olivier and Suzanne came in behind them.

Camille introduced his friend to the company. Grivet pursed his lips. He hated Laurent, whose salary had gone up too quickly, he thought. In any case the introduction of a new guest was an important matter, and the Raquins' guests could not accept a stranger without a certain reserve.

Laurent behaved very amiably. He grasped the situation, and wanted to please and be accepted at once. He told stories, enlivened the evening with his hearty laugh, and won the friendship even of Grivet.

That evening Thérèse showed no desire to go down to the shop. She stayed sitting in her chair until eleven, playing and chatting, avoiding Laurent's eyes. Moreover Laurent took no notice of her. The man's sanguine temperament, his loud voice, his fat laughter, the keen, powerful aroma given off by his whole person, threw the young woman off her balance and plunged her into a sort of nervous anguish.

6

From that day onwards Laurent came to the Raquins' nearly every evening. He lodged in a tiny furnished room at eighteen francs a month in the rue Saint-Victor, opposite the Port aux Vins; it was scarcely six square metres in area and had a sloping ceiling with a window in it that opened like a lid on to the sky. Laurent went home to this garret as late as possible. Before he met Camille, as he had not enough money to hang about in cafés, he used to sit on at the little eating house where he had his evening meal, smoking two or three pipes and drinking a three-sou coffee and rum. Then he would slowly make his way back to the rue Saint-Victor, strolling along the embankments and sitting on seats when the weather was warm.

So for him the shop in the Passage du Pont-Neuf was a delightful haven, warm, quiet, full of friendly talk and kind attentions. He saved the three sous on his rum and coffee, and drank freely of Madame Raquin's excellent tea. There he stayed until ten, half asleep, digesting his meal and feeling quite at home, and he only left after helping Camille to shut up the shop.

One evening he brought his easel and a box of paints, as he proposed to start work on Camille's portrait the following day. A piece of canvas was bought and the most careful preparations made. At length the artist set to work in the couple's bedroom where, he said, the light was better.

It took him three evenings to sketch in the head. He laboriously drew his charcoal over the canvas with thin, niggling little strokes, and his stiff, lifeless sketch was oddly reminiscent of the primitive masters. He copied Camille's face as a pupil copies a model, with hesitant hand and a clumsy precision that made it look disagreeable. On the fourth day he put some little dabs of paint on his palette and began to paint with the tip of his brush, stippling the canvas with little muddy dots and making short and crowded hachurings as though he were using a pencil.

At the end of each sitting Madame Raquin and Camille went into raptures. Laurent said that more time was needed and that the likeness would come.

From the beginning of work on the portrait Thérèse never left the bedroom-turned-studio. She left her aunt alone behind the counter, and at the slightest excuse went upstairs and gazed at Laurent painting, oblivious of all else.

Always serious and subdued, paler and quieter than ever, she sat there and watched the brushes moving. Not that the sight seemed to amuse her much; she came to this room as though drawn by force, and stayed as though nailed to the spot. Occasionally Laurent would turn round and smile at her, asking if the picture was to her liking. She scarcely answered a word, but quivered and relapsed into her solemn ecstasy.

On getting back at night to the rue Saint-Victor, Laurent argued at length with himself whether or not he should become Thérèse's lover.

'That young woman', he told himself, 'will be mine whenever I like. She is always there, right on top of me, scrutinizing me, measuring me, weighing me up. She's all quivering, her face is strange, quiet but passionate. What she wants is a lover, that's a certain fact; you can see it in her eyes. And I must say Camille isn't much of a specimen.'

Laurent laughed to himself at the thought of his friend's pallid skinniness, then went on:

'That shop is getting on her nerves. I go there because I don't know where else to go.

If it weren't for that you wouldn't often catch me in the Passage du Pont-Neuf! Damp, miserable hole. Must be the death of a woman. . . . She likes me, I'm sure, so why not me rather than somebody else?'

He broke off and gave himself up to complacent visions, gazing intently at the Seine flowing by.

'Well, here goes,' he exclaimed; 'the first chance I get I kiss her. . . . I bet she falls straight into my arms!'

But then he walked on again, a prey to indecisions.

'She really is plain, though,' he thought. 'Long nose, big mouth. Besides, I'm not in the least in love with her. I might get myself into a spot of bother. Mustn't rush things.'

Laurent, who was extremely prudent, turned these thoughts over in his mind for a full week. He worked out all the possible developments in an affair with Thérèse and only decided to embark on the enterprise when he had satisfied himself that it was really in his interests to do so.

As he saw it, Thérèse was decidedly plain and he did not love her, but then she would not cost anything, and the women he picked up cheap were certainly no more beautiful, nor did he love them either. Already economy was advising him to take his friend's wife. And then again, it was a long time since he had satisfied his appetites; money being tight, his flesh was going hungry, and he did not want to miss a chance to indulge it a little. And finally, such a liaison as this, when you came to think of it, could not lead to any trouble, for Thérèse would be anxious to keep everything dark, and he could easily drop her whenever he wanted to; and even supposing that Camille found out everything and took it badly, he could knock him down with a single punch if he got awkward. From every point of view the proposition appealed to him as easy and attractive.

From then onwards he lived in quiet confidence, biding his time. He had decided to go straight ahead when the first chance offered. He visualized a future of cosy evenings, with all the Raquins ministering to his enjoyment: Thérèse slaking the burning thirst of his passions, Madame Raquin coddling him like a mother, and Camille, with his conversation, saving him from getting too bored in the shop of an evening.

The portrait was nearly finished, but still chances did not present themselves. Thérèse was always present, subdued and uneasy, but Camille never went out of the room, and Laurent despaired of being able to get him out of the way for an hour. But the day came when he had to declare that he would finish the portrait on the morrow. Madame Raquin announced that they would all dine together to celebrate the painter's work.

The next day, when Laurent had applied the final brushstrokes to the canvas, the whole family gathered round to exclaim what a perfect likeness it was. It was a miserable daub, dirty grey in colour with large bluish patches. Even the brightest colours went dull and muddy when Laurent used them, and in spite of himself he had overdone the pallid colouring of his model, making his face take on the greenish look of a drowned man, and this sinister resemblance was rendered all the more striking by the grimacing draughtsmanship which twisted the features. But Camille was delighted, saying that on the canvas he looked distinguished.

When he had thoroughly admired his own face he said that he was going to get two bottles of champagne. Madame Raquin went downstairs to the shop. The artist was left alone with Thérèse.

She had remained crouching there, looking vaguely in front of her. She seemed to be waiting, tense. Laurent hesitated, looking at the canvas, playing with his brushes. Time was short, Camille might come back, the chance might never recur. Suddenly he turned round and faced Thérèse. They looked at each other for a few seconds.

Then with a violent movement Laurent stooped, took the young woman, and held her against his breast. He pushed her head back, crushing her lips beneath his own. She made one wild instinctive effort to resist and then yielded, slipping down on to the floor. Not a single word was exchanged. The act was silent and brutal.

7

From the outset the lovers felt their liaison to be inevitable, fatal, quite natural. At the first meeting they talked in lovers' language, kissed each other freely and without embarrassment or awkwardness, as though their intimacy had been going on for years. They were quite at ease in their new situation, perfectly tranquil and shameless.

They arranged how they should meet. As Thérèse could not go out, it was decided that Laurent would come to her. In a clear and businesslike way she explained what she had thought out. Their meetings would take place in the room she shared with her husband. Her lover would come by way of the side passage leading from the arcade, and Thérèse would open the door for him. Meanwhile Camille would be at the office and Madame Raquin down in the shop. The very effrontery of the scheme guaranteed its success.

Laurent fell in with it. With all his prudence he had a sort of animal daring, the daring of a man with big fists. His mistress's quiet calm was an invitation to come and sample a passion offered so brazenly. He thought up an excuse, got two hours' leave from his chief and hastened to the Passage du Pont-Neuf.

As soon as he entered the arcade he began to feel intense sensations of pleasure. The vendor of artificial jewellery was sitting right opposite the door to the side passage, and he had to wait until she was busy with a workgirl wanting to buy a ring or some brass earrings. Then he quickly slipped into the passage and climbed the narrow, dark steps, steadying himself against the damp, sticky walls. He kicked against the stone steps, and at the sound of each kick a burning sensation ran through his chest. A door opened, and there on the threshold, dazzling in the whitish light, he saw Thérèse, in her petticoat, with her hair caught back in a heavy knot behind her head. She shut the door and flung her arms round his neck. There was about her a scent of white linen and newly-washed flesh.

To his surprise, Laurent found she was beautiful. He had never really seen this woman. Lissom and strong, Thérèse held him close, throwing back her head, and flashes of fire and passionate laughter passed across her face. This face was transfigured by love, its expression was wild and yet caressing, her lips were moist, her eyes shining; she was radiant. Writhing and sinuous, she was beautiful with a strong beauty born of passionate abandon. It was as though her face had been lit up from within and fire leaped from her flesh. Her boiling blood and taut nerves radiated warmth, something keen and penetrating.

From the very first kiss she showed herself adept in the arts of love. Her unsated body threw itself frantically into pleasure; she was emerging as from a dream, she was being born into passion. She was passing from the weakly arms of Camille into the vigorous embrace of Laurent, and this approach of a virile man was the sudden shock that aroused her from the sleep of the flesh. All the instincts of this highly-strung woman burst forth with unparalleled violence; her mother's blood, the African blood that burned in her veins, now began to rush and beat furiously through her thin and still almost virgin body. She paraded this body, offering herself with supreme shamelessness. And long spasms ran through her from head to foot.

Laurent had never known a woman like this, and it left him amazed and ill at ease. His women did not as a rule receive him with such transports; he was accustomed to cool and apathetic embraces, tired and sated unions. Thérèse's moans and paroxysms almost frightened him, at the same time as they excited his erotic curiosity. When he left her he was reeling like a drunken man. But the next day, when he was back in his normal mood of prudent caution, he wondered whether he would return to this mistress whose kisses set him on fire. At first he made up his mind definitely to stay at home. Then he had moments of weakness. He wanted to forget the sight of Thérèse in her nudity and her sweet and sensual caresses, but she was always there, implacable, holding out her arms. The physical discomfort this vision caused him became unbearable.

And so he gave in, fixed another meeting, and returned to the Passage du Pont-Neuf.

From that day onwards Thérèse became part of his life. He did not yet accept her, but submitted to her. He had hours of panic and moments of caution, and in fact the affair was an unpleasant upheaval, but his fears and misgivings could not stand up to his desires. The meetings went on with increasing frequency.

Thérèse had none of these doubts. She gave herself without reserve, going straight where her passion led. This woman, bowed down by circumstances and now at last rising again, was laying her whole self bare and explaining her development.

At times she would throw her arms round Laurent's neck, press herself against his breast, and say in a voice still gasping with passion:

'Oh, if you only knew what I have been through! I was brought up in the steamy atmosphere of a sickroom. I slept with Camille at night, and I would get as far away from him as I could, for the stale smell of his body made me feel sick. He was nasty and awkward and wouldn't take any medicines that I refused to share with him, and so to please my aunt I had to drink some of each of them. I don't know why it didn't kill me. They have made me ugly, my poor darling, they have stolen everything I possessed, and you can't love me as I love you.'

She kissed Laurent through her tears, and went on with smouldering hate:

'I don't wish them any harm. They took me in and brought me up, saved me from want. But I would rather have been abandoned than have their hospitality. I longed desperately for the open air; as a tiny child I dreamed of roaming on the roads, barefoot in the dust, begging my way, living the gipsy life. I have been told that my mother was the daughter of a tribal chief in Africa. I have often thought about her and realized that I belonged to her by blood and instinct. I would have liked to be with her always and cross the sandy wastes on her back. Oh what a childhood I had! I still feel sick and furious when I remember the long days I spent shut in a room, with Camille snuffling away. I used to squat in front of the fire, dully watching the infusions simmering and feeling my limbs going numb. And I couldn't move, because my aunt was cross if I made a noise. Later on I had some really deep happiness in the little house by the water, but I had already got feeble by then; I could hardly walk, and fell over when I tried to run. And then they buried me alive in this horrible shop.'

Thérèse was breathing hard, her arms tightly embracing her lover. She was taking her revenge, and her thin, delicate nostrils quivered nervously.

'You'd never believe how nasty they made me. They have turned me into a hypocrite and a liar. They have so smothered me in their middle-class refinement that I don't know how there can be any blood left in my veins. I lowered my eyes, put on a dismal, silly expression, just like them; I was just as dead-and-alive as they were. When you first saw me I looked half-baked, didn't I? Solemn, crushed flat, dazed. No hope left in anything — I thought that one day I should throw myself into the Seine. But before I caved in like that, how many furious nights I went through! At Vernon, in my cold bedroom, I used to bite my pillow to stifle my cries, hit myself, call myself a coward. My blood boiled, and I could have torn myself to pieces. Twice I meant to run away, just go straight ahead into the sunshine, but my courage failed me, for they had turned me into a docile creature with their cloying charity and sickening kindness. So I told lies, and I have told lies ever since. And there I stayed, ever so gentle and quiet, while I dreamed of hitting and biting.'

She paused and brushed her moist lips against Laurent's neck, then went on:

'I can't think now why I ever agreed to marry Camille. I didn't object, out of a sort of scornful indifference. The boy struck me as pitiable. When I played with him I could feel my fingers sink into his limbs as though they were putty. I took him because my aunt offered him, and I never intended to put myself out for him. . . . And in my husband I found the same sickly little boy I had already slept with at the age of six — just as fragile,

91

just as peevish, and still with the same stale smell of an invalid child that used to upset me so all those years ago. . . . I am telling you all this so that you won't be jealous. . . . A sort of nausea caught me in the throat as I remembered all the medicines I had swallowed, and I kept away from him and had some terrible nights. But you, you . . .'

She raised her body away from him, bending backwards, her fingers held in Laurent's strong hands, looking down on his broad shoulders and massive neck.

'You, well, I love you, and did the day Camille pushed you into the shop. You may not think anything of me, perhaps, because I gave myself all at once, body and soul. . . . Really I don't know how that happened. I am proud and violent, and I felt like hitting you that first day when you kissed me and threw me on to the floor in this very room. . . . I don't know how I loved you, it was more like hate. The sight of you infuriated me and I couldn't bear it; when you were there my nerves were strained to breaking point, my mind went blank, and I saw red. Oh, what a torture it was! And I went out of my way to meet this torture, I waited for you to come, moved round and round your chair so as to walk through your breath and brush my clothes along yours.

Your blood seemed to radiate warmth as I passed you, and it was this sort of cloud of fire surrounding you that drew me on and held me close to you in spite of all my inner resistance. . . . You remember when you were painting here: a sort of fate pulled me to your side, and I breathed your air with agonizing delight. I realized that it looked as though I was throwing myself in the way of your kisses, and I was ashamed of being enslaved. I felt I should collapse if you touched me. But I gave into my cowardice, shivering with cold while waiting for you to deign to take me in your arms.'

She stopped, gasping as though proud and avenged, holding Laurent, drunk with passion, on her breast. And in this bare and chilly room there were enacted scenes of burning lust, sinister in their brutality. Each fresh meeting brought still more frenzied ecstasies.

On her part she seemed to revel in daring and shamelessness. Not a single moment of hesitation or fear possessed her. She threw herself into adultery with a kind of furious honesty, flouting danger, and as it were, taking pride in doing so. When her lover was due to come, the only precaution she would take was to tell her aunt she was going upstairs to rest, but when he was up there she would walk about, talk, and behave in a normal manner, never bothering about avoiding noise. Sometimes, in the early days, Laurent was terrified.

'For God's sake,' he would whisper, 'don't make so much noise. Madame Raquin will come up.'

'Who cares?' she laughed. 'You're always all of a tremble. She is glued to her counter, so why should she come up here, do you think? She'd be too afraid of being robbed. . . . Besides, let her come up if she wants to. You can hide. To hell with her! I love you.'

These words hardly reassured Laurent, whose passion had not yet stifled his native peasant caution. But soon, out of force of habit, he accepted without undue terror the risks of these meetings in broad daylight, in Camille's room, a couple of yards from the old woman. His mistress kept on assuring him that danger passes by those who face up to it, and she was right. The lovers could never have found a safer place than this room where nobody would ever come looking for them. So there they satisfied their passion in unbelievable peace of mind.

And yet one day Madame Raquin did come up, fearing that her niece was ill, for she had been upstairs nearly three hours.

Thérèse carried her audacity to the point of not bolting the door between the bedroom and the dining-room.

When Laurent heard the old woman's heavy step on the wooden stairs he lost his head and began frantically looking for his waistcoat and hat. Thérèse began to laugh at the comic figure he was cutting. She seized him by the arm, bent him down at the foot of the bed, and whispered with perfect self-possession:

'Stay there . . . don't move.'

She threw over him all the male clothes that were lying about and spread on top of the lot a white petticoat she had taken off. This was done with deft and accurate movements and no loss of her calm. Then she lay down, with hair loose, half naked and still flushed and palpitating.

Madame Raquin opened the door quietly and tiptoed up to the bed. The younger woman pretended to be asleep. Under the white petticoat Laurent was in a sweat.

'Thérèse,' asked the old lady with some concern, 'are you ill, my dear?'

Thérèse opened her eyes, yawned, turned over, and answered in a plaintive tone that she had an atrocious migraine. She begged her aunt to let her sleep on. The old lady left as she had come, without making a sound.

The two lovers, quietly laughing, took each other again with passionate violence.

'So you see,' said Thérèse in triumph, 'there's nothing to be afraid of here. . . . All these folk are blind, they're not in love.'

Another day she had a queer idea. At times she acted as though she were mad and wandering in her mind.

François the tabby cat was sitting upright in the middle of the room. Dignified and motionless, he stared with his round eyes at the two lovers, appearing to examine them carefully, never blinking, lost in a kind of devilish ecstasy.

'Just look at François,' said Thérèse to Laurent; 'you'd think he understands and is going to tell Camille the whole story to-night. . . . I say, wouldn't it be funny if he started talking in the shop one of these days; he knows a thing or two about us.'

The idea that François might talk tickled the young woman mightily. Laurent looked at the cat's big green eyes and felt a shudder run through him.

'This is how he'd do it,' Thérèse went on. 'He'd stand up, and pointing one paw at me and the other at you, would call out: "Monsieur and Madame embrace each other very hard in the bedroom. They haven't both-ered about me at all, but as their criminal goings-on make me sick, will you please have them both put in prison and stop them upsetting my siesta!" '

Thérèse joked like a child, putting on cat-like movements, poking out her fingers like claws, and doing feline undulations with her shoulders. François remained as still as a statue and contemplated her. Only his eyes seemed alive, and two deep wrinkles at the corners of his mouth made him look like a stuffed animal suddenly grinning.

Laurent felt chilled to the bone. Thérèse's foolery struck him as ridiculous. He got up and put the cat out of the door. The truth was that he was scared. His mistress's hold on him was not yet complete, and there still remained some of the uneasiness he had felt when she had first kissed him.

8

Laurent's evenings in the shop were perfectly
happy. He usually came back from the office
with Camille. Madame Raquin had developed a motherly fondness for him, and knowing he was hard-up, underfed, and sleeping in
a garret, she had told him once and for all
that there would always be a place for him at
their table. She loved the fellow with that gar-
rulous affection old women show for people
from their old home who bring memories of
the past.

The young man freely availed himself of
this hospitality. After the office, and before
coming home with him, he would usually
take a turn along the river with Camille, and
this intimacy suited them both, for they felt
less dull as they strolled along and talked.
Then they would make up their minds to go
home and eat Madame Raquin's supper.
Laurent would open the shop door as
though he owned the place, straddle the
chairs, smoke and spit, in fact make himself
quite at home.

Thérèse's presence did not upset him in

the least. He treated her with straightforward friendliness, joked, paid her conventional compliments, without moving a muscle of his face. Camille laughed away, and as his wife only answered in monosyllables he firmly believed that they disliked each other. One day he even criticized Thérèse for what he called her coolness towards Laurent.

Laurent's guess had turned out to be correct: he was now the wife's lover, the husband's friend, and the mother's spoilt boy. Never before had he enjoyed such gratifications of his appetites; he basked in the endless delights supplied by the Raquin family. Moreoever his position in the family was quite normal, he thought; he felt neither anger nor remorse as he talked to Camille in the language of intimate friendship. He did not even watch his words and gestures, so certain was he of his own prudence and self-control, for the selfishness with which he enjoyed his bliss saved him from making any slip. In the shop his mistress simply became a woman like any other, whom you did not kiss and who meant nothing to you. The reason why he did not kiss her in front of everybody was simply that he was afraid of not being allowed to come any more, and that was all that stopped him. Apart from that he would not have cared two pins about hurting Camille and his mother. What the discovery of his liaison might lead to never entered his head. He simply thought he was acting as anybody else would have done in his position, namely as a poor and hungry man. Hence his blissful tranquillity, prudent audacities, and detached and facetious attitudes.

Thérèse, more highly-strung and nervous, was obliged to play a part, and she played it to perfection, thanks to the cunning hypocrisy with which her upbringing had endowed her. For close on fifteen years she had lied, repressing her burning desires and devoting her implacable will-power to appearing outwardly dull and half-awake. With only a slight effort she could assume the death-mask that froze her face. When Laurent came in it was to find her serious, sullen, longer-nosed and thinner-lipped than ever, looking ugly, ill-tempered, and unapproachable. She did not overdo her effects, however, but played her usual part and avoided calling attention to herself by more marked surliness. For her part, she derived a bitter enjoyment from deceiving Camille and Madame Raquin. She did not wallow in the complete satisfaction of her desires with no thought for duty, as Laurent did, but on the contrary she knew she was doing wrong, and felt wild urges to rise from the table and kiss Laurent full on the lips to show her husband and aunt that she was not just a silly gawk, but had a lover.

At times waves of excitement went to her head, and good actress though she was she could not then help bursting into song, so long as her lover was not present and she was not afraid of giving herself away. These sudden fits of mirth delighted Madame Raquin, who accused her niece of being too serious. Thérèse bought pots of flowers for the window of her room and had the walls repapered, and she wanted a carpet, curtains, and rosewood furniture, all for Laurent.

Nature and circumstances seemed to have made this woman for this man and to have thrust them in each other's way. Between them, with her nervous tension and hypocrisy and his sanguine nature and animal existence, they made a couple held together by powerful bonds, for they completed and protected each other. As they sat at the table in the evenings in the pale lamplight, the strength of their alliance could be judged by the solid, smiling face of Laurent opposite the mute, impenetrable mask of Thérèse.

Those were cosy, quiet evenings, with friendly talk breaking the silence in the soft, warm shadows. When the meal was over they drew closer together round the table and chattered about the day's countless little bits of news, memories of yesterday, and hopes for tomorrow. Camille loved Laurent as much as he was capable of loving anybody in his smug, self-centred way, and Laurent seemed to return quite as much affection; indeed between them there was a constant exchange of protestations of loyalty, kindly acts, and understanding looks. In this tranquil atmosphere Madame Raquin, with her placid face, spread her own peacefulness among her children. You would have thought it was a gathering of old friends who knew the very secrets of each other's hearts and who confidently entrusted themselves to the good faith of their friendship.

As motionless and peaceful as the others, Thérèse looked on at these respectable pleasures and smiling relaxations, but inwardly laughed savagely and jeered at them with all her being, while keeping her cold, impassive face. She reminded herself, with exquisite pleasure, that a few hours earlier she had been in the next room, lying half-naked and dishevelled on Laurent's breast; she recalled every detail of the afternoon's wild passion and dwelt on them one by one in her memory, contrasting that thrilling orgy with the dead-and-alive scene before her eyes. Ah, how she was deceiving these worthy souls, and how happy she was to deceive them with such triumphant impudence! And just over there, a yard or two away, on the other side of that thin partition, she regularly had a man, she wallowed in the delicious agonies of adultery. And now her lover was pretending to be a stranger, some friend of her husband's, some poor fool of a visitor from outside who was no concern of hers. This atrocious farce, these deceptions, this comparison between the burning embraces of the day and the assumed indifference of the evening, made her blood tingle anew.

If Madame Raquin and Camille happened to go downstairs, Thérèse would leap up and without making a sound crush her lover's lips beneath her own with brutal energy, and there she would stay, gasping and unable to breathe, until she heard the creak of the wooden stairs. Then with a swift movement she would resume her former position and put on her impenetrable face again, while Laurent would calmly take up the conversation with Camille where it had broken off. It was like a lightning flash of passion, swift and blinding in a leaden sky.

On Thursdays the evening was a little more lively. These evening parties bored Laurent to death, but he made a point of never missing one, for as a precaution he wanted to be known and respected by Camille's friends. So he had to listen to the drivelling tales of Grivet and old Michaud; Michaud always told the same stories of murder and theft, while Grivet held forth about his underlings and superiors in the department. The young man sought refuge with Olivier and Suzanne, whose idiocy struck him as less appalling. And he asked for the dominoes as quickly as possible.

It was on Thursday evenings that Thérèse arranged the days and times of their next meetings. During the confusion of leaving, while Madame Raquin and Camille were escorting the departing guests to the door, she would sidle up to Laurent, whisper and squeeze his hand. Sometimes, when everybody's back was turned, she would even kiss him, out of a sort of bravado.

This life of alternating excitement and calm went on for eight months. The lovers lived in perfect bliss. Thérèse was no longer bored, and had nothing left to wish for; Laurent, sated, coddled, heavier than ever, had only one fear, that this delectable existence might come to an end.

9

One afternoon, as Laurent was on the point of leaving his office to hurry off to Thérèse, who was expecting him, he was summoned to see his chief, who told him that from then onwards no time off would be allowed. He had been having far too much leave of absence, and the company was determined to dismiss him if he ever took time off again.

And so, tied to his stool, he fumed in despair until evening. He had to earn his living, he could not risk the sack. That evening Thérèse's angry face was a torment. He did not know how to explain his broken promise, but while Camille was shutting the shop he darted up to her:

'We can't see each other any more,' he whispered, 'my boss won't give me any more time off.'

Camille was already coming back. Laurent had to go without any further explanation, leaving Thérèse staggered by this curt statement. Exasperated and refusing to admit that her pleasures could be upset, she spent a sleepless night turning over plans for impossible assignations. On the following Thursday she only had a minute's talk with Laurent at the most. They were all the more on edge because they had no idea where they could meet to talk things over and come to some arrangement. She made a new appointment with her lover, and for the second time he failed to keep it. From then on she was obsessed with a single idea: to see him at all costs.

Laurent had not been able to come anywhere near Thérèse for a fortnight, and he realized how necessary this woman had become to him; habits of lust had created new appetites, sharp and imperative ones. He had long ceased to feel any misgivings while in his mistress's arms, and now he sought her embraces with the pertinacity of a famished animal. A deep-seated lust had been dormant in his system, and now that he was deprived of his woman this passion burst forth with blind fury: he loved to the point of frenzy. In his sanguine animal nature everything seemed to be unconscious; he obeyed his instincts and let himself be dictated to by the demands of his body. A year before he would have burst out laughing if he had been told that he would be so enslaved by a woman that it threatened his comfort. All unrecognized, the hidden forces of lust had worked away within him until they had subjected him, bound hand and foot, to Thérèse's fierce caresses. And now he was afraid of forgetting prudence, and dared not go to the Passage du Pont-Neuf for fear of doing something rash. He was no longer in control of himself, for little by little his mistress, with her cat-like suppleness and sinewy flexibility, had worked her way into every fibre of his being. For him this woman was a necessity of life, like food and drink.

He would certainly have done something silly had he not received a letter from Thérèse asking him to stay indoors the following evening. She promised to come at about eight.

When they came out of the office he got rid of Camille, alleging that he was tired and going straight home to bed. Similarly Thérèse played her part after dinner, mentioned a customer who had moved away without paying, and acted the part of the relentless creditor, declaring that she was going to demand her money. The customer lived in the Batignolles district. Madame Raquin and Camille thought it was a long journey with little chance of success, but they were not surprised, and let Thérèse go without demur.

She rushed to the Port aux Vins, slipping on the wet cobbles, colliding with passers-by, bent on getting there quickly. Her face was moist and her hands burning; she might have been drunk. She was breathless and wild-eyed by the time she reached the sixth floor and saw Laurent leaning over the banisters, waiting for her.

She went into his garret, which was so narrow that her wide skirt more than filled it. With one hand she tore off her hat, and leaned almost swooning against the bed.

Through the open skylight the cool evening air poured down on the burning couch. The lovers stayed there a long time, as though in the depths of some cave. Suddenly Thérèse heard the Pitié clock strike ten. She would have liked to be deaf, but she struggled unwillingly to her feet and looked round the garret, which she had not yet seen. She found her hat, tied the ribbons, and then sat down, saying dolefully:

'I must go.'

But Laurent was on his knees before her, taking her hands in his.

'See you sometime,' she said, but she did not move.

'No, not sometime,' he cried, 'that's too vague. What day will you come again?'

She looked him in the eyes.

'Do you want the truth? Well, I don't really think I shall be here again. I've no excuse, and I can't invent one.'

'Then we must say good-bye.'

'No. That I won't do!'

She said this with terrified anger; then added in a softer voice, without knowing what she was saying, and without rising from her chair:

'I am going.'

Laurent was preoccupied. He was thinking about Camille.

'I have nothing against him,' he finally said, without naming him, 'but he really is too much of a nuisance. . . . Couldn't you get him out of our way, send him on a journey, anywhere, so long as it's a long way away?'

'Send him on a journey, I like that!' she shook her head. 'Do you think a man like that agrees to go on journeys? There is only one journey you don't come back from. . . . But no, he will bury us all; these people always at their last gasp never die.'

There was a silence. Laurent dragged himself closer on his knees, holding her tight, with his head on her breast.

'I had been letting myself dream,' he said; 'I wanted to spend a whole night with you, and go off to sleep in your arms and be

awakened in the morning by your kisses. . . .
I would like to be your husband. . . . You understand, don't you?'

'Yes, yes,' she answered, shuddering.

And she suddenly bent over Laurent's
face and covered it with kisses. The ribbons
of her hat scratched against his stiff beard;
she forgot that she was fully dressed and
would crease her clothes, but sobbed, and
gasped through her tears:

'Don't say things like that, or I shall never
find the strength to go, but shall stay here.
No, you must give me courage — say that we
shall see each other again. You need me,
don't you? And some day we shall find a way
to be together for good.'

'Well, then, come back; come back tomorrow,' said Laurent, whose hands were
shaking as they crept up her body.

'But I can't. I've told you already, there's
no excuse.'

And she went on, wringing her hands.

'Oh, it's not the scandal I'm afraid of. If
you like, as soon as I get home I'll tell
Camille that you are my lover and then
come back here for the night. . . . But it's
you I'm worrying about; I don't want to
upset your life, I want to make it happy.'

The young man's instinctive prudence
came back into play.

'You are right,' he said, 'we mustn't act like children. Oh, if only your husband were to die. . . .'

'If my husband were to die,' she slowly repeated.

'We could get married, have nothing more to be afraid of and enjoy each other to our hearts' content. What a lovely, sweet life it would be!'

But she leapt to her feet. The colour had drained from her cheeks. She studied her lover with dull eyes; her lips were twitching.

'People do sometimes die,' she finally murmured, 'only it's dangerous for the survivors.'

No answer from Laurent.

'You see,' she went on, 'none of the known ways are any good.'

'You didn't get my meaning,' he said calmly. 'I'm not a fool, and I want to love you, in peace. . . . I was thinking that accidents happen every day, a foot may slip, a tile may fall . . . see what I mean? In that case the only guilty party is the wind.'

His voice sounded strange. He smiled and added in caressing tones:

'Now don't you worry. We shall love each other all right, and live happily. As you can't come to me, I shall fix things up somehow. If we go for months without seeing each other, don't forget me, but remember that I am working for our happiness.'

As she was opening the door to go, he seized her in his arms.

'You do belong to me, don't you?' he went on. 'You swear to give yourself, body and soul, any time I want you?'

'Yes,' she cried, 'I belong to you, do what you like with me.'

For a moment they stood there, fierce and silent. Then she tore herself away, and without looking back ran out of the room and down the stairs. Laurent listened until her footsteps died away.

When there was nothing more to be heard he went back and threw himself on to the bed. The sheets were still warm. This narrow cell, still filled with the heat of her passion, stifled him. He still seemed to be breathing something of her; she had, as she passed, permeated everything with her penetrating scent of violets, and now all that was left to hold in his arms was the intangible phantom of his mistress writhing round him and burning him with renewed and unsatisfied lust. He left his skylight open, hoping for some cool air as he lay on his back, with arms bare and hands open, turning over his thoughts as he looked at the dark blue square of sky framed by the opening.

Until dawn the same idea went round and round in his mind. Before Thérèse had come he had never thought of murdering Camille, but now, under the pressure of facts, exasperated by the thought that he might never see his mistress again, he had put this man's death into words. Thus it was that a new corner of his unconscious nature had been revealed: in the frenzy of adultery he had begun to entertain the thought of murder.

Calmer now, and alone in the peaceful night, he examined the question of murder. The idea of death, thrown off wildly between two kisses, now came back with implacable clarity. Racked by insomnia and tormented by the pungent scent left by Thérèse, Laurent was now setting traps, working out the chances of a mishap, going over the advantages he would reap from being a murderer.

All his interests urged him into crime. He reflected that his father, the Jeufosse peasant, was in no hurry to die, and that he might have to stay on in a job for another ten years, eating in coffee-shops and living womanless in a garret. And it was an infuriating thought. On the other hand, with

Camille dead he was at once Thérèse's husband, Madame Raquin's heir, had left his job, and was free to bask in the sun. Thereupon he gave himself up to the pleasure of dreaming of this lazy life, with nothing to do but eat and sleep and quietly wait for his father's death. But when reality stood out in the midst of this dream he came up against Camille, and he clenched his fists as if to knock him down.

Laurent desired Thérèse; he wanted her to himself and always at hand. Unless he removed the husband the wife slipped from his grasp. She could not come back; she had said so herself. Of course he might have kidnapped her and taken her off somewhere, but in that case they would die of starvation. No, it was less risky to kill the husband; no scandal would be raised, he would merely be pushing one man out of the way so as to take his place. His brutal peasant logic found this method excellent and natural, and his native prudence, even, recommended the speedy way.

He lay sprawling on his bed, sweating, flat on his stomach with his greasy face buried in the pillow where Thérèse's hair had been. He took the linen between his parched lips and inhaled its faint perfume, and there he remained, breathless and gasping, while

114

bars of fire darted across his closed eyelids. How could he kill Camille? Then, when he could breathe no more, he turned over again in one bound on to his back, and with eyes wide open and the cold air blowing on his face from the skylight, searched among the stars in the blue-black square of sky for some advice on killing, some plan for murder.

None came. As he had said to his mistress, he was not a child or a fool, and he would have nothing to do with daggers or poison. He wanted something subtle, with no risk attached to it, some sort of sinister snuffing-out, with no cry, no terror, just a simple disappearance. However fiercely passion might shake him and thrust him onwards, his whole being insisted upon caution. He was too soft and comfort-loving to jeopardize his tranquillity. He was considering murder in order to get a quiet and happy life.

Gradually sleep overcame him. The cold air had blown the warm, scented ghost of Thérèse out of the garret, and now, exhausted but relieved, he let a kind of soft and vague numbness steal over him. As he was dropping off, he decided to wait for a favourable opportunity, and in his last moments of fleeting consciousness he was lulled by the thought: 'I'll kill him, I'll kill him.' Five minutes later he was at rest, breathing with serene regularity.

Thérèse had reached home at eleven without ever realizing how she got to the Passage du Pont-Neuf, for her head was on fire and her mind strained to breaking-point. She felt she was still running down Laurent's stairs, for the words she had heard were still echoing in her ears. Madame Raquin and Camille were anxious and fussing, but she answered their questions curtly, saying she had been on a fruitless errand and had stood for an hour on the pavement waiting for a bus.

When she got into bed the sheets struck cold and damp. Her feverish body shivered with distaste. Camille went straight off to sleep and for a long time she looked at the pasty face resting stupid and gaping on the pillow. She drew away, for she felt an urge to push her clenched fist into his mouth.

10

Nearly three weeks went by. Laurent came back to the shop every evening; he looked worn and ill, with faint bluish circles round his eyes, and his lips were colourless and chapped. However, he was still heavy and stolid, still looked Camille straight in the eyes and treated him in the same open friendly way. Madame Raquin's kindly attentions to the friend of the family had redoubled since she had noticed him sinking into a sort of sleepy sickness.

Thérèse had put on her silent and sulky mask again, and was more motionless, inscrutable, and tranquil than ever. You would have said that Laurent did not exist as far as she was concerned; she scarcely gave him a glance and seldom spoke to him, treating him with complete indifference. Madame Raquin's kind heart was hurt by this attitude, and she sometimes said to the young man: 'Don't take any notice of my niece's unfriendliness. I know her, and if her face seems cold she has a warm heart, full of every sort of affection and kindness.'

The lovers had no more meetings. Since the evening in the rue Saint-Victor they had not been alone together. In the evenings when they sat opposite each other, to all appearances indifferent strangers, tempests of passion, fear, and desire raged beneath the untroubled surface of their faces. Thérèse had fits of temper, cowardice, or cruel sarcasm, and Laurent times of sombre brutality or agonizing indecision. They dared not peer down into their own natures, down into the feverish confusion that filled their minds with a kind of dense, acrid mist.

When they had a chance, behind a door, they silently clutched each other's hands almost to breaking-point in a rough, hurried embrace, as though they would have liked to tear off bits of each other's flesh in their fingers. For this gripping of hands was the only way they had left of appeasing their desires. They put their whole bodies into it. They asked for nothing else. They were biding their time.

One Thursday evening, before they sat down to play, the Raquins' guests had their usual little gossip. One of the great topics was to talk to old Michaud about his former duties and draw him out on the subject of the strange and sinister adventures he must have been involved in. Grivet and Camille would then listen to the tales of the ex-superintendent with the scared and gaping expression of children listening to *Bluebeard* or *Tom Thumb*. It was both terrifying and entertaining.

On that particular evening, having recounted a horrible murder with details that had given his audience the creeps, Michaud added with a shake of the head:

'And a great deal never comes out at all. . . . How many crimes remain undiscovered! How many murderers escape human punishment!'

'What!' said Grivet in amazement, 'do you really believe there are foul creatures at large in the streets who have committed murder and not been arrested?'

Olivier smiled superciliously.

'My dear sir,' he said in his crushing tone, 'if they have not been arrested it means that they are not suspected of being murderers.'

This argument did not seem to convince Grivet. Camille came to his rescue.

'I share the opinion of Monsieur Grivet,' he said pompously. 'I like to be able to think we are efficiently policed and that I shall never rub shoulders with a murderer on the pavement.'

Olivier interpreted these words as a personal attack.

'Of course the police are efficient,' he exclaimed in hurt tones. 'But we really can't do the impossible. There are criminals who have learned crime at the devil's own school and would escape from God himself. Don't you think so, Father?'

'Yes, yes,' old Michaud agreed. 'Now when I was at Vernon — perhaps you will recollect this, Madame Raquin — a carter was done to death on the main road. The corpse was found in a ditch, hacked to pieces. The criminal has never been run to earth. He is still alive today, perhaps he is a neighbour of ours, and perhaps Monsieur Grivet will run into him on his way home.'

Grivet went as white as a sheet. He dared not look round for fear that the carter's murderer was behind him. But all the same, fear was a delicious sensation.

'Oh, no, really!' he stammered, not quite knowing what he was saying; 'really, no, I won't believe that. . . . I know a story too. Once there was a servant who was imprisoned for having stolen some table silver from her employers. Two months later they were felling a tree and found the silver in a magpie's nest. The thief was a magpie! The servant was released. . . . So you see the guilty are always punished,' he ended triumphantly.

'And so,' sneered Olivier, 'the magpie was put in prison.'

'That's not what Monsier Grivet meant,' Camille chimed in, annoyed to see his chief being laughed at. . . . 'Give us the dominoes, Mother.'

While Madame Raquin was away getting the box, the young man went on, addressing Michaud:

'So you admit the police are powerless! There are murderers walking about in broad daylight!'

'Oh yes, unfortunately,' answered the superintendent.

'It's immoral,' concluded Grivet.

During this conversation Thérèse and Laurent had kept quiet. They had not even smiled at Grivet's silliness. They sat with elbows on the table, slightly pale, with expressionless eyes, listening. But once their eyes had met, dark and blazing. And little beads of sweat formed at the roots of Thérèse's hair, and icy draughts sent imperceptible shivers down Laurent's skin.

11

Sometimes on a fine Sunday Camille forced Thérèse to go out with him for a little walk in the Champs-Élysées. She would rather have stayed in the damp and dark shop, for she got tired and bored with being dragged along the pavements on her husband's arm, having to stop in front of shop windows with silly wonderment, silly comments, and silly silences. But Camille insisted, for he loved showing off his wife, and when he met one of his colleagues, especially one of the chiefs, he was proud to exchange greetings while escorting his lady. Then, too, he walked for the sake of walking, hardly saying a word, stiff and unnatural in his Sunday best, dawdling, brainless, and vain. Thérèse hated being arm in arm with such a man.

When they were going out, Madame Raquin accompanied her children to the end of the Passage, then kissed them goodbye as though they were setting out on a long journey, with endless advice, urgent warnings.

'Above all,' she would say, 'do be careful

about accidents . . . this city of Paris is so full of traffic! Promise me you won't get into a crowd.'

At last she let them go, but stood watching them for a long time. Then back she went to the shop, for her legs were getting bad and prevented her walking any distance.

Sometimes, on rare occasions, the couple went out of Paris, to Saint-Ouen or Asnières, and had a meal of fried fish in one of the riverside restaurants. These were high days and holidays, and were discussed for a month beforehand. Thérèse agreed more readily, indeed almost joyfully, to these outings which kept her in the open air until ten or eleven at night. Saint-Ouen with its green islands reminded her of Vernon, for it stirred into new life the wild love of the Seine which had possessed her when she was a girl. She would sit on the shingle and dip her hands into the water, and in the blazing sun, tempered by cool breezes from beneath the shady trees, she felt she was alive. While she tore and dirtied her dress on stones and mud, Camille would daintily spread out his handkerchief and squat beside her, taking infinite precautions. Recently they had almost always taken Laurent with them, and he enlivened the outings with his laughter and peasant vitality.

One Sunday, Camille, Thérèse, and Laurent set out for Saint-Ouen about eleven, after an early lunch. The excursion had been planned for a long time, and was to be the last of the season. Autumn was on the way, and in the evenings cold winds made the air quite shivery.

On this particular morning the sky still had all its blue serenity, and it was hot in the sun and quite warm in the shade. It was decided that they must take advantage of the last rays of summer.

The three got into a cab, to the accompaniment of moanings and fussy forebodings from the old lady. They crossed Paris, got out of the cab when they reached the fortifications, and then made for Saint-Ouen by the road. It was noon, and the dusty road, fully exposed to the sun, was as blindingly white as snow. The scorching air was heavy and caught the throat. Thérèse trotted along on Camille's arm, sheltering under her sunshade whilst her husband fanned his face with a huge handkerchief. Laurent brought up the rear, and though the sun shone straight on his neck he seemed quite unaffected as he whistled and kicked the stones, but now and again there was a fierce glint in his eyes as he watched his mistress's swinging hips.

When they reached Saint-Ouen they began at once to look for a clump of trees and a carpet of green grass in the shade. They crossed to an island and plunged into a copse. Dead leaves covered the ground with a russet carpet that rustled crisply underfoot. The tree-trunks rose upwards like clustered Gothic columns and the branches came down as low as their foreheads, so that all they could see was the coppery vault of dying leaves and the black and white shafts of the aspens and oaks. They were in the wilds, in a melancholy retreat, a narrow, silent, cool glade. Round them on all sides was the murmuring of the Seine.

Camille had selected a dry spot and sat down, after lifting his coat-tails. Thérèse had thrown herself down on the leaves with much rustling of skirts, and lay half buried in the folds of her dress, which went up all round her, showing one of her legs up to the knee. Laurent, lying flat on his stomach with his chin buried in the ground, looked at this leg as he listened to his friend holding forth against the government, declaring that all the islands in the Seine ought to be turned into parks, with seats, gravel paths, and clipped trees, like the Tuileries.

They stayed in this woodland spot for nearly three hours, waiting for the sun to get less hot so that they could go on a country ramble before dinner. Camille talked away about his office and told feeble stories, and then he grew somnolent, lay back and went off to sleep, having first covered his eyes with his hat. For some time Thérèse had been pretending to be asleep, with closed eyes.

Thereupon Laurent stealthily crept towards her, thrust out his lips and kissed her shoe and ankle. The leather and the white stocking burned his mouth as he kissed them. The sharp scent of the earth mingled with the faint perfume from Thérèse ran through him, kindling his blood and exacerbating his nerves. For a month past his life had been infuriatingly chaste, and this walk in the sun along the Saint-Ouen road had set him on fire. And now here he was, buried in a hidden retreat, deep amid the sensual shade and silence, yet unable to hold close to his heart the woman who was already his. Her husband might wake up and see them, and all his prudent calculations would be foiled. Always the obstacle was this man. And so the lover, flat on the ground and hidden by her skirts, lay shaking with exasperation as he pressed silent kisses upon the shoe and white stocking. Thérèse might have been dead for all the movement she made. Laurent thought she was asleep.

He stood up and leaned against a tree, for his back ached. And then he saw her staring up into the air with wide, shining eyes. Her face, framed by her raised arms, looked white, matt, stiff, and cold. She was lost in thought. Her staring eyes were like a dark chasm in which nothing but blackness could be seen. She never moved or looked towards Laurent standing beside her.

Her lover studied her and was almost frightened to see how impassively she received his caresses. Her dead-white face, floating among the billows of her skirts, filled him with a sort of panic mingled with keen desire. He would have liked to stoop and close those great open eyes with a kiss. But Camille was sleeping there too, almost lying on her dress. The poor creature, with his twisted body and looking so skinny, was gently snoring, his face half covered by his hat, below which could be seen an open mouth distorted by sleep into a stupid grimace; the pasty flesh of his girlish chin was flecked by a sparse gingerish stubble, and as his head was thrown backwards his wrinkled and scrawny neck could be seen, in the middle of which his prominent, brick-red Adam's apple bobbed up and down with each snore. Lying sprawled out like that, Camille was exasperating and contemptible.

Laurent, looking at him, suddenly lifted his foot. He would smash in that face with one jab of his heel.

Thérèse stifled a cry, went white, and shut her eyes. She turned her face away as if to avoid being splashed by the blood.

But Laurent remained like that for several seconds, with his heel poised above the face of the sleeping Camille. Then he slowly brought his leg down and moved a few paces away. He had realized that that would be a fool's way of committing murder. That smashed-in head would have put the police force on his trail. The only object in getting rid of Camille was to marry Thérèse, for he meant to live on quite openly, when once the murder was committed, like the carter's murderer in old Michaud's story.

He moved to the water's edge and stared vacantly at the river flowing by. Then suddenly he went back into the copse. At last he had hit on a plan, invented a simple murder free of danger to himself.

He woke up the sleeping man by tickling his nose with a straw. Camille sneezed and got up, thinking it a great joke. He liked Laurent for these funny tricks that made him laugh. He then shook his wife, who was still keeping her eyes shut, and when Thérèse had got to her feet and shaken the dead leaves off her creased skirt, the three of them made their way out of the clearing, snapping the twigs as they went.

Leaving the island, they wandered off along roads and paths crowded with parties in their Sunday best. Girls in gay-coloured frocks ran along between hedges, a crew of oarsmen sang as they passed, processions of worthy couples, elderly folk, office workers and their wives sauntered along beside the ditches. Every path seemed to be a noisy and populous street. Only the sun sinking towards the horizon kept its spacious tranquillity as it cast immense sheets of pale light on the reddening trees and white roads. A penetrating chill was beginning to come down from the quivering sky.

Camille no longer had Thérèse on his arm, for he was chatting to Laurent, laughing at his friend's jokes and feats of strength as he jumped over ditches or lifted big boulders. The young woman walked on the other side of the road, head forward, stooping now and again to pick a blade of grass. When she found herself behind she would stop and look from a distance at her husband and her lover.

'Hallo, aren't you hungry?' Camille shouted back at length.

'Of course I am,' she replied.

'Well, come on then!'

She was not hungry, but she was tired and uneasy. She did not know what was in Laurent's mind, and she was so apprehensive that her legs were giving way beneath her.

The three went back to the water front and looked for a restaurant. They took a table on a sort of wooden terrace belonging to an eating-house that reeked of fat and wine. The place was full of shouting, singing, and the clatter of crockery, and in each private and public dining-room there was some club outing or other shouting away, and the thin partitions added a vibrating sonority to the din. The stairs shook as the waiters ran up.

Out on the terrace the river breezes dispelled the odours of burnt fat. Thérèse leaned over the balustrade and looked at the river front. To right and left stretched a double row of cafés and booths, and looking through the scant yellow foliage you could make out bits of white tablecloth, black coats, and bright coloured skirts; people were going up and down bareheaded, running and laughing, and the dismal strains of the barrel organ were mingled with the bawling of the crowd. A smell of fried fish and dust hung in the still air.

Below Thérèse some tarts from the Latin Quarter were dancing in a ring on a worn patch of grass, singing a nursery round. Their hats slipped to their shoulders, their hair had come down, and they were holding hands, playing like little girls. They seemed to have recovered a note or two of their childish voices, and on their pallid faces, crushed by brutish kisses, glowed delicate virgin blushes. Their wide open, brazen eyes were shining with sentimental moisture. Some students, smoking their clay pipes, were watching their gyrations and throwing in a few suggestive remarks.

And beyond all this the serene beauty of evening was falling over the Seine and its hills, vague bluish vapours bathing the trees in transparent mist.

'Well,' Laurent shouted down the staircase, 'waiter, what about our dinner?'

Then, as if changing his mind:

'I say, Camille, suppose we go for a row before we start the meal? That would give them time to roast the chicken for us. We can't just do nothing for an hour while we wait.'

'Just as you like,' Camille answered without enthusiasm; 'but Thérèse is hungry.'

'No, no, I can wait,' she said hastily, for Laurent was looking hard at her.

They all went down again. As they passed the counter they booked a table and settled the menu, saying that they would be back in an hour. As the landlord also hired out boats they asked him to come and unfasten one. Laurent chose a narrow skiff which terrified Camille by its fragility.

'The devil!' he said; 'we musn't move about in that thing. We should have a lovely dip if we did.'

The truth of the matter was that he was horribly afraid of water. At Vernon when he was a child his delicate health had not allowed him to go paddling in the Seine, and when his school-friends dashed off and dived straight into the river he lay down between two warm blankets. Laurent had become a daring swimmer and indefatigable oarsman, but Camille had kept the terror that women and children have of deep water. So he tapped one end of the boat with his foot as though to test its strength.

'Come on, get in,' laughed Laurent. 'You're always nervous.'

Camille stepped over the side, staggered along, and took a seat in the stern. When he could feel a floor beneath him he put on a confident air and cracked jokes to show how brave he was.

Thérèse had stayed on the bank, solemn

and still beside her lover as he held the painter. He stooped and whispered rapidly, 'Now be careful, I'm going to throw him in. Just do as I say . . . I'll see to everything.'

She went horribly pale and stood there as though rooted to the ground. Her body stiffened and her eyes were staring.

'Come on, get in the boat,' Laurent murmured.

She did not move. A terrible battle was raging inside her. With all her strength she strained her will-power, for she was afraid of bursting into tears and falling to the ground.

'Aha!' shouted Camille. 'Laurent, just look at Thérèse. She's the one who's afraid! Will she? won't she?'

He had now spread himself on the stern seat, with his elbows on the sides of the boat, and was lolling about and showing off. Thérèse gave him a strange look; the poor creature's sneers acted like a whip and lashed her into making up her mind. She suddenly jumped into the boat, but stayed in the bows. Laurent took the oars, the boat left the bank and slowly headed for the islands.

Dusk was falling. The trees cast great shadows and the water was black near the banks. In midstream there were broad trails of pale silver. Soon they were in the middle of the Seine, and from there all the noises on the shore sounded faint, and the singing and shouting, by the time it reached them, was vague and melancholy, muted and sad. No more smells of frying and dust; the air blew fresh, and it was chilly.

Laurent stopped rowing and let the boat drift with the current. Before them rose the great russet mass of the islands. The two banks, dark brown flecked with grey, stretched away like two broad bands that joined on the horizon. Water and sky looked as though they had been cut out of the same whitish material. Nothing is more depressingly calm than an autumn twilight. The sun's rays shine palely in the chilly air, the aged trees shed their leaves. The countryside, dried up by the hot summer days, feels death approaching with the first cold winds as they mournfully sing in the sky of the end of hope. Night comes down from above bearing shrouds in its shadows.

They fell silent, all three. Sitting in the drifting boat they watched the last gleams leave the topmost branches. The islands were drawing near. The great russet masses were darkening, and now with the coming of dusk the whole landscape was becoming simpler: the Seine, the sky, the islands, and the hills were now nothing but brown and grey shapes disappearing into a milky haze.

Camille, who by now was lying flat on his belly with his head dangling over the water, dipped his hands into the stream.

'Golly, it isn't half cold!' he cried. 'It wouldn't be very nice to take a header into that brew.'

Laurent made no answer. For a minute or two he had been anxiously scanning both banks. His big hands came forward on to his knees and his lips tightened. Thérèse sat stiff and motionless with her head slightly back, waiting.

The boat was about to drift into a narrow, dark channel between two islands. From the further side of one of them came the distant song of a boat's crew who must be rowing upstream. Behind them the river was empty.

At that moment Laurent stood up and put his arms round Camille's waist. The latter burst out laughing.

'No, don't, you're tickling me. No funny tricks. Look here, that'll do, you'll make me fall in.'

Laurent tightened his grip and gave a jerk. Camille turned and saw the terrible expression on his friend's face, which was contracted with hate. Without quite under-

135

standing, he was seized with a vague fear. He wanted to shout out, but a brutal hand closed round his throat. With the instinct of an animal at bay he got to his knees and clung to the side of the boat. For some seconds he continued to struggle in this way.

'Thérèse! Thérèse!' he appealed in muffled, hissing tones.

She looked on, clinging with both hands to a seat of the creaking, dancing boat. She could not shut her eyes, for an awful muscular stiffness kept them wide open and staring at the horrible struggle. She was rigid and speechless.

'Thérèse! Thérèse!' the wretched man called again, now at his last gasp.

The final appeal made Thérèse burst into sobs. Her nerves gave way and the paroxysm she had dreaded threw her to the bottom of the boat, where she lay in a heap, twitching and half-dead.

Meanwhile Laurent was still tugging at Camille, with one hand closed round his throat. He finally wrenched him away from the boat with his other hand and held him poised like a child in his strong outstretched arms. As Laurent's head was thrown back, leaving his neck exposed, his victim, crazed with terror, twisted round, bent forward, and sank his teeth into it. The murderer stifled a howl of pain and hurled Camille into the river, but the teeth tore off a fragment of flesh.

Camille fell with a shriek. He came to the surface two or three times, but his cries were fainter each time.

Laurent did not waste a second. He turned up his coat collar to hide the wound and then taking the unconscious Thérèse in his arms, capsized the boat with a kick, and fell into the Seine. He held her above water and shouted for help in heartrending tones.

The rowers whom he had heard singing beyond the point of the island came up at full speed. They realized that there had been a mishap and rescued Thérèse, whom they laid on a seat, and Laurent, who started bitterly lamenting his friend's death. He jumped back into the water, he hunted for Camille in places where he could not possibly be, he came back in tears, wringing his hands and tearing his hair. They tried to calm and console him.

'It's all my fault,' he moaned; 'I never ought to have let the poor chap dance about as he was doing. All three of us got together on the same side of the boat at the same time, and we capsized. . . . As he fell in he begged me to save his wife.'

As always happens in such cases, two or three of the young fellows in the boating party claimed to have witnessed the accident.

'Oh yes, we saw you,' they said, 'and, God knows, a rowing-boat isn't as firm as a floor. . . . Oh, poor little thing, what an awful awakening she is in for!'

They took up their oars again, and with the other boat in tow took Thérèse and Laurent back to the restaurant where their dinner was ready. In no time at all the whole of Saint-Ouen knew about the accident. The young men gave eye-witness descriptions. A sympathetic crowd stood outside.

The proprietor and his wife were kindly folk and they put their wardrobe at the disposal of the victims. When Thérèse came to she had a fit of hysterics, uttering piercing screams, and had to be put to bed. Thus nature herself added her share to the sinister performance that had been staged.

When Thérèse had calmed down Laurent entrusted her to the restaurant people, for he intended to return to Paris alone in order to break the dreadful news to Madame Raquin with the utmost tact and consideration. The truth of the matter was that he was afraid of Thérèse's excitable condition, and he preferred to give her time to think things over and study her part.

It was the boating party that ate Camille's dinner.

12

In the dark corner of the omnibus taking him back to Paris, Laurent put the finishing touches to his plan. He was almost sure he could escape undetected, and was filled with that grim joy tinged with anxiety, the joy of crime accomplished. At the Clichy barrier he changed into a cab and had himself driven to old Michaud's in the rue de Seine. By then it was nine in the evening.

He found the ex-superintendent at table with Olivier and Suzanne. His reason for going there was to cover himself if suspicion lighted on him, and also to avoid having to go and tell Madame Raquin the awful story himself. He had a strange dread of this meeting, expecting such an intensity of sorrow that he was afraid he would not put enough tears into his own performance; and besides, this grief of a mother was painful even though he was not deeply concerned.

There was a question in Michaud's eyes as he saw Laurent come in wearing rough garments much too small for him. Laurent told him about the accident in a broken voice as though gasping with grief and exhaustion.

'And so I have come to you,' he concluded, 'because I didn't know what to do about these two poor women so cruelly bereaved. . . . I haven't had the courage to go to his mother on my own. . . . Do please come with me.'

While he was speaking Olivier looked searchingly at him, and the directness of his gaze terrified Laurent. The murderer had gone deliberately into this den of police folk, hoping to shield himself by sheer audacity. But he could not help flinching beneath their scrutiny, and saw suspicion where there was only amazement and pity. Suzanne, altogether more delicate and frail, was half swooning. Olivier, who hated the thought of death, but whose feelings were not involved, assumed an expression of pained surprise while closely examining Laurent's face out of force of habit and not for one moment suspecting the sinister truth. Old Michaud, for his part, uttered exclamations of horror, commiseration, astonishment, fidgeted on his chair, clasped his hands, rolled his eyes heavenwards.

'Oh, dear me,' he said in a choking voice, 'dear me, what a dreadful thing! You go out and die, just like that, in the twinkling of an eye. Horrible! and poor Madame Raquin, his poor mother, what are we going to say to her? Yes, indeed, you did well to come and fetch us. . . . We'll come along with you.'

He got up and trotted round the room looking for his hat and stick, and while doing so made Laurent go over all the details of the catastrophe once again; and once again he greeted each phrase with exclamations.

They all went downstairs. At the end of the Passage du Pont-Neuf Michaud stopped Laurent.

'Don't you come,' he said, 'your presence would be just the kind of brutal statement of the truth we must try to avoid. The unhappy mother would at once suspect the worst and force us to come out with it sooner than we should. . . . You wait for us here.'

This arrangement was a relief to the murderer, who shrank from the thought of going into the shop in the passage. He at once felt much calmer and began to walk up and down the pavement in complete peace of mind. At times he forgot what was going on in there and looked at shop windows, whistled through his teeth and turned round to look at women who brushed past him. He spent a full half-hour like this in the street, feeling more and more his usual self.

He had had nothing to eat since morning. Hunger suddenly gripped him and so he went into a baker's shop and stuffed himself with cakes.

Meanwhile a heartrending scene was going on in the shop in the passage. In spite of old Michaud's precautions and his soothing and affectionate words, the moment came when Madame Raquin realized that something terrible had happened to her son. She at once demanded to be told the truth, and her wild despair and the violence of her weeping and wailing broke down her old friend. And when she knew the truth her grief was tragic. She sobbed quietly, spasms jerked her backwards in a paroxysm of terror and anguish that left her gasping for breath, though now and again a shrill scream rose out of the depths of her pain. She would have grovelled on the floor had not Suzanne thrown her arms round her waist and wept on her lap with her white face looking up at her. Olivier and his father stood silent and uneasy, looking the other way, unpleasantly affected by a scene so disturbing to their egoism.

But the wretched mother saw her son rolled along in the muddy waters of the Seine, his body stiff and horribly swollen; while at the same time she saw him as a tiny child in his cradle when she used to drive away death as it hovered over him. More than ten times she had given birth to him anew, and she loved him for all the loving care she had lavished on him for thirty years. And now he had died far away from her, suddenly, in cold, dirty water, like a dog. And that reminded her of all the warm blankets she had wrapped him in. So much attention, such a cosy, sheltered childhood, how she had petted and loved him, and all to see him miserably drowned in the end! At these thoughts Madame Raquin felt her throat contract so tightly that she hoped she was going to die herself, choked with grief.

Old Michaud left hurriedly, leaving Suzanne to look after the old lady, and he and Olivier went and joined Laurent so as to go with all speed to Saint-Ouen.

Scarcely a word was exchanged on the way, each having buried himself in a corner of the cab that jolted them over the cobbles, and they sat silent and motionless in the darkness. Now and again the rays of a street lamp cast a fleeting beam of light upon their faces. The sinister event that had brought them together enveloped them in a kind of mournful apathy.

At length they reached the riverside restaurant, where they found Thérèse in bed, with burning hot hands and head. The proprietor whispered that the young lady had a high temperature. In reality Thérèse, feeling weak and frightened, was terrified of confessing to the murder in an attack of nerves, and she had deliberately chosen to be ill. So she maintained a fierce silence, keeping her lips and eyelids firmly shut, refusing to see anybody and afraid to speak. Holding the sheet up to her chin and half burying her face in the pillow, she withdrew into herself and anxiously listened to everything being said round her. But all the time in the reddish light showing through her closed lids she could see Camille and Laurent struggling on the edge of the boat, she could see her husband's form, ghastly white and larger than life, rising straight up above the slimy water. This relentless vision added fuel to the fire in her blood.

Old Michaud tried to speak to her and console her, but she turned away impatiently and fell into a fresh fit of sobbing.

'Leave her alone, sir,' said the proprietor; 'the slightest sound gives her the shudders. You see, what she wants is rest.'

In the main dining-room downstairs a policeman was taking down particulars of the accident. Michaud and his son went down, and Laurent after them. When Olivier had made himself known as a senior official at the Préfecture the matter was all settled in ten minutes. The men from the other boat were still there, going over the drowning in the minutest detail, describing the way the three fell in, claiming to be eye-witnesses. If Olivier and his father had entertained the slightest suspicion, that suspicion would have vanished with such witnesses. But they had never doubted Laurent's veracity for a single moment; on the contrary they introduced him to the policeman as the victim's best friend, and took care to see that his report stated that the young man had plunged into the water to rescue Camille Raquin. The following day the papers described the accident with a wealth of detail: the unhappy mother, the inconsolable widow, the noble and courageous friend, it was all there in the complete news-item, which did the rounds of the Paris press and then went and faded away in local provincial rags.

When the report was finished, Laurent felt joy and warmth fill his body with new life. From the moment when his victim had sunk his teeth into his neck, he had been as it were stiff and taut, acting automatically according to a prearranged plan. The instinct of self-preservation alone had driven him along, dictating his words and gestures.

146

But now, with the certainty of getting off scot-free, his blood began to course calmly and gently through his veins again. The police had passed quite close to his crime and the police had seen nothing; they had been taken in and had acquitted him. He was safe. At the thought of this he broke out into a sweat of relief, and a warm glow restored the suppleness to his body and mind. He went on playing the part of the heartbroken friend with incomparable skill and aplomb. In reality he was enjoying a purely animal sensation of pleasure; he was thinking of Thérèse lying in the upstairs room.

'We can't leave that poor young woman here,' he said to Michaud. 'She may be in for a serious illness, and we really must get her back to Paris. Come along, we must persuade her to come with us.'

Upstairs he talked to Thérèse himself and begged her to get up and let herself be taken back to the Passage du Pont-Neuf. When she heard his voice she started, opened her eyes wide and stared at him, dazed and shuddering. She sat up painfully but answered never a word. The men went out, leaving her alone with the wife of the proprietor. When she was dressed she made her way downstairs unsteadily and was helped into the cab by Olivier.

The journey was made in silence. With consummate daring and impudence Laurent slipped his hand along Thérèse's skirt and grasped her fingers. He was sitting opposite her in the moving shadows, and could not see her face, which she kept sunk on her chest. But having seized her hand he held it tight and kept it in his all the way to the rue Mazarine. He could feel her hand trembling, but it was not withdrawn; on the contrary, every now and then he felt its sudden, affectionate pressure. And their hands remained clasped, burning hot, and their moist palms stuck together and their fingers gripped each other's until each fresh movement hurt. It seemed to Laurent and Thérèse that their blood-stream passed from the one to the other by way of their united hands, which became a blazing furnace in which their life reached boiling-point. In the strained darkness and silence this frantic gripping of hands was like a crushing weight dropped on Camille's head to keep him down under water.

The cab stopped and Michaud and his son got out first. Laurent leaned across and whispered to his mistress:

'Be strong, Thérèse. We have a long time to wait. . . . Don't forget.'

She had not yet spoken. Now she opened

her lips for the first time since her husband's death.

'Oh, I shan't forget,' she said with a shudder, in a voice hardly louder than a breath.

Olivier offered his hand to help her down. This time Laurent did go into the shop. Madame Raquin was lying down and violently delirious. Thérèse dragged herself to her bed and Suzanne had scarcely time to undress her. Feeling reassured because everything seemed to be turning out as he wished, Laurent took himself off and slowly made his way home to the garret in the rue Saint-Victor.

It was past midnight. There was a cool breeze blowing in the silent and empty streets, and the young man could hear no sound but his own footsteps on the pavement. The coolness filled him with a sense of well-being, and the silence and darkness with fleeting sensations of pleasure. He slackened his pace.

At last he was free of his crime. He had killed Camille. The matter had been closed and no more would be heard of it. Henceforth he was going to live in peace, and wait for the right time to take possession of Thérèse. The thought of this murder had sometimes stifled him, but now it was accomplished his chest felt free, he could breathe easily, he was cured of the ills with which hesitation and fear had afflicted him.

He was really a little stupefied, for his limbs and mind were heavy with fatigue. He went home and slept soundly, but during his sleep slight nervous twitchings passed across his face.

13

Laurent awoke next morning in excellent spirits. He had slept well. The cold air from the skylight made his sluggish blood tingle. He hardly remembered the scenes of the previous day, and had it not been for the smarting pain in his neck he might have thought he had gone to bed at ten after an uneventful evening. But the bite made by Camille was like a red-hot brand burning into his skin, and when he paused to think about the pain of it he felt it intensely. It was like a dozen needles slowly penetrating his flesh.

He pulled down his shirt collar and looked at the wound in the nasty, cheap mirror on the wall. It was a red hole as wide as a two-sou piece, where the skin had been torn away and the flesh showed pinkish with dark spots. Thin trickles of blood had run down to his shoulder and congealed. Against the whiteness of his neck the bite looked a deep, dull brown; it was on the right side, below the ear. Laurent stooped over and stretched his neck so as to see, and the greenish mirror gave his features a hideous grimace.

He rinsed himself freely when he had had a satisfactory inspection, and told himself that the wound would skin over in a few days. Then, without hurrying, he dressed and made his way to the office as usual. There he told the story of the accident in heartbroken tones, and when his colleagues had read the newspaper account as well, he became a real hero. For a whole week the employees of the Orleans Railway could talk of nothing else; they were as proud as could be that one of their number had been drowned. Grivet never stopped talking about the folly of venturing in mid Seine when it is so easy to look at the water from the bridges.

One nagging worry remained in Laurent's mind. The authorities had not been able to take official cognizance of Camille's decease. Thérèse's husband was well and truly dead, but his murderer would have liked to discover the body so that a formal certificate could be issued. On the day after the accident there had been a fruitless search for the body of the drowned man, and it was thought that probably it had lodged in some cavity under the banks of the islands. Salvage men were busily combing the Seine in the hope of claiming the reward.

Laurent set himself the task of looking into the Morgue every morning on his way to the office. He had sworn he would see the job through. Though it made him heave with disgust, and in spite of the shudders that sometimes ran right through him, he went regularly for over a week and examined the faces of all the drowned persons laid out on the slabs.

When he entered he was nauseated by a sickly smell, the smell of washed flesh, and chill shivers ran over his skin; the dampness of the walls seemed to make his clothes weigh heavier on his shoulders. He made straight for the window separating the onlookers from the corpses, glued his pale face to the glass and looked. Rows of grey stone slabs stretched out in front of him. Here and there, on the slabs, lay naked bodies, making patches of green and yellow, white and red; for some of the bodies had kept their flesh virgin white in the rigidity of death, but others were like heaps of rotting, bleeding meat. On the wall at the back were hanging pitiful tatters: skirts and trousers contorted against the bare plaster. At first Laurent could only see a general impression of dingy grey slabs and walls on which the garments and corpses made red and black blotches. There was a murmur of running water.

153

Gradually he could make out the bodies, and then he passed from one to the next. He was only concerned with the drowned, and when there were several swollen and bluish from immersion he studied them eagerly, trying to recognize Camille. Often the flesh of the faces was coming away bit by bit, the bones had pierced the softened skin, and the whole face was a mere flabby pulp. This made Laurent hesitate, and he examined the bodies in the hope of recognizing the emaciation of his victim. But all drowned corpses are fat, and he saw enormous bellies, blown-up thighs, and great round arms. He was baffled. He shuddered in front of these greenish chunks of flesh that seemed to be jeering at him with horrible grins.

One morning he had a real fright. For some moments he had been looking at a drowned man short of stature and terribly disfigured. The flesh was so soft and decomposed that the running water was flaking it away bit by bit. The jet playing on the face was boring a hole to the left of the nose. And then all of a sudden the nose flattened out and the lips came away, showing the white teeth. The drowned head burst out laughing.

Each time he thought he recognized Camille, Laurent's heart burned within him. He was desperately anxious to find his victim's body, yet cowardly fears came over him when he imagined that the body was there in front of him. His visits to the Morgue gave him shivers and nightmares that left him gasping. He shook off his fears, told himself not to be childish and tried to be strong, but, try as he would, his flesh rebelled, and each time, as soon as he found himself in this dark and sickly-smelling hall, his whole being was seized with nausea and terror.

When he reached the last row of slabs and there were no cases of drowning, he sighed with relief and his disgust lessened somewhat. He then became a mere sightseer, and found a strange pleasure in looking violent death in the face, with its lugubriously weird and grotesque attitudes. It was an interesting show, especially when there were women displaying their bare breasts. This brutal display of naked bodies spattered with blood, sometimes with holes in them, held him spellbound. One day he saw a young woman of twenty, a buxom, working-class girl, apparently asleep on her stone slab, her fresh, plump body taking on most delicate hues with the pallor of death. She was half smiling, with her head a little to one side and her bosom was thrust forward in a provocative manner. You might have taken her for a harlot sprawling in abandon had there not been a dark stripe round her throat like a necklace of shadow. It was a girl who had hanged herself out of unrequited love. He lingered over her for a long time, running his eyes up and down her body, lost in a sort of fearful desire.

Every morning, all the time he was there, he could hear the tramp of the public going in and out.

The Morgue is within the reach of every purse; passers-by, rich and poor alike, treat themselves to this free show. The door is open, anyone can enter. Some connoisseurs make a special detour so as not to miss one of these displays of death, and when the slabs are bare people go out muttering, feeling let down and swindled. When the slabs are occupied and there is a nice show of human flesh, the visitors jostle each other and indulge in cheap thrills, shudder with horror, crack jokes, applaud or whistle just as they would at the theatre, and finally go away satisfied, declaring that the Morgue has been a good show today.

Laurent soon got to know the regulars by sight: a mixed lot who came for communal weeping or giggling. Workmen would look in on their way to work, with a loaf and their tools under their arms; they found death ever so funny. Among them would be the wags who made the gallery titter by passing some comic remark about each corpse's expression — those who had died in fires would be called stokers, the hanged, the murdered, the drowned, or bodies hacked about or crushed would each call forth some breezy witticism — and in rather unsteady voices they would venture some joke or other in the eerie silence of the hall. Then there were the shabby, genteel, thin, desiccated, and elderly, people simply out for a walk who dropped in for the sake of something to do and gazed at the corpses with vacant eyes and the distaste of the respectable and refined. Women came in large numbers: young work-girls, fresh and rosy in white linen and neat skirts, who slipped quickly from one end of the windows to the other, staring with wide, attentive eyes as though looking at the display windows of a big shop; and also poor women, pathetic and bewildered, and fashionably-dressed ladies gliding elegantly by in their silk dresses.

One day Laurent saw one of these ladies standing rooted a foot or so from the window, holding a cambric handkerchief to her nostrils. She was wearing a fine grey silk skirt and flowing mantle of black lace, her face was veiled and her gloved hands were small and beautifully shaped. She was surrounded by a delicate aroma of violets. She was looking at a corpse. A few feet from her, on a stone slab, was laid out the body of a strapping young fellow, a stonemason who had met sudden death by falling from a scaffolding; his chest was well developed, his muscles strong and taut, his flesh white and firm; death had turned him into a marble statue. The lady went on studying him and, as it were, turning him over with her eyes, weighing him up. The sight of this man enthralled her. She raised the corner of her veil, took one last look, and went away.

Sometimes gangs of small boys came in, mere children of twelve to fifteen, who rushed along the windows and only stopped in front of female corpses. They leaned on the glass with their hands and ran their impudent eyes over the bare breasts, nudging each other and passing smutty remarks, learning vice at the school of death. Young louts have their first women in the Morgue.

After a week of it Laurent felt sick. At night he dreamed about the corpses he had seen in the morning. This daily horror and suspense, which he forced himself to go through, so upset him in the end that he made up his mind to go only twice more.

The very next day, as he went in, he felt a violent blow in the chest: there, in front of him, on a slab, was Camille, laid out on his back with his head raised and looking at him through half-closed eyes.

The murderer moved slowly towards the window as though compelled, unable to take his eyes off his victim. It did not upset him; all he could feel was a cold sensation inside and a slight tingling of the skin. He would have expected to tremble more. There he stood quite still for a full five minutes, unconsciously taking it in, unconsciously impressing upon his memory each horrible line, each gruesome colour of the picture in front of him.

Camille looked revolting. He had been in the water for a fortnight. His face still seemed firm and rigid, and the features were preserved, but the skin had taken on a muddy, yellowish hue. The thin, bony, and yet slightly puffy face was grinning and lolling to one side, with the hair sticking to the temples; the lids were raised and showing the tallow-coloured eyeballs, the lips twisted towards one side into a frightful sneer, and the blackened tip of the tongue stood out against the whiteness of the teeth. The skin of the whole head seemed tanned and stretched, and its expression of pain and fear was all the more terrible because it had kept its human appearance, whereas the body had deteriorated horribly and was simply a heap of decomposing flesh. The arms looked as though they were coming loose, the collar bones were sticking through the skin of the shoulders, black ribs banded the greenish chest, and the left side had an open hole in it, jagged and dark red at the edges. The whole torso was rotting away. The legs were firmer and stretched out straight, but covered with filthy stains. The feet were coming adrift.

Laurent contemplated Camille. He had not so far seen such an appalling case of drowning. And in addition to everything else, the corpse had a shrunken look, it seemed skinny and miserable as though in its decomposition it had contracted into quite a tiny heap. You could have guessed that he was a twelve-hundred-franc employee, feeble and sickly, brought up by his mother on herb-tea. The puny body, reared in warm blankets, was now shivering on the cold stone.

When Laurent at last managed to tear himself away from the painful curiosity that held him motionless and gaping, he went out and walked rapidly along the embankment. And as he walked he repeated to himself: 'That's what I've made of him. He's beastly.' A pungent smell seemed to be following him, the smell that the putrefying body must be giving off.

He went and saw old Michaud and told him that he had recognized Camille on a slab in the Morgue. The formalities were completed, the drowned man was buried, and a death certificate issued. From now on Laurent was at peace, and joyfully threw himself into the task of forgetting his crime and the annoying and painful scenes which had followed.

14

The shop in the Passsage du Pont-Neuf remained shut for three days, and when it reopened it seemed darker and damper than ever. The goods on display were yellow with dust and seemed to be sharing the mourning of the house, for everything was at sixes and sevens in the dingy windows. Behind the linen caps hanging on their rusty rods, Thérèse's face looked more deathly pale, more ashen, and her stillness was sinister in its calm.

All the neighbours were full of sympathy. The imitation jewellery woman pointed out to all her customers the young widow's emaciated profile as an interesting and harrowing sight.

During those three days Madame Raquin and Thérèse had kept to their beds without speaking or even seeing each other. The old woman, sitting propped with pillows, stared vaguely in front of her with vacant eyes. Her son's death had been like a blow on the head that had knocked her out. For hours and hours she stayed quiet and inert, lost in the depths of her despair, and then at times she would have a fit of crying, shouting, and delirium. In the other room Thérèse seemed to be asleep; she had turned her face to the wall and pulled the coverlet over her eyes, and there she lay, stiff and silent, and never a sob disturbed the bedclothes covering her. It was as though she were concealing in the darkness of the bed the thoughts that held her motionless. Suzanne, who was looking after both of them, shuffled softly from the one to the other, bending her waxen face over the two beds; but she could never make Thérèse turn towards her instead of shaking herself petulantly, nor control Madame Raquin, whose tears began to flow as soon as a voice startled her out of her inertia.

On the third day Thérèse pushed back the bedclothes and sat up in bed with a sort of sudden feverish decision. She pushed her hair away from her eyes, paused for a moment with her hands to her temples, her eyes staring, still apparently lost in thought. Then she jumped down on to the carpet. Her limbs were aching and red with fever, and her skin, mottled with large livid patches, was crinkled in places as though there were no flesh beneath. She had aged.

Suzanne happened to be coming in; she was amazed to find Thérèse up, and in her calm and doleful tones advised her to go back to bed and get some more rest. She paid no attention, but found her clothes and put them on with quick, fumbling movements. When she was dressed she went and looked at herself in the glass, rubbed her eyes, and passed her hands over her face as though to wipe something away. Then without a word she ran across the dining-room and went in to see Madame Raquin.

The old lady was in one of her moments of dazed calm. When Thérèse came in she turned and followed the young widow with her eyes as she came over and stood in front of her in heavy silence. For a few seconds the two women contemplated each other, the niece with growing anxiety and the aunt with painful efforts to remember. Remembering at last, Madame Raquin held out her trembling arms, flung them round Thérèse's neck, and cried:

'My poor child, my poor Camille!'

She was weeping, and her tears dried on the burning skin of the young widow, who hid her own dry eyes in the folds of the sheet. Thérèse remained bending over, letting the old mother have her cry out. Ever since the murder she had been dreading this first meeting, and she had stayed in bed herself in order to put it off and gain time to work out quietly the terrible part she had to play.

When she saw that Madame Raquin had calmed down, she busied herself about the room and suggested that she had better get up and go down to the shop. The old woman had almost relapsed into childishness, but the sudden entry of her niece caused an improvement that restored her memory and consciousness of people and things round her. She thanked Suzanne for her kindness and spoke quite rationally again, if somewhat weakly, for her grief now and again got the better of her. She watched Thérèse moving about and would suddenly begin to cry, call her, and kiss her, tearfully saying that she had nobody else left in the world.

That evening she agreed to get up and try to eat something. And then Thérèse was able to see what a terrible shock her aunt had had. The poor old woman's legs had become so bad that she could only drag herself to the dining-room with the help of a stick, and when she got there the walls seemed to be reeling round her.

But the very next morning she wanted the shop opened, for she was afraid of going out of her mind if she stayed alone in her room. She lumbered heavily down the wooden staircase, pausing to put both feet on each step, and took her seat behind the counter. From that day on she remained tied to her place, a figure of serene grief.

By her side Thérèse dreamed and waited. The shop settled down to its usual dark monotony.

15

Every few days Laurent would look in during the evening. He stayed down in the shop and had half an hour's talk with Madame Raquin, then would go off without having looked direct at Thérèse at all. The old lady regarded him as the rescuer of her niece, a noble soul who had done his utmost to save her son. She welcomed him with tender affection.

One Thursday evening he happened to be there when old Michaud and Grivet came in. It was exactly eight. The clerk and the ex-superintendent had each thought independently that they could now take up their beloved routine once again without being indelicate, and they arrived at the same minute as though worked by the same spring. Behind them came Olivier and Suzanne.

They all went upstairs to the dining-room. Madame Raquin, who had not expected visitors, hastened to light the lamp and make tea. When they were all seated round the table with cups in front of them, and the domino box had been emptied, the wretched mother, suddenly finding herself back in the past, looked at her guests and burst into tears. There was an empty place, her son's.

This outburst chilled and vexed the company. Each face had worn an expression of selfish contentment, and these people felt ill at ease, for they had not kept the slightest memory of Camille alive in their hearts.

'Now, now, my dear lady,' cried Michaud, with a hint of impatience, 'you really mustn't upset yourself like this. You'll make yourself ill.'

'We are all mortal,' asserted Grivet.

'Your tears won't bring your son back,' said Olivier sententiously.

'Oh, please!' murmured Suzanne, 'don't make us feel unhappy.'

But Madame Raquin only sobbed the louder and could not hold back her tears.

'Come, come,' Michaud went on, 'you must try to be brave. You must realize that we are all here to cheer you up. Hang it all, don't let us be miserable, let's try and forget. . . . Now, we are playing for a penny a game, aren't we? Is that all right?'

She choked back her tears with a supreme effort, realizing, possibly, how smugly self-centred her guests were. She dried her tears but was still very shaken. The dominoes shook in her poor hands and the tears held back beneath her lids prevented her from seeing. They played.

Laurent and Thérèse had watched this little scene with serious, expressionless faces. He was delighted that the Thursday evenings were starting again, for he urgently needed them to attain his ends. And besides, without knowing quite why, he felt more at ease surrounded by these few acquaintances, and had the courage to look straight at Thérèse.

She, pale and remote in her black dress, seemed to him endowed with a beauty he had never known before. He was happy to meet her eyes and see them looking bravely and steadily into his. She still belonged to him, body and soul.

16

Fifteen months went by. The keen emotions of the first hours softened with each passing day, life became calmer and more relaxed, and the old routine was resumed with weary listlessness and that monotonous flatness which is the aftermath of great crises. And at first Laurent and Thérèse let themselves drift into the new way of life that was transforming them. They were undergoing a mysterious process of change which would have to be analysed most subtly if each gradation were to be noted.

Soon Laurent called at the shop every evening as of old, but he no longer had a meal there or camped out for the whole evening. He came at half past nine and went off after shutting up the shop. He seemed to be doing a duty by coming and helping the two women. If he did not do his job one day, he would apologize the next as humbly as a servant. On Thursdays he helped Madame Raquin to light the fire and do the honours of the house. He was unobtrusively attentive in a way that quite charmed the old lady.

Thérèse calmly watched him as he busied himself about her. She had lost her pallor and looked better; her expression was more cheerful and less strained. But just occasionally she nervously compressed her lips, making two deep lines that gave her face a strangely grief-stricken and scared look.

The lovers made no further attempt to see each other alone. They never arranged a single meeting or even exchanged a furtive kiss. For the time being murder had cooled the voluptuous fevers of their flesh, and by killing Camille they had succeeded in slaking the wild and unquenchable desires which they had failed to satisfy even when crushed in each other's arms. Crime seemed an acute enjoyment that made their embraces boring and sickening.

And yet they could have found a thousand opportunities for the untrammelled life of love, the dream of which had spurred them on to murder. Madame Raquin was no obstacle, for she was helpless and hardly knew where she was. The house belonged to them, they could come and go just as they liked. But love had lost its appeal, their appetite had gone, and so there they stayed quietly chatting, looking at each other with neither blush nor tremor, having apparently forgotten the frantic embraces which had formerly bruised their bodies and made their bones crack. They even avoided being alone together, for they had nothing to say to each other and each was afraid of appearing to have cooled off. When they shook hands the touch of each other's skin gave them a sort of uneasiness.

Of course they both thought they knew what kept them so indifferent and nervous in each other's presence. They put their coolness down to prudence. According to them their calmness and abstinence were the hall-mark of superior wisdom, and they pretended that this tranquillity of the flesh and slumber of the heart were intentional. Also they regarded the distaste and uneasiness they felt as a lingering fear, a barely conscious fear of punishment. At times they forced themselves to hope, and strove to recover the burning dreams of earlier days, and they were quite amazed to find that their imaginations were sterile. Then they clung to the idea of their coming marriage; if they reached their goal, with all fears gone, each belonging to the other, they would surely recover their old passion and turn the dreamed-of delights into realities. This hope calmed them and prevented their exploring fully the void that had opened up within them. They persuaded themselves that they were still in love as of old, and they longed for the hour that would make their happiness complete by joining them for ever.

Thérèse had never been so much at peace. She certainly was getting better. All the implacable determination of her character was relaxing.

At night, alone in her bed, she was happy; no longer were the thin face and puny body of Camille beside her to tantalize her flesh and fill her with unsatisfied desires. She felt like a little girl again, virginal among the white bed-curtains, at peace in the quiet shadows. Her big, slightly chilly room appealed to her, with its lofty ceiling, dark corners, and convent atmosphere. She even came to like the high black wall opposite her window, and through a whole summer she spent hours every evening just looking at the grey stones of the wall and narrow strips of starry sky cut up by chimneys and roofs. The only times she thought about Laurent were when a nightmare woke her with a start, and then sitting up, trembling and wide-eyed, clutching her nightdress round her, she told herself that she would not have these sudden frights if she had a man lying by her side. She thought of her lover as a watchdog to protect her, and never a tremor of desire disturbed her cool, calm flesh.

By day, in the shop, she took an interest in outside things and came out of herself, no longer living in a state of brooding revolt and harbouring thoughts of hatred and revenge. Now she disliked day-dreaming and felt the need of something to see and do. From morning till night she watched the people going through the Passage, and the noise and bustle entertained her. She was becoming inquisitive and talkative, in fact a woman, for until then all her actions and ideas had been those of a man.

In the course of her watching she noticed a young fellow, a student, who lived in some lodging-house near by and passed the shop several times a day. He was pale and handsome, with long, poetic hair and a military moustache. She thought he looked distinguished, and was in love with him for a whole week, and as lovesick as a schoolgirl. She took to reading novels and compared the young student with Laurent, whom she found very coarse and heavy. Reading opened up new and romantic horizons she had never known before; so far she had only loved with her blood and nerves, but now she began to love with her mind. Then one day the student vanished, having probably changed lodgings. In a few hours she forgot all about him.

She joined a subscription library and developed passions for all the heroes of the stories she read. This sudden love of reading had a strong influence upon her temperament; she developed a nervous sensitivity that made her laugh or cry without cause. The balance which was beginning to be established in her was disturbed, and she fell into a sort of vague dreaminess. Sometimes the thought of Camille would upset her and she would begin to feel renewed desire for Laurent, but desire full of fear and misgivings. All this threw her back into her earlier distress; sometimes she tried to find a way of marrying her lover at that very moment, but sometimes she thought of running away so as never to set eyes on him again. The novels she read told of chastity and honour, and put an obstacle between her instincts and her aspirations. She was still the indomitable creature who had been prepared to struggle with the Seine and who had flung herself headlong into adultery, but now she also realized the meaning of goodness and gentleness; she understood the meek face and passive attitude of Olivier's wife, and knew that it was possible to be happy without killing your husband. And so she lost any clear conception of what she was herself, and lived in a cruel state of indecision.

In the same way Laurent went through various phases of calm and upheaval. At first he enjoyed a deep peace of mind, relieved of a crushing burden. Now and again he questioned himself with amazement, thinking he must have had a bad dream, and he wondered whether it was really a fact that he had thrown Camille into the river and then seen his corpse on a slab in the Morgue. The recollection of his crime was strangely surprising; never would he have thought himself capable of murder, and now all the caution and cowardice in him shuddered, and cold sweat broke out on his forehead at the very thought that his crime might have been discovered and he could have been guillotined. It made him feel the cold steel of the knife at his throat. So long as he had been active he had gone straight ahead with his natural tenacity and a blind animal instinct. But now he could look round, and seeing the chasm he had just crossed he grew faint with terror.

'Really, I must have been drunk,' he thought; 'that woman had intoxicated me with love. Good God, what a bloody fool I've been! I was risking the guillotine, doing a thing like that. . . . Anyway, it has all gone off all right. But if it had to be done again I wouldn't embark on it.'

Laurent let himself go and went soft, became more cautious and timid than ever. He got fat and sloppy. Looking at his big, lumpy body with apparently no bones or sinews in it, nobody would have dreamed of accusing him of violence or cruelty.

He went back to his old habits, and for several months was a model employee, doing his job with exemplary dullness. He took his evening meal in a cheap restaurant in the rue Saint-Victor, cutting up his bread into small slices, chewing slowly, spinning the meal out as long as possible, after which he lolled back against the wall and smoked his pipe. You might have taken him for a fat and jolly family man. In the daytime not a single thought passed through his head, and at night he slept a heavy dreamless sleep. His face was pink and plump, his belly full and his head empty. He was happy.

His flesh was apparently dead, and he scarcely gave a thought to Thérèse. When he did think of her it was as one thinks of a woman one will eventually marry, at some unspecified date. He looked forward to his wedding day without impatience, forgetting the bride and dwelling upon the new position he would then occupy. For then he would leave the office, do a little amateur painting, and just be a gentleman of leisure.

These hopes led him back every evening to the shop in the Passage, in spite of the vague uneasiness that came over him every time he went in.

One Sunday, being bored and at a loose end, he went and looked up his old school friend, the young painter he had lived with for quite a time. The artist was working on a picture he intended to submit to the Salon and which represented a nude Bacchante lying sprawled on some drapery. At one end of the studio a model was lying with her head thrown back, torso twisted and haunch raised high. The woman sometimes laughed and thrust forward her bosom, stretching her arms for a rest. Laurent had taken a seat opposite her, and as he smoked his pipe and chatted to his friend he kept his eyes on her. This spectacle set his pulse racing and excited his nerves. He stayed there until evening and then took the woman home with him. He kept her as his mistress for nearly a year. The poor girl thought he was a handsome man and fell in love with him. She went off every morning, posed as a model all day, and came back each evening at the same time, feeding, clothing, and keeping herself out of her own earnings, without costing Laurent a penny, and he never bothered to find out where she had come from or what she had been doing. This woman was one more steadying influence in his life, and he accepted her as a useful and necessary thing for keeping his body quiet and healthy. He never knew whether he loved her, and it never occurred to him that he was being unfaithful to Thérèse. He felt fitter and happier, that was all.

Meanwhile Thérèse was out of mourning. She was wearing gay colours, and one evening Laurent discovered that she was looking younger and prettier. But he still felt slightly awkward with her, and for some time he had thought she was overwrought, given to strange whims, laughing or crying for no reason. Her instability alarmed him because up to a point he could guess what her struggles and worries must be. And being terrified of disturbing his own tranquillity, he began to hesitate, for after all he was getting along quite nicely, satisfying his appetites in sensible moderation, and he was afraid of jeopardizing the balance of his life by tying himself to an excitable woman whose passion had driven him crazy once already. Not that he worked all this out consciously, but he instinctively sensed the upheavals to which he would be a prey if he possessed Thérèse.

The first shock he received to shake him

out of his lethargy was the realization that he must really think about getting married, for Camille had been dead nearly fifteen months. It did occur to him for a moment that he might not get married at all, but throw Thérèse over and keep the model, whose undemanding and inexpensive love was good enough for him. But then he reflected that it was absurd to have killed a man for nothing, and when he thought of the crime itself and the terrible efforts he had made to be sole possessor of the woman who was still arousing his passions, it seemed to him that the murder would be pointless and shocking if he did not marry her now. To throw a man into the water in order to steal his widow, to wait fifteen months, and then decide to live with a tart who hawked her body round all the studios, really did seem ridiculous, and made him smile. And was he not bound to Thérèse by ties of blood and horror? Vaguely he could feel her crying out and writhing within him, and he belonged to her. Besides, he was afraid of his accomplice; if he did not marry her perhaps she might go and tell the authorities everything, out of revenge and jealousy. These thoughts throbbed in his head and brought back his feverish condition.

It was at this juncture that the model suddenly left him. One Sunday she did not return; no doubt she had found a warmer and more comfortable place to roost. Laurent was only moderately upset, but he had got used to having a woman lying by his side at night, and he was conscious of a sudden gap in his life. A week later his passions rebelled. He took to spending whole evenings in the shop again, watching Thérèse with fleeting glints in his eyes. She was still palpitating from her long bouts of novel-reading, and met his glances with languishing and provocative looks.

And so, after a full year of sated and indifferent waiting, they had both come back to the torments of desire. One evening, while shutting the shop, Laurent held back Thérèse in the Passage.

'Do you want me to come to your room tonight?' he asked passionately.

'No, no, let's wait,' she said, with a start of fear; 'let's be prudent.'

'I've waited a pretty long time as it is, it seems to me,' he went on. 'I'm sick of it, I want you.'

Thérèse looked at him wildly; her hands and face were burning hot. She seemed to hesitate and then said in a rush:

'Let's get married, and then I'll belong to you.'

17

As he left the Passage, Laurent's mind was on edge and his body restless. Thérèse's burning breath and her consent had filled him with the old lusts again. He went along the embankment, walking hat in hand so as to let all the winds of heaven blow freely on his face.

When he reached the door of his lodging-house in the rue Saint-Victor he suddenly felt afraid of going upstairs and being alone. A childish panic, quite inexplicable and unforeseen, made him terrified of finding a man hiding in his attic. He had never been subject to such scares before. He did not even attempt to explain the strange repugnance that came over him, but went into a wine-house and stayed there an hour, until midnight, sitting motionless and silent at a table, automatically drinking large glasses of wine. As his thoughts dwelt on Thérèse, he worked himself up into a temper with her for refusing to have him in her room that very night, for he felt that with her he would not have been afraid.

It was closing time and he was turned out,

but he went back to ask for some matches. The concierge's office was on the first floor, which meant that he had to negotiate a long passage and go up a few stairs before he could get his candle. The passage and short staircase were pitch dark and terrified him. Usually he went through this dark bit gaily enough, but that evening he dared not ring the bell, for he told himself that in a certain recess made by the cellar doorway there might be assassins lurking, ready to leap at his throat as he went by. Eventually he did ring, lit a match, and made up his mind to venture into the passage. The match went out. He stood still, breathing hard, not daring to run away, striking matches on the damp wall, his hand shaking with anxiety. He thought he could hear voices and foot-steps somewhere ahead. The matches broke off in his fingers. At last he managed to light one. The sulphur began to sizzle, igniting the wood with a slowness that redoubled Laurent's terrors, and in its dim bluish light and the dancing shadows he thought he could make out monstrous shapes. Then the match caught and the light became white and clear. Much relieved, he advanced very cautiously so that the flame should not go down. When the cellar door had to be passed, he hugged the wall opposite because the patch of darkness filled him with dread. He scurried up the two or three stairs to the office, and having taken his candle he felt he was safe. He went up the remaining flights more slowly, holding his candle aloft so as to light up all the dark corners he had to pass. The huge, weird shadows that dart about when you carry a light on a staircase filled him with uneasiness as they reared up or suddenly slid away in front of him.

He reached the top floor, opened his door, and shut himself inside as quickly as possible. The first thing he did was to look under the bed and search the room meticulously in case anybody was hiding. He shut the skylight, because somebody might get in that way. Having taken these precautions he felt calmer; he undressed, astonished at his own cowardice and finally smiling at his childishness. He had never been nervous before and could not understand this sudden fit of the horrors.

He went to bed. When he was between the warm sheets his thoughts returned to Thérèse, for his terror had driven her from his mind. Although he kept his eyes tightly shut and tried to go to sleep, his mind insisted on being active, forcing ideas upon him, linking these ideas together, and continually pointing out the advantages he would reap by marrying as soon as possible. Now and again he turned over, saying to himself: 'Let's stop thinking and get to sleep. I've got to be up at eight and go to work.' And he endeavoured to drop off. But back the ideas came one by one, his deliberations began their obstinate grinding all over again, and soon he was once again in a sort of intense meditation that set out in his mind the reasons why his marriage was essential, the arguments that first his desires and then his caution produced for and against possessing Thérèse.

Realizing that he could not sleep and that insomnia was keeping his flesh in a state of excitement, he turned on to his back, opened his eyes wide, and let his mind dwell upon his recollections of the young woman. The delicate balance had been upset and the old, hot lust possessed him again. He thought of getting up and going back to the Passage du Pont-Neuf, where he could get the passage gate opened, knock at the little side door, and Thérèse would let him in. The thought sent the blood racing to his neck.

His hallucination was astonishingly clear. He saw himself walking quickly along the streets and past the houses, and said to himself: 'I'll take this boulevard, pass the crossroads, and get there quicker.' Then the gate of the Passage squeaked, he went along the narrow arcade, all dark and deserted, congratulating himself on being able to go up to Thérèse without being seen by the woman who sold artificial jewellery; then he imagined himself in the side passage, on the little staircase up which he had gone so often. Having arrived he experienced the keen pleasure of earlier days, lived once again through the delicious terrors and agonizing thrills of adultery. His memories turned into present realities involving all his senses: he could smell the fusty smell of the passage and touch the sticky walls, see the murky shadows lingering. And he panted as he climbed each step, stopped to listen, already satisfying his desire as he nervously approached the woman he coveted. At last he was scratching at the door, it opened, and there was Thérèse waiting for him, all white in her underclothes.

His thoughts passed before him like real, visible objects. His eyes, staring into the darkness, really saw. When he had come to the end of his journey through the streets, entered the Passage, climbed the back stairs, and seemed to be really seeing Thérèse, pale and eager, he leaped out of bed, muttering: 'I must go, she is waiting for me.' But the sudden movement dispelled the hallucination, the tiled floor struck cold, and fear overcame him. For a moment he stood quite still, barefoot, listening. He thought he heard a noise on the landing outside. If he went to Thérèse he would have to go past that cellar door again downstairs, and the very thought sent a shiver down his spine. Terror seized him again, irrational, overwhelming terror. He looked round his room suspiciously, saw whitish streaks of light here and there, and then softly, but with hasty and anxious precautions, got back into bed, curled himself up and hid, as though trying to dodge some weapon, some threatening dagger.

The blood had rushed to his neck and made it smart. He put up his hand and his fingers could feel that scar made by Camille's bite. It had almost passed out of his mind, and now he was horrified as he rediscovered it on his skin, for it seemed to be gnawing away at his flesh. Although he at once took his hand away so as not to feel it, he could feel it still, eating a hole into his neck. So he tried to scratch it carefully with his nail, but that made the terrible itch far worse. He thrust both his hands between his drawn-up knees to stop himself from clawing the skin off. And so he remained, stiff, tense, with his neck on fire, and his teeth chattering with fear.

Then his thoughts fastened on to Camille with a dreadful determination. So far the drowned man had not troubled Laurent's nights. And now the thought of Thérèse brought with it the spectre of her husband. The murderer dared not open his eyes again for fear of seeing his victim in some corner of the room. A moment came when his bed seemed to be jerking in a curious way, and he imagined that Camille was hiding underneath and was shaking it up and down so as to tip him out and bite him. Wild-eyed, his hair standing on end, he clung to his mattress, for the jerks seemed to be increasing in violence.

But then he realized that the bed was not moving at all, and suddenly recovered himself. He sat up and lit his candle, calling himself a fool, and drank off a glassful of water to steady his nerves.

'It was a mistake to go to that wine-shop,' he thought. 'I don't know what's the matter with me tonight. Idiotic. I shall be washed-out at the office today. I should have gone straight to sleep as soon as I turned in, and not chewed over all sorts of things in my mind. That's what's kept me awake. Let's go to sleep.'

He blew out his light once more and buried his head in the pillow, feeling a little calmer and determined to stop thinking and stop being afraid. Exhaustion was beginning to relax his nerves.

But instead of falling into his usual heavy, profound slumber, he slipped into an uneasy drowsiness as if he were just numbed, or lost in a soft delicious insensitiveness. As he dozed he was still conscious of his body, and his mind was still awake in his dormant flesh. He had put away the thoughts as they came, and had defended himself against wakefulness, but when he dropped off and his strength and will-power deserted him, back crept his thoughts one by one and regained possession of his flagging consciousness. The dreams started again. Once more he made the journey to Thérèse down the stairs, past the cellar at the run, out into the open, along all the streets he had already taken in thought when still awake, into the Passage du Pont-Neuf, up the back stairs until he scratched at the door. But instead of Thérèse, instead of the young woman half undressed, with naked breast, it was Camille who opened the door, Camille as he had seen him in the Morgue, greenish and horribly disfigured. The corpse held out its arms to him, uttering a hideous cackle and poking out a bit of black tongue between its white teeth.

Laurent woke up with a start, screaming, bathed in icy sweat. He pulled the blanket up over his eyes, swearing angrily at himself. Once again he willed himself to go to sleep.

He did go to sleep once again, slowly, as before, and the same exhaustion came over him; and as soon as his will-power had once again escaped his control in the unguarded state of half-sleep, off he started on the same journey, back where his obsession took him, back to Thérèse, and again the drowned man opened the door to him.

The terrified wretch sat up. He would have given anything in the world to drive away this pitiless dream. Oh, for a leaden sleep to smash down his thoughts! So long as he kept awake he had enough strength to ward off the ghost of his victim, but as soon as he lost control of his mind, his mind led him to horror by first leading him to voluptuous enjoyment.

He made yet another bid for sleep. But then came a succession of delicious drowsings and sudden, appalling awakenings. With insane obstinacy he kept going to Thérèse and coming up against Camille's body. More than ten times he took the same road, his body, hot and excited, had the same sensations, went through the same actions with meticulous exactness, and more than ten times the drowned man came into his arms just as he was putting them out to seize his mistress and hold her close to him. But this same sinister culmination which awoke him each time, gasping and terror-stricken, did nothing to slake his desire, and a few minutes later, as soon as he was dropping off to sleep again, his lust forgot the loathsome corpse that was lying in wait and sought yet again a woman's warm, lithe body. For a whole hour he lived through this succession of nightmares, through this bad dream constantly recurring but constantly unexpected, which shattered him with a more terrible awakening each time.

One of these shocks, the last, was so violent and painful that he decided to get up and not go on with the struggle. Day was dawning, and a dismal grey light came in through the window which made a whitish, ashen square of sky above him.

Laurent dressed slowly, smouldering with rage, furious at not having slept and at having let himself give in to a panic he now dismissed as childish. He pulled on his trousers, stretched and rubbed his limbs and passed his hands across a face ravaged and bloated after a sleepless night.

'I ought not to have dwelt on all that. I should have gone to sleep,' he kept on telling himself, 'and I'd have been fresh and bright now. . . . Oh, if only Thérèse had been willing last night, if she had slept with me . . .'

The thought that Thérèse would have prevented his being frightened calmed him somewhat, but what he really dreaded was having to go through other nights like the one he had just endured.

He gave his face a rinse and combed his hair. This perfunctory toilet cooled his head and dispelled his last terrors. His mind was working clearly now, and the only thing amiss was great weariness in all his limbs.

'And yet I'm not a coward,' he mused as he finished dressing; 'I don't care a damn about Camille. It's ridiculous to think the poor devil is under my bed. Now I suppose I am going to think about that every night. I really must hurry up and get married. With Thérèse holding me in her arms I shan't worry overmuch about Camille. She'll kiss my neck, and kiss away that awful smarting. Let's have a look at it now.'

He went to the mirror, stretched his neck, and had a look. The scar was pale pink. On making out the toothmarks of his victim, Laurent felt a little disturbed and the blood

192

came surging up to his head. Thereupon he perceived a strange phenomenon. The mounting blood turned the scar purple and it became a vivid blood red, standing out against his white, fleshy neck. At the same time he felt a sharp pricking sensation, as though needles were being stuck into the wound. He hastily pulled up the neck of his shirt.

'Oh well,' he went on, 'Thérèse will put that right. A few kisses will do the trick. What a fool I am to think about these things!'

He put on his hat and went downstairs, feeling he wanted to breathe some air and stretch his legs. As he passed the cellar door he smiled, but all the same he tested the strength of the hook that secured it. When he was outside he walked slowly along the empty pavements in the cool morning air. It was about five.

Laurent had a most unpleasant day. In the afternoon at the office he had to struggle against overwhelming sleepiness. His head was heavy and aching and nodding in spite of himself, and he would raise it with a jerk when he heard one of his supervisors coming. This struggle and these sudden jumps into wakefulness tired him out and filled him with intolerable anxiety.

But exhausted though he was, he was determined to see Thérèse that evening. He found her overwrought and worn out like himself.

'Poor Thérèse had a bad night,' explained Madame Raquin after he had taken a seat. 'She seems to have had nightmares and dreadful sleeplessness. Several times I heard her call out. This morning she was quite ill.'

While her aunt was speaking Thérèse stared intently at Laurent. Possibly they guessed that their terrors were shared, for the same nervous twitch ran over their faces. They sat there opposite each other until ten o'clock, talking about nothing in particular, but reading each other's minds and imploring each other with their eyes to hurry on the moment when they could join forces against the drowned man.

18

Thérèse also had been haunted by Camille's ghost during that dreadful night.

Laurent's urgent plea for a meeting, coming after more than a year of indifference, had suddenly whipped up her senses. Her flesh had begun to tingle when, alone in bed, she had realized that their marriage must take place soon, and then, as she tossed in insomnia, she had seen the drowned man rise up before her. Like Laurent, she had writhed in desire and horror, like him she had told herself that she would have no more of these fears and sufferings when she held her lover in her arms.

The man and the woman had both experienced, at the very same time, a kind of nervous upheaval that had thrown them back into their monstrous lusts, gasping and terror-stricken. There had sprung up between them a relationship in blood and sensuality; they shuddered with the same shudders, their hearts, like brothers in suffering, ached with the same anguish. Thenceforth they had but a single body and soul for enjoyment and suffering. This participation or interpenetration is a psychological and physiological fact which often comes into existence between people flung violently together by severe nervous shocks.

For over a year the chain riveted to their limbs and binding them together was in no way irksome to Thérèse and Laurent. During the stage of numbness following the acute crisis of the murder itself, in the satiety and longing for peace and quiet of the succeeding days, these two prisoners could imagine they were free and that the iron bond no longer tied them to each other; the slack chain hung loose on the ground, and for their part they were resting, overcome by a sort of contented lassitude. They tried to find love elsewhere and to establish a prudent, balanced way of life. But now that the facts of the case had driven them to begin exchanging words of passion again, the chain jerked tight and the shock was so violent that they realized that they were tied to each other for ever.

And so the very next day Thérèse quietly set to work to bring about her marriage to Laurent. It was a difficult undertaking, fraught with peril. The lovers were terrified of doing something imprudent and arousing suspicion by letting the interest they had in

Camille's death become too suddenly apparent. Realizing that no mention of a marriage could possibly come from them, they evolved a very subtle plan consisting of getting others, that is to say Madame Raquin and the Thursday guests, to offer them what they dared not ask for themselves. The only thing needed was to put into the heads of these good people the notion of Thérèse's remarrying, and above all to make them think that the notion came from them and was their very own.

It was a long comedy needing skilful acting. Thérèse and Laurent had each undertaken the part best suited to them, and the slightest words and acts were nicely calculated and carried out with extreme circumspection. In reality their nerves were strained and on edge with burning impatience. They lived in a continual state of nervous excitement, and it was only their extreme cowardice that forced them to keep outwardly smiling and peaceful.

The reason why they were so anxious to get it over quickly was that they could now no longer remain alone and apart. Every single night the drowned man came and visited them, and insomnia laid them on a bed of blazing coals and turned them over with red-hot tongs. They were living in a state of exacerbation that kindled fresh desires in their blood each night by setting up before their eyes the most appalling hallucinations. When darkness fell Thérèse could no longer find the courage to go up to her room, and she went through cruel torments every time she had to shut herself up until morning in that big room where, as soon as she blew out her candle, weird gleams of light appeared and a population of ghosts came out. In the end she left her candle alight and tried not to go to sleep, so as to keep her eyes wide open all the time. But when exhaustion lowered her eyelids she saw Camille in the darkness and opened her eyes again with a jerk. In the morning she dragged herself along, worn out after having dozed for only an hour or two in broad daylight. And Laurent had become decidedly timorous ever since that night when he had lost his nerve going past the cellar door. Until then he had lived in blissful confidence, like an animal, but now the slightest sound made him tremble and blanch like a little boy. A tremor of fear had suddenly afflicted his limbs and refused to let him go. At night he suffered even more than Thérèse, for fear shook that great soft, flabby body of his to its depths. As he saw daylight fade, he would be filled with cruel apprehension. More than once he made up his mind not to go home at all, but spent whole nights tramping about the deserted streets. One night, in sheets of rain, he stayed under a bridge until dawn, and crouching there, frozen to death, afraid to get up and climb to the embankment, for nearly six hours he watched the murky water flow by in the grey shadows; but now and again he flung himself flat on the wet ground in terror, for there, under the arch, he thought he could see long lines of drowned corpses drifting downstream. When weariness forced him home, he double-locked himself in and tossed about until dawn with frightful bouts of fever. The same nightmare came back persistently; he thought he was falling out of the warm, passionate arms of Thérèse into the cold slimy ones of Camille; he dreamed that his mistress was clasping him in a hot embrace and immediately afterwards that the drowned man was hugging him to his putrefying chest in a grip of ice. These sudden alternations of sensual pleasure and nausea, these successive contacts with hot, passionate flesh and flesh cold and softened by slimy ooze, left him gasping, shuddering, choking with terror.

Each day the lovers' terrors grew fiercer, each day their nightmare visions battered and maddened them still more. They could see no other remedy for insomnia than each other's embraces, but out of prudence they dared not arrange a meeting. They were waiting for their wedding-day as a day of salvation to be followed by a night of bliss.

Thus they looked forward to their union with all the longing they felt for a peaceful night's sleep. During the period of indifference they had hesitated, each one forgetting the various selfish and passionate factors which, having led them to commit murder, had since seemed to have melted into air. But now they were once again burning with lusts, and they rediscovered in the selfishness and sensuality of their natures the original reasons that had made them kill Camille, namely to taste the joys they thought a regular marriage would assure them. Yet this supreme decision to unite openly was due to an indefinable despair. Deep down within them was fear. Their very desires were quivering with apprehension. They were, so to speak, hanging over each other as though over a chasm, fascinated by its horror; there they were, each peering down into the other, unable to move, unable to speak, while stabbing ecstasies, making their minds whirl and their limbs melt into nothingness, filled them with a mad desire to fall into perdition. But faced by the present moment, with their anxious waiting and timorous desires, they felt the urgent necessity to shut their eyes and dream of a future of amorous felicity and peaceful enjoyment. The more they trembled at the sight of each other and sensed the horror of the abyss into which they were about to hurl themselves, the more they sought to renew the promise of bliss and to set out the irrefutable facts that inevitably pointed to their marriage.

Thérèse only wanted to marry because she was frightened and her organism demanded Laurent's violent love-making. She was a prey to a nervous crisis that had unhinged her, and the truth was that she was scarcely using her reason at all, but throwing herself into passion with a mind unbalanced by the novels she had been reading and a body inflamed by the cruel insomnia that had kept her awake for weeks on end.

Laurent, coarser-grained by nature, though giving in to his panics and desires, nevertheless was determined to reason out his decision. In order to prove to himself that his marriage was a necessity and that at last he was going to be absolutely happy, and so as to dispel the vague misgivings he was beginning to feel, he went over all the old calculations once again. Since his father, the peasant of Jeufosse, was apparently determined never to die, he reflected that his heritage might be a long time coming, and he was even afraid it might give him the slip and go into the pocket of one of his cousins, a hefty fellow who tilled the soil much to old Laurent's satisfaction. And he himself would always be poor, living without women in some garret, sleeping badly and eating even worse. Besides, he had no intention of working all his life, and life at his office was beginning to get decidedly on his nerves, for the unimportant jobs entrusted to him were getting altogether too much for his laziness. The upshot of his reflections always was that the height of all happiness consists in doing nothing. At this juncture he remembered that the reason why he had drowned Camille was to marry Thérèse and do nothing for ever after. No doubt the desire to have his mistress to himself had played a large part in turning his thoughts to the crime, but he had been led to murder perhaps even more by the prospect of putting himself in Camille's place, being looked after like him, enjoying perpetual bliss. If he had been egged on by passion alone he would never have shown so much craven prudence, but the fact was that by committing murder he had been trying to secure a life of calm and idleness, with permanent satisfaction of his appetites. All these thoughts, whether openly admitted or so far unconscious, now came crowding in, and to keep his courage up he repeatedly told himself that the time had come to reap the expected harvest from Camille's death. He reviewed the advantages and joys of his future existence: no more office, a life of delicious ease with food, drink, and sleep *ad lib*, a passionate woman always available to keep the balance of his sexual requirement nicely adjusted; in due course he would come into Madame Raquin's forty-odd thousand francs, for the poor old girl was failing day by day. In fact he would achieve for himself a happy animal existence and forget everything else. Since they had decided on marriage, Laurent had gone over this time and again, and he tried to think of still more advantages, and was delighted when he thought he had delved into his self-interest and found a new argument for marrying the drowned man's widow. But try as he would to find hope, dream as he might about a future glutted with slothful delights, he still felt sudden chills run over his skin, and there were still moments when a feeling of dread choked the joy in his throat.

19

Meanwhile, the well-concealed work of Thérèse and Laurent was beginning to bear fruit. Thérèse had put on a gloomy, despairing look which soon worried Madame Raquin, who wanted to know what was upsetting her niece so much. Thereupon Thérèse played the part of the inconsolable widow with consummate skill, mentioning depression, lassitude, and nervous pains, but all in a vague way, without going into details. When her aunt plied her with questions she answered that she was quite well and had no idea what was upsetting her in this way, making her cry for no reason she could see. Prolonged fits of breathlessness, wan heart-rending smiles, heavy silences pregnant with a sense of emptiness and despair, and so on. The young woman, so withdrawn into herself and apparently succumbing to some unknown disease, ended by really alarming Madame Raquin. She had nobody left in the world but her niece, and every night prayed God to preserve this child to close her eyes in death. This last love of her old age was not unmixed with selfishness. When it occurred to her that she might lose Thérèse and die alone in that dank shop in the Passage, it seemed as though a blow had been struck at the feeble props that helped her to go on living, and from then onwards she kept a ceaseless watch over her niece, studied her languors with terror, and wondered what she could do to cure her of her mute despair.

The circumstances being so serious, she thought she ought to ask the advice of her old friend Michaud. So one Thursday evening she kept him back in the shop and confided her fears.

'Well, of course,' the old chap answered with the brutal frankness of his former profession, 'I've noticed for a long time that Thérèse has been moping, and I know perfectly well why her face is so colourless and looks so miserable.'

'Do you really?' said the old lady; 'then tell me at once. If only we could cure her!'

'Oh, the remedy is simple enough,' Michaud laughed. 'Your niece is bored with being alone in her bedroom at night for nearly two years. She wants a husband; you can see it in her eyes.'

The ex-superintendent's crude directness hurt Madame Raquin. She thought that the wound, which had never stopped bleeding within her since the dreadful accident at Saint-Ouen, must be just as fresh and painful in the young widow's heart. With her son dead and gone there did not seem any other conceivable husband for her niece. And here was Michaud declaring with a coarse laugh that Thérèse was sickening for want of a husband.

'Marry her off as soon as may be,' he said as a parting shot, 'unless you want to see her dry up altogether. That's my opinion, dear lady, and it's the right one, mark my words.'

Madame Raquin could not reconcile herself at once to the idea that her son was already forgotten. Old Michaud had not even mentioned his name and had talked about Thérèse's supposed illness as though it were a joke. The wretched mother realized that she alone kept the memory of her dear son alive in her heart. It seemed as though Camille had just died for the second time, and she wept. But when she had had a good cry and tired herself out with her sorrow, she found that she could not help thinking about Michaud's words, and began to get used to the idea of buying a little happiness at the cost of a marriage which, to her over-scrupulous mind, amounted to killing her son over again. And when she found herself alone with Thérèse sitting opposite, dismal and depressed in the chilly silence of the shop, her heart failed her. She was not one of those stiff and withered souls who find keen enjoyment in a life of eternal misery; on the contrary, she fitted in with others, gave herself freely, and was demonstrative; in fact her temperament was altogether that of a nice, comfortable, jolly old lady, and it made her live a life of active kindliness. Since her niece had grown so quiet and had been sitting there pale and languid, life had not been worth living and the shop seemed to her like a tomb. She wanted to be surrounded by warm affection, see a bit of life round her, be coddled, in fact she wanted something cosy and gay to help her wait peacefully for death. These unconscious desires made the suggestion of Thérèse's remarriage acceptable to her, and she even forgot her son a little, and into the state of living death in which she existed there came a kind of awakening, with new desires and new things to occupy her mind. Now she was looking for a husband for her niece, and that took up all her thoughts, for the choice of a husband was a very serious matter, since the poor old thing was even more concerned for herself than for Thérèse; she wanted to get her married in such a way as to be happy herself, being terrified that the young widow's new husband might come in and upset the last days of her old age. It was a frightening thought that she was about to bring a stranger into her daily life, and it was the only thing that held her back from discussing marriage openly with her niece.

While Thérèse, with the consummate hypocrisy instilled into her by her upbringing, was acting the part of apathy and depression, Laurent had assumed that of the sympathetic and obliging fellow. He was full of little kindnesses for the two women, but especially for Madame Raquin, whom he overwhelmed with delicate attentions. Gradually he made himself indispensable in the shop, and he alone brought a little cheerfulness into that dark hole. If he was not there in the evening the old lady would look about uneasily as though she had lost something, or she was almost afraid of being alone with Thérèse and her miseries. It must be said that if Laurent did stay away one evening, he only did so in order to consolidate his power; normally he came every evening straight from the office and stayed until the Passage was closed for the night. He ran errands, fetched and carried little things for Madame Raquin, who was not good on her legs, and finally he would take a seat and talk. He had developed a stage voice, soft yet carrying, which he used for flattering the old dame's ears and heart. In particular he seemed very disquieted about Thérèse's health, in a friendly way, like a kindly man hurt by the sufferings of others. More than once he took Madame Raquin to one side and terrified her by seeming to be extremely alarmed himself by the changes, nay, the ravages he said he could see in the young woman's face.

'We shall lose her before long,' he murmured tearfully. 'It's no use trying to deceive ourselves, she is very ill. Alas for our poor bit of happiness, our nice quiet evenings!'

Madame Raquin was horrified as she listened. Laurent even carried his audacity to the length of talking about Camille.

'You see,' he went on, 'my poor friend's death has been a terrible blow to her. She has been going downhill for two years, ever since that dreadful day when she lost Camille. Nothing will ever console her or cure her. We must just resign ourselves.'

These barefaced lies made the old woman weep bitter tears. Any reminder of her son threw her off her balance and confused her vision. Each time she heard Camille's name pronounced she gave way to a fit of sobbing, and so lost control of herself that she would have embraced anybody who mentioned her beloved child. Laurent had noticed the emotional confusion into which this name threw her; it gave him the power to make her cry at will, and break her down with an emotion that prevented her seeing things clearly; and he took advantage of this power and kept her continually grief-stricken and pliable in his hands. Every evening, although an inner revulsion made him feel sick, he turned the conversation on to the rare qualities, the tender heart, and the intelligence of Camille, and sang his victim's praises with complete cynicism. Sometimes when he caught Thérèse's eyes looking strangely into his, a shudder ran through him, for he himself was coming to believe all the good he was saying of the drowned man; and then he would fall silent, suddenly filled with an appalling jealousy, fearing that the widow really loved the man he had thrown into the river, whose praises he was now singing with the conviction of a man possessed. Throughout the conversation Madame Raquin was in tears and unaware of anything going on round her. In the midst of her tears she thought that Laurent had a loving and generous heart, for he alone remembered her boy, he alone still talked of him in a voice unsteady with emotion. And she would dry

210

her tears and gaze at the young man with infinite tenderness, loving him like her own
child.

One Thursday evening, Michaud and
Grivet were already in the dining-room
when Laurent came in and went up to
Thérèse, asking her about her health with
gentle concern. He sat by her for a moment,
acting for the benefit of those present his
part of affectionate and anxious friend. As
the two young people were sitting together
and exchanging a few words, Michaud, who
was watching them, leaned over and whispered to the old lady, pointing at Laurent:

'Look, there's the husband for your niece.
Fix that marriage up with all speed. We'll
help you if need be.'

Michaud smiled a knowing smile, thinking that Thérèse could do with a virile husband. Madame Raquin was as it were suddenly enlightened, and she saw in a flash all
the advantages she would reap personally
from the marriage of Thérèse and Laurent.
It could only tighten still more the bonds
that already united her, her niece, and her
son's friend, the kindly soul who came in
and cheered them up in the evenings. She
would not be bringing a stranger into her
home and running the risk of being unhappy; on the contrary, while giving

Thérèse a man to support her she would be adding another joy to her old age and would find a second son in the man who had shown her a son's love for three years now. And besides, it seemed to her that by marrying Laurent, Thérèse would be less disloyal to Camille's memory. There are strange delicacies in the religions of the heart. Madame Raquin, who would have wept to see a stranger kiss her son's widow, felt no objection to the idea of handing her over to the embraces of his former friend. She thought it was keeping it in the family, as the saying goes.

All that evening, as her guests played dominoes, the old lady watched the couple with an indulgent expression that led them to guess that their play-acting had succeeded and that the climax was at hand. Before leaving, Michaud had a brief word with Madame Raquin in an undertone, then pointedly took Laurent's arm, declaring that he would go part of the way home with him. As he went, Laurent threw a quick glance at Thérèse, a glance full of urgent meaning.

Michaud had undertaken to spy out the land. He found that the young man was very attached to both ladies, but most surprised at the suggestion of a marriage between

Thérèse and himself. Laurent went on to say, in a voice faltering with emotion, that he loved his poor friend's widow like a sister, but that marrying her would seem just like sacrilege. The ex-superintendent stuck to his point, giving a hundred good reasons why he should consent; he even spoke of self-dedication and went so far as to say that duty commanded him to give back a son to Madame Raquin and a husband to Thérèse. Little by little Laurent let himself be talked over, pretending to give in to his emotion and to accept the idea of marriage as an inspiration straight from heaven, dictated by self-dedication and duty, as Michaud had put it. When the old man had obtained a definite 'yes' he left his companion, rubbing his hands, believing that he had won a great victory and congratulating himself upon having been the first to think of a marriage which would bring back all the old zest to Thursday evenings.

While Michaud was having this out with Laurent as they slowly walked along by the river, Madame Raquin was having an almost identical conversation with Thérèse. She kept her niece back for a minute when she was about to retire for the night, pale and delicate-looking as usual, and questioned her in an affectionate tone, begging her to tell her frankly what was behind this overwhelming depression of hers. But getting only vague answers she went on to the emptiness of widowhood, gradually drawing nearer to the precise suggestion of a second marriage, and finally asking her outright whether she did not secretly want to marry again. Thérèse protested that nothing was further from her mind and said that she would stay faithful to Camille. Madame Raquin began to cry. She pleaded against the promptings of her own heart, pointing out that despair cannot last for ever, and then, when the young woman exclaimed that she could never put anyone in Camille's place, she suddenly mentioned Laurent. Thereupon she broke into a torrent of words about the suitability and advantages of such a union, laying bare her soul, and saying aloud what she had been thinking all the evening. With naïve selfishness she painted a picture of the happiness of her closing years with her two beloved children. Thérèse listened with bowed head, resigned, docile, and ready to satisfy her smallest wish.

'I love Laurent as a brother,' she said in mournful tones when her aunt had finished. 'As it is your wish, I will try and love him as a husband. I want to make you happy. I had hoped that you would leave me to weep in peace, but I will dry my tears since your happiness is at stake.'

And she kissed the old lady, who was overcome with confusion at having been the first to forget her son. As she went to bed Madame Raquin sobbed bitterly, accusing herself of being less steadfast than Thérèse and wanting this marriage for selfish reasons, whereas the young widow consented in a simple spirit of abnegation.

Next morning Michaud and his old friend had a brief word with each other in the Passage outside the shop door, told each other how their schemes had worked, and agreed to go in for direct action and force the pair to become officially engaged that very evening.

Michaud was already in the shop by five o'clock when Laurent came, and as soon as he had sat down the ex-superintendent whispered into his ear:

'She accepts.'

This bald statement was overheard by Thérèse, who sat there with pale face, staring brazenly at Laurent. The lovers looked at each other for several seconds, as though consulting, and realized that they had to accept the situation without hesitation and settle things straight away. So

Laurent stood up, went over and took the hand of Madame Raquin, who was struggling to hold back her tears.

'Mother dear,' he smiled, 'I discussed your happiness with Monsieur Michaud last night. Your children want to make you happy.'

The poor old woman, hearing herself called 'Mother dear', let her tears burst forth. She grabbed Thérèse's hand and thrust it into Laurent's, but could not utter a word.

A shudder ran through the lovers as they felt their bodies come into contact. Their fingers remained tightly entwined in a burning, nervous grip. Then he stammered:

'Thérèse, do you want us to give your aunt a happy, peaceful life?'

'Yes,' she murmured, 'we have a duty to fulfil.'

Laurent looked very pale as he turned to Madame Raquin and went on:

'When Camille fell into the river he called out to me: "Save my wife, I leave her in your care." By marrying Thérèse I believe I am carrying out his last wishes.'

Hearing these words, Thérèse let go of Laurent's hand. It was as though she had been hit in the chest. Her lover's impudence appalled her, and she stared at him wild-

216

eyed whilst Madame Raquin managed to say through her sobs:

'Yes, yes, my dear boy, you marry her and make her happy, and my son will thank you from the depths of the grave.'

Laurent felt himself coming over faint, and leaned against the back of a chair. Michaud, also moved to tears, pushed him towards Thérèse, saying:

'Kiss each other, and this will be your engagement.'

As his lips touched the widow's cheeks he felt strangely ill at ease, and she backed away quickly, as though her lover's two kisses had burned her. These were the first caresses he had given her before witnesses, and all her blood rushed to her face. This woman, to whom modesty was unknown and who had never once blushed in all her sexual orgies, now felt fiery red.

But once this ordeal was over, the two murderers breathed again. Their marriage was settled, and at long last they were within reach of the goal they had been aiming at for so long. It was all arranged that same evening, and the following Thursday Grivet, Olivier, and his wife were told of the forthcoming marriage. As he broke the news Michaud rubbed his hands with delight, saying:

'It was all my idea, I brought them to-gether. You'll see what a fine couple they'll make!'

Suzanne went and kissed Thérèse without a word. The poor, pale, lifeless creature had taken a liking to the gloomy, intense widow, and loved her with a sort of respectful awe, like a child. Olivier complimented aunt and niece, and Grivet ventured a few spicy jokes that did not go down too well. But all in all the company was thrilled and delighted, de-claring that all was for the best. In fact they already fancied themselves at the wedding.

Thérèse and Laurent maintained a digni-fied and carefully studied attitude, showing an affectionate and considerate friendship, but not more than that. They seemed to be accomplishing an act of supreme self-ded-ication. Nothing in their faces gave the slightest hint of the terrors and desires that were shaking them to the core. Ma-dame Raquin looked on them with wan smiles and comfortable, grateful kindli-ness.

There were a few formalities to be ob-served. Laurent had to write and ask his fa-ther's consent. The old peasant at Jeufosse, who had almost forgotten he had a son in Paris, answered in four lines to the effect that he could marry and be hanged if he wanted to, and made it clear that, since he was determined not to give him a single sou, he left him free to dispose of his own person and commit all the follies in the world. The way this permission was granted worried Laurent considerably.

When she read this unnatural father's letter Madame Raquin was moved, in a burst of kind-heartedness, to do a foolish thing. She settled her capital of over forty thousand francs on her niece, thus depriving herself of everything in favour of the young couple, entrusting herself to their kindness of heart, and wishing to derive all her happiness from them alone. Laurent contributed nothing to the common fund, and he even made it clear that he would not stay in his job indefinitely, but might take up painting again. It must be added that the little family's future was secure, for the income from the forty-odd thousand francs, plus the profits from the haberdashery business, would support three people quite comfortably. They would have just enough to keep them happy.

The wedding preparations were speeded up and the formalities cut down as much as possible. It was as though everybody was in a hurry to push Laurent into Thérèse's bedroom. The longed-for day came at last.

20

That morning Laurent and Thérèse awoke in their respective rooms with the same deeply joyful thought that their last night of terror was over. No more sleeping alone; henceforth they were going to defend each other against the drowned man.

Thérèse looked about her and broke into a strange smile as she measured the big double bed with her eyes. She rose and dressed slowly, waiting for Suzanne, who was to come and help prepare the bride.

Laurent sat up in bed and stayed in that position for several minutes, bidding his farewells to this attic of his which struck him as beastly. At last he was about to leave this kennel and have a wife of his own. It was December and he shivered, but as he jumped out on to the floor he told himself that he would be nice and warm that night.

A week earlier Madame Raquin, knowing how hard up he was, had slipped into his hand a purse containing five hundred francs, all her savings. The young man had made no bones about pocketing it, and had fitted himself out with new clothes. The old lady's money had also enabled him to give Thérèse the customary presents.

His black trousers and coat and his white waistcoat, together with a shirt and tie of the finest quality, were laid out on two chairs. Laurent used plenty of soap and made his body smell sweet with Eau de Cologne, then proceeded to dress with meticulous care, for he wanted to look handsome. As he was putting on his collar, a stiff and high one, he felt a sharp pain in his neck. The stud kept slipping out of his fingers and he lost his temper, for it seemed as though the starched linen was cutting him. He raised his chin to have a look and there were Camille's tooth-marks fiery red. The collar had grazed the scar. Laurent bit his lips and went pale. The sight of this mark discolouring his neck was frightening and annoying at this particular moment. He crumpled up the collar and took out another which he put on with infinite care. Then he finished dressing. As he went down the stairs his new clothes kept him quite stiff, and he dared not turn his head round because his neck was imprisoned in starched linen. With his every movement an edge of the linen pinched the wound that the drowning man's teeth had made in his flesh. The sharp jabs kept on hurting him as he got into the carriage and set off to call for Thérèse and take her to the town hall and the church.

On the way he picked up a fellow employee of the Orleans Railway, and old Michaud, who were to be his witnesses. When they reached the shop everybody was ready: Grivet and Olivier, Thérèse's witnesses, and Suzanne, who were gazing at the bride like little girls gazing at dolls they have just dressed. Madame Raquin, although no longer able to walk, wanted to be with her children all the time, and so she was hoisted into a carriage and off they went.

Everything went off well at the town hall and the church. The quiet and modest bearing of bride and bridegroom was noticed with approbation. They pronounced the solemn word 'yes' with an emotion that even Grivet found touching. But they were in a kind of dream. As they were calmly seated or kneeling side by side they could not help being racked by frantic thoughts, and they avoided each other's eyes. When they got back into the carriage they felt greater strangers than before.

It had been decided that the wedding dinner should be a purely family affair and held in a little restaurant up in Belleville. The only guests were the Michauds and

Grivet. The party drove all round the Boulevards, killing time until six, and then repaired to the eating-house, where a table for seven had been laid in a private room painted yellow and reeking of dust and wine.

The meal could have been merrier. The bridal pair were serious and preoccupied. Ever since the morning they had been haunted by peculiar sensations that they did not even try to understand. From the outset they had been dazed by the speed of the formalities and the ceremony that had tied them together for ever. Then the long ride on the Boulevards had lulled them into drowsiness and it seemed to have gone on for months and months; nor had they minded letting themselves drift along the monotonous streets, looking at the shops and people with unseeing eyes, and overcome by a stupefying numbness that they tried to shake off with bursts of forced laughter. It was with a back-breaking fatigue and a growing feeling of stupor that they had reached the restaurant.

Sitting opposite each other at table they wore a set smile but were constantly relapsing into dull dreaminess; they ate, answered questions, and moved their limbs automatically. But the same series of intangible thoughts kept on coming back into their listless, exhausted minds. They were married, but not conscious of any difference, and this struck them as most astonishing. In their imagination they were still separated by a chasm, and every now and then they wondered how they could ever cross it. They thought they were back at the stage before the murder, when a material obstacle still stood between them, and then all of a sudden they recollected that they would be sleeping together that very night, in a few hours' time, and looked at each other in amazement, not quite understanding why it should be allowed. Far from feeling united, they thought that they had been roughly torn asunder and hurled in opposite directions.

As the circle of fatuously grinning guests expected to hear them 'dear' and 'darling' each other, they tried to relieve the general embarrassment, but stammered and blushed and could not make up their minds to treat each other as lovers in public.

The long wait had worn out their desire, and all the past had disappeared. Their violent sexual appetites had gone, and they were even unaware of the joy they had felt that morning, the deep satisfaction that had come over them at the thought that they would never be afraid again. Now they were just tired out and dazed with everything that was happening, and the day's doings were going round and round in their heads, monstrous and incomprehensible. So there they were, silent and smiling but without any expectation or hope. Yet deep down in their bewilderment there lurked a mysterious, painful anxiety.

And Laurent, each time he moved his neck, felt a smarting, pinching sensation in his flesh where his collar cut and caught Camille's tooth-marks. While the mayor was reading out the marriage law or the priest was holding forth about God, in fact every minute of the long day, he had felt the drowned man's teeth biting into his flesh. At times, he imagined that a trickle of blood must be running down his chest and would at any moment stain the whiteness of his waistcoat.

Madame Raquin was inwardly grateful to the couple for their decorum. Boisterous jollity would have jarred on the poor mother; her son, she felt, was there, invisible, giving over Thérèse into Laurent's hands. Grivet was not of the same opinion; he thought the wedding was dull, and was vainly trying to liven it up, in spite of warning looks from Michaud and Olivier which rooted him to his chair each time he was by way of rising to make a silly speech. But he did manage to get to his feet once, and proposed a toast:

'I drink to the children of Monsieur and Madame,' he said with a suggestive leer.

They had to acknowledge the toast. Thérèse and Laurent had turned very pale at Grivet's remark. It had never occurred to them that they might have children, and the thought sent an icy chill through them. They nervously clinked glasses, looking at each other in bewilderment, frightened at being there face to face.

The meal was over early and the guests wanted to accompany the bridal pair to the nuptial chamber. It was hardly more than half past nine when the party reached the shop in the Passage. The artificial jewellery woman was still in her cubbyhole by her blue-velvet-lined box. She looked up at them with interest and smiled at the newly-weds. They caught her eye and were terrified. Perhaps this old woman had known all about their meetings long ago and had watched Laurent stealing into the side passage.

Thérèse retired almost at once with Madame Raquin and Suzanne. The men stayed in the dining-room while the bride was preparing for the night. Laurent was lolling about, not feeling the slightest impatience, but amiably listening to the coarse jokes of old Michaud and Grivet who, now that the ladies were no longer present, were having a really good time. When Suzanne and Madame Raquin emerged from the nuptial chamber and the old lady, deeply moved, told Laurent that his wife was ready, a shudder ran through him and for a moment he stood still in a panic. Then he hastily shook the proffered hands and went in to Thérèse, holding on to the door like a drunken man.

21

Laurent carefully shut the door behind him, then stood leaning against it for a moment looking into the room, ill at ease and embarrassed.

A good fire was blazing in the hearth, setting great patches of golden light dancing on the ceiling and walls, illuminating the whole room with a bright and flickering radiance against which the lamp on the table seemed but a feeble glimmer. Madame Raquin had wanted to make the room nice and dainty and everything was gleaming white and scented, like a nest for young and virginal love. She had taken a delight in decorating the bed with some extra pieces of lace and filling the vases on the mantelpiece with big bunches of roses. The air was soft, warm, and fragrant, everything breathed peace and restfulness, with a kind of lulling sensuality. The crackling of the fire broke the expectant silence with little staccato sounds. It was like a quiet retreat for happiness, a sequestered nook, warm, scented, shut off from all outside clamour, one of those retreats specially made for the pleasures of the senses, with their need for mystery.

Thérèse was sitting on a low chair to the right of the fireplace, her chin cupped in her hand, staring at the flames. She did not look round when Laurent came in. Her lacy petticoat and bodice showed up dead white in the light of the blazing fire. The bodice was slipping down and part of her shoulder emerged pink, half hidden by a tress of her black hair.

Laurent moved forward a step or two without a word, and took off his coat and waistcoat. In his shirtsleeves he looked once again at Thérèse who still had not moved. He seemed to hesitate and then, seeing the bare shoulder, he stooped down tremulously to press his lips to the bit of bare flesh. But she freed her shoulder by quickly turning round, and stared at Laurent with such a strange expression of fear and repugnance that he backed away, thrown off his balance as though he too were terrified and revolted.

He sat down opposite her on the other side of the fire, and there they stayed for five whole minutes without a word or a movement. Now and then the wood spurted jets of ruddy flame, and then the murderers' faces were touched with fleeting gleams of blood.

It was nearly two years since the lovers had been together in the same room without witnesses and able to give themselves up to each other. They had never met to make love since the day Thérèse had gone to the rue Saint-Victor and taken with her the idea of the murder. Some instinct of prudence had kept their bodies apart. The most they had allowed themselves had been an occasional handclasp or a stolen kiss. After Camille's murder, new desires had seized them, but they had kept them under control, waiting for the wedding night, promising themselves frantic enjoyment when they could have it with impunity. And now at last their wedding night had come, and here they were, face to face, overcome with sudden uneasiness. They had only to stretch out their arms and crush each other in a passionate embrace, and lo! their arms seemed flabby as if they were already worn out with love-making. The oppression of the day weighed more and more heavily upon them, and they looked at each other with no desire but only timid awkwardness, irked at staying silent and cold. Their fevered dreams were turning into a weird reality; the mere fact that they had succeeded in killing Camille and marrying, that Laurent's lips had touched Thérèse's shoulder, was enough to cool their lust to the point of nausea and horror.

They began desperately searching in themselves for something of the passion that had possessed them long ago. Their bodies now seemed to be devoid of muscles or nerves, but their embarrassment and fear increased, and it made them feel self-conscious to be sitting like this tongue-tied and dismal opposite each other. They wished they could find the strength to embrace till their bones cracked, so as not to appear idiotic in their own eyes. Well! they now belonged to each other, they had killed a man and played out a grisly comedy so as to be free to wallow in shameless gratification at all hours of the day and night, and here they now were on either side of a fireplace, numb and exhausted, with minds unhinged and flesh dead! Such a dénouement really seemed ludicrously horrible and cruel. And so Laurent tried to talk of love and bring back memories of the past, drawing upon his imagination to revive his caresses.

'Thérèse,' he said, bending towards her, 'don't you remember our afternoons in this room? I used to come in by that door, but today I have come by this one. We are free, we are going to be able to make love in peace.'

But his voice was hesitant, lifeless. She, crouching on her low chair, went on watching the flames, lost in dreams, not listening. He went on:

'Don't you remember? I used to dream that I wanted to stay a whole night with you, fall asleep in your arms, and wake up next morning to your kisses. Now I am going to make that dream come true.'

Thérèse started as though with surprise at hearing a voice muttering in her ear. She turned to Laurent on whose face the fire happened to be casting a beam of ruddy light, and she looked at that blood-red countenance and shuddered.

Even more disturbed and anxious he went on:

'We have managed it, Thérèse, we have smashed all the obstacles and we belong to each other. The future is ours, isn't it? A future of quiet happiness and contented love. There's no Camille now . . .'

He stopped short; his throat was parched, he was gasping for breath and could not go on. Camille's name had struck Thérèse like a blow in the stomach. The two murderers sat staring stupidly at each other, pale and trembling. The golden beams of the fire were still dancing on the ceiling and walls, the warmth brought out the scent of the roses, and the burning wood made little cracking noises in the silence.

Memories had been let loose. The ghost of Camille had been called up and had taken its seat between the newly married pair in front of the blazing fire. Mixed with the warm air they were breathing they sensed the damp, cold smell of the drowned man; feeling that there was a corpse just near them, they gazed at each other without daring to move. Thereupon the whole terrible story of the crime passed before their mind's eye. The mere name of their victim sufficed to overwhelm them with the past and force them to live all over again through the emotions of the murder. They never opened their mouths, but looked at each other, and each went through the same nightmare and read in the other's eyes the same dreadful story. The exchange of horrified looks, and the unspoken account of the murder they were about to give each other, filled them with an acute, unbearable foreboding. Their strained nerves might give way at any moment, and then they might shriek and maybe start fighting. In an effort to thrust these memories aside, Laurent jerked himself roughly out of the horrible spell compelling him to look into Thérèse's eyes, walked up and down the room, took off his shoes and put on some slippers, then came and sat down again by the fire and attempted to launch into small talk.

Thérèse understood what he wanted to do and made herself answer his questions. They chatted about the weather, trying to force themselves to carry on a light conversation. Laurent stated that it was hot in the room. Thérèse said that all the same a certain amount of draught did come under the door to the back stairs. They turned and looked at the door with a sudden shiver of fear. So he hastily talked about the roses, the fire, in fact anything he could see, and she with a great effort found monosyllables to prevent the conversation from petering out. They had moved away from each other and were now trying to behave casually, to forget who they were and treat each other like strangers thrown together by some chance encounter.

And yet, in some strange way and in spite of themselves, even while they were speaking, each guessed the thoughts that the other was concealing beneath the banality of their empty words. Their minds came back irresistibly to Camille, and their eyes went on with the story of the past, a continuous, silent conversation going on independently of the haphazard one spoken aloud. The odd words they said were meaningless, disconnected, contradictory, their whole being was concerned with the silent exchange of nightmare memories. When Laurent was talking about the roses or the fire or something or other, Thérèse understood perfectly that he was reminding her of the struggle in the boat and the gentle splash as Camille fell into the water, and when Thérèse answered yes or no to some trivial question Laurent understood that she meant she did or did not recall some detail of the crime. And thus they conversed, heart to heart and with no need for words, while talking about something else. Without even being conscious of the words they were saying, they followed out their secret thoughts sentence by sentence, and if they had suddenly gone on aloud, the thread of their understanding would not have been broken. This sort of thought-reading, this obstinacy of their memories in constantly thrusting the vision of Camille before them, was gradually driving them frantic; they realized that they were reading each other like books, and that unless they stopped talking the words would rise unbidden to their lips and name the drowned man and describe his murder. So they shut their mouths tight and broke off the conversation.

But still, in the ensuing unbearable silence, the two murderers went on conversing about their victim. Their eyes seemed to bore into each other's flesh and plunge clear, sharp sentences into each other like knives. At times they thought they heard themselves speaking aloud, for their senses were becoming confused and their sight turning into a sort of strange, sensitive hearing; their thoughts could be read clearly on their faces and so took on a weird, strident tone that shook their whole organism. They would not have understood each other any better had they screamed at the top of their voices: 'We have killed Camille, and his corpse is here between us, turning our limbs to ice.' And so their terrible exchange of secrets went on and on, ever louder and more obvious, in the warm, quiet air of the bedroom.

Laurent and Thérèse had begun the silent story with the day of their first sight of each other in the shop, and their memories had followed one by one in sequence: the hours of ecstasy, the moments of hesitation and anger, the terrible moment of the murder. It was at that point that they had shut their mouths and stopped talking about one thing and another for fear of suddenly naming Camille in spite of themselves. But their thoughts had not stopped at the murder, but had taken them on through the anguish of the terror-stricken wait that had followed. And so they came to the thought of the drowned corpse laid out on the slab at the Morgue. Laurent's eyes told Thérèse all his horror, and she, at the end of her tether and forced by a hand of iron to open her lips, suddenly went on with the conversation aloud:

'So you saw him at the Morgue?' she asked, without naming Camille.

He seemed to be waiting for the question, which he had read a moment before on her white face.

'Yes,' was all he could manage to say.

They shuddered, drew nearer the fire, and held out their hands to warm them as if an icy wind had suddenly blown through the warm room. They stayed crouching and huddled up for a minute or two, and then Thérèse went on softly:

'Did he look as though he had suffered a lot?'

Laurent could not answer, but made a terrified movement as though to push a horrible sight away. He jumped up, walked over to the bed, and came back brutally, with arms open.

'Give me a kiss,' he said, offering his neck.

Thérèse had risen to her feet, deathly pale, and stood there in her nightgown, leaning back with one elbow on the marble mantelpiece. She looked at his neck and saw a pink patch on his white skin. His pulse was beating fast, and the blood enlarged the patch and turned it fiery red.

'Kiss me, kiss me,' he repeated, his face and neck aflame.

She leaned farther and farther backwards to avoid a kiss, and, putting a finger on the mark made by Camille's teeth, asked her husband:

'What's that? I didn't know you had that wound.'

Her finger felt as though it were boring into his throat, and he jumped back with a little cry of pain.

'That?' he stammered. 'Er . . . that . . .'

He tried to hedge, but could not lie to her, and had to tell the truth.

'Camille bit me, you know . . . in the boat. It's nothing, it's healed up. Come on, kiss me, kiss me.'

The poor wretch proffered his burning neck. He wanted her to kiss it on the wound, reckoning on her kiss to soothe the thousand stings torturing his flesh. Chin up, neck thrust forward, he stood offering himself, but, almost lying along the marble mantelpiece, she made a gesture of utter disgust and cried in an imploring voice:

'Oh no! not there . . . there's blood there.'

She sank on to the low chair, trembling, and buried her face in her hands. Laurent stood there dazed, his jaw dropped, and he stared at Thérèse uncomprehendingly. And then, like a wild beast, he suddenly seized her head in his huge hands and thrust her lips against his neck on Camille's tooth-marks, and for a moment held the woman's head pressed tightly to his skin. Thérèse limply abandoned herself, moaning softly, for she was suffocating against his neck. But when she had struggled out of his embrace she wiped her mouth hard and spat in the fire. She had not uttered a word.

Ashamed of his brutality, Laurent began slowly pacing up and down between the bed and the window. It was only the horrible smarting pain that had made him force a kiss from Thérèse, but when her lips had struck cold on the burning scar the pain had felt worse still. The kiss he had forced from her had finished him. Not for anything in the world would he have gone through it again, the shock had been too painful. And as he looked at the woman he had got to live with, who was cringing and shuddering over the fire with her back to him, he told himself over and over again that he did not love her now, nor she him. For close on an hour she stayed huddled up and he went on walking up and down without a word. Each of them was facing the terrifying fact that their passion was dead, that by killing Camille they had killed their own desire. The bright fire gradually died into a great mass of red-hot embers, while the heat in the room became intolerable and the flowers drooped and filled the heavy air with their strong, heady perfume.

Suddenly Laurent seemed to have a hallucination. As he turned round on his way back from window to bed he saw Camille in a shadowy corner between the fireplace and the wardrobe. His victim's face was green and twisted just as he had seen it on the slab in the Morgue. He stayed rooted to the carpet, half swooning and holding on to a table. The low gasp that escaped him made Thérèse look up.

'There! there!' he shrieked.

He pointed to the dark corner where he could see the ghastly face of Camille. His fear infected her, and she came over and stood close to him.

'It's his portrait,' she whispered very softly, as though the painted face of her first husband could hear her.

'His portrait?' repeated Laurent, his hair standing on end.

'Yes, you know, the one you painted. Aunt

should have moved it into her room today, but she must have forgotten to take it down.'

'Yes, of course . . . his portrait . . .'

The murderer did not at once recognize his own canvas. In his panic he forgot that these botched features and hideous, splodged colours that frightened him so much were his own handiwork. Fear now made him see the picture as it really was, mean, badly put together, muddy, showing a grinning corpse-face against a black background. The dreadful ugliness of his own work overwhelmed him, especially the white eyes floating in indeterminate yellow sockets that reminded him exactly of the putrefying eyes of the drowned man in the Morgue. For a moment he stood there panting, thinking that Thérèse was lying to reassure him. Then he made out the frame, and gradually recovered some composure.

'You go and take it down,' he muttered.

'Oh no, I'm frightened,' she answered with a shudder.

Laurent's trembling came back. Now and again the frame disappeared, and all he could see was the pair of white eyes staring hard at him.

'For God's sake take it down,' he implored his wife.

'No, no.'

'We'll turn it to the wall, and then it won't frighten us.'

'No, I can't.'

Cowardly and cringing, he began pushing her towards the picture, hiding behind her to avoid the drowned man's gaze. But she freed herself, and he, making up his mind to brazen it out, went up to the picture, raised his hand, and felt for the hook. But the portrait looked at him with such a scornful, evil, and prolonged stare that Laurent, try as he might to outstare it, had to give in and fell back beaten, murmuring:

'No, you're right, Thérèse, we can't. Your aunt will take it down tomorrow.'

He started walking up and down again, but keeping his head lowered, feeling that the portrait was following him with its eyes. He could not help throwing an occasional glance at it, and sure enough the eyes of the drowned man could always be seen, staring flat and dull out of the darkness. The idea that Camille was there in the corner spying on him, witnessing his wedding night, scrutinizing them both, quite unhinged him with terror and desperation.

A thing that would have made anybody else smile made him lose his head completely. As he was by the fireplace he heard a sort of scratching sound. He blanched, for the scratching seemed to come from the portrait, and he imagined that Camille was coming out of his frame. Then he realized that the sound was coming from the little door on to the back stairs. He glanced at Thérèse, who was giving way to panic again.

'There's somebody on that staircase,' he whispered. 'Whoever could come that way?'

She did not answer. They were both thinking of the drowned man, and an icy sweat broke out on their foreheads. They fled to the other end of the room, expecting to see the door fly open and let the corpse fall in on the floor. The noise went on, but fainter and more erratic, as though their victim were scraping the wood with his nails so as to get in. For nearly five minutes they dared not move. And then at last there came a miaow. Laurent went across, realizing that it was Madame Raquin's tabby cat; he had been inadvertently shut up in the room and was trying to get out by shaking the little door with his claws. François was afraid of Laurent and bounded on to a chair, where with bristling fur and legs stiff he stood looking at his new master with a hard, cruel stare. Laurent disliked cats, and François almost frightened him, for at this moment of tension and fear he thought the cat was going to leap up at his face, and avenge

Camille. The creature must know everything: there was understanding in his round,
strangely dilated eyes, and he had to lower
his own before the fixity of that animal stare.
He was about to give François a kick when
Thérèse cried out:

'Don't you hurt him!'

Her cry affected him in a strange way. An
absurd idea came into his head.

'Camille has entered that cat's body,' he
thought; 'I shall have to kill the brute. . . . It
looks like a human being.'

But he did not kick him, for fear of hearing François speak in Camille's voice. Then
he remembered Thérèse's jokes in the days
of their passion, when the cat used to watch
their embraces, and he told himself that the
animal knew far too much and would have
to be thrown out of the window. But he had
not the courage to put his idea into practice.
So François remained at the ready, claws
out and back arched in sulky hostility, following his enemy's every movement with
lofty calm. The metallic gleam of his eyes
disconcerted Laurent, and he hastened to
open the door into the dining-room,
through which the cat fled with a squeaky
miaow.

Thérèse had once again sat down in front
of the dead fire, and Laurent resumed his

walking from bed to window. And thus they waited for dawn, never dreaming of going to bed, for their bodies and hearts were quite dead. One desire alone possessed them: to get out of that suffocating room. To be shut up together and have to breathe the same air was a real torture; they would have liked somebody else there to interrupt their privacy and save them from the cruel embarrassment they were in, staying there opposite each other without speaking, without the possibility of reviving their passion. Their long silences were a torment — silences fraught with bitter, desperate recriminations, unspoken accusations that they could hear distinctly in the noiseless air.

Daylight came at last, dismal and grey, with a penetrating chill.

When the room was filled with pale light Laurent shivered but felt calmer. He looked squarely at Camille's portrait and saw it for what it was, a banal and childish daub, and took it down with a shrug of the shoulders, thinking how silly he had been. Thérèse had got to her feet and was rumpling the bed to deceive her aunt and make it look as though they had enjoyed a night of happiness.

'Now look here,' Laurent said roughly, 'I hope we shall get some sleep tonight. This sort of nonsense can't go on.'

Thérèse gave him a serious look, full of meaning.

'You must realize I didn't get married so as to sit up all night. . . . We're just a couple of babies. . . . You upset me. The way you looked was enough to give anybody the creeps. Try and be a bit cheerful tonight and not scare the life out of me.'

He put on a laugh, though he did not know what he was laughing at.

'I'll try,' she said softly.

Such was their wedding night.

22

The nights that followed were even worse. The murderers had wanted to be together at night to defend each other against the drowned man, and now, by some strange development, since they had been together they shook with fright even more. They infuriated each other, got on each other's nerves, went through agonies of pain and terror merely from exchanging a single word or look. If the least bit of conversation started between them, or if they were alone together for the minimum of time, they saw red and went hysterical.

Thérèse's highly-strung nature had acted in a strange way upon the stolid, sanguine one of Laurent. Formerly, when their passion was at its height, the differences between their temperaments had bound this man and this woman closely together, establishing a kind of balance between them in which each, as it were, completed the other's organism. The lover contributed his blood and the mistress her nerves, they lived in each other, needing each other's embraces to regulate the mechanism of their being. But something had gone out of gear. Thérèse's overwrought nerves had taken control, and suddenly Laurent had found himself thrown into a state of nervous hypersensitivity; under her sensual influence his own temperament had turned into that of a girl in a highly neurotic condition. It would be interesting to study the modifications that sometimes take place in certain organisms as results of predetermined circumstances. These modifications originate in the body but rapidly spread to the brain and thence to the whole individual.

Before meeting Thérèse, Laurent had been a typical peasant, heavy, stolidly canny and full-blooded, eating, drinking, and sleeping like an animal. All day long and in all the things of daily life he drew steady, placid breaths, was on the smug side and tending towards the fat and dull. Only occasionally did he feel slight stirrings of desire deep down in his heavy flesh. It was these stirrings that Thérèse had magnified into horrible convulsions of lust. In that great, fat, flabby body of his she had planted an astonishingly sensitive nervous system. Formerly Laurent had enjoyed life in a more sanguine than nervous manner, but now he suddenly found a less coarse-grained sensuality. A new, poignant nervous existence was revealed to him by his mistress's first kisses. This existence magnified his sensual pleasures and gave his joys so keen an edge that at first he was almost frantic and madly gave himself up to crises of ecstasy that his flesh alone had never given him before. Then a strange process took place in him; the nervous side developed and took precedence over the sanguine, and this single fact modified his whole nature. He lost his calm ponderousness and ceased living in a state of somnolence. He reached a stage in which nerves and blood were nicely balanced, and this was a stage of deep enjoyment and perfection of life. But then the nerves became predominant, and he fell into the agonies that torture those whose minds and bodies are disturbed.

This was how Laurent had come to tremble at the sight of a dark corner, like a cowardly child. This haggard, shuddering creature, the new individual who had just emerged from the lumping, oafish peasant, was now going through the fears and anxieties of nervous temperaments. All these circumstances — Thérèse's wild embraces, the tension of the murder, and panic-stricken expectation of the resulting sensual pleasure — had combined to drive him out of his mind, intensifying his senses by sudden, repeated shocks to the nerves. Insomnia had followed inevitably, and with it hallucinations. And then Laurent had sunk into the intolerable life of ceaseless terror in which he was now floundering.

His remorse was purely physical. Only his body, strained nerves, and cowering flesh were afraid of the drowned man. Conscience played no part in his terrors, and he had not the slightest regret about killing Camille; in his moments of calm, when the spectre was not present, he would have committed the murder over again had he thought his interests required it. In the daytime he laughed at his own fears, promising himself that he would be strong and nagging at Thérèse for upsetting him; according to him Thérèse was the one who was trembling, it was Thérèse alone who made the awful scenes at night in the bedroom. But then as soon as night came and he was shut in with his wife, cold sweat broke out on his skin and he was shaken by childish panics. So he had regular attacks of nerves which recurred every evening, bedevilling his senses and making him see the green, disgusting face of his victim. They were like attacks of some fell disease, a sort of murder-hysteria, for the term disease or nervous disorder was really the only suitable one for Laurent's panics. His face became contorted, his limbs went stiff, and his sinews stood out in knots. His body went through agonies, but the soul was not involved at all. The wretched man did not feel the least repentance; Thérèse's passion had inflicted some terrible malady upon him, but that was all.

Thérèse, too, was suffering from deep-seated disturbances, but in her case all that happened was an undue stimulation of her normal nature. Since the age of ten she had been subject to nervous disorders, partly due to the way she had grown up in the nasty, overheated atmosphere of little Camille's sickroom. Storms had gathered within her, powerful streams had collected that were to burst forth later as veritable floods. Laurent had been to her what she had been to him, a brutal shock. From the moment of their first embrace her uncompromising and voluptuous temperament had developed with furious energy, and she had lived for nothing but passion. Giving herself up more and more to her burning desires, she had ended in a dazed and morbid state. The facts of real life overwhelmed her; everything drove her into unreason. And in her terrors she showed more womanly weakness than her new husband,

for she had vague feelings of remorse, regrets she would not admit to; she sometimes
had an impulse to fall on her knees and pray
to Camille's ghost, implore his forgiveness,
and swear to appease him by repentance.
Probably Laurent noticed these attacks of
cowardice, for when they were stricken by a
common terror he would lay the blame on
her and treat her harshly.

For the first few nights they could not go
to bed at all, but sat by the fire waiting for
daylight, or walked up and down as on their
wedding night. The thought of lying side by
side on that bed filled them with horrified
repugnance. They tacitly agreed to avoid
embraces, and never even looked at the
bed, which Thérèse rumpled every morning. When exhaustion overcame them they
dozed for an hour or two in armchairs, only
to wake up with a jerk when some nightmare reached its sinister climax. On waking
with stiff and aching limbs, faces blotched
with livid patches, and shivering with anguish and cold, they stared at each other
uncomprehendingly, amazed to find themselves there, subject to strange attacks of
modesty in front of each other, feeling
ashamed of letting their revulsion and
terror be seen.

Of course they fought as hard as they

could against sleeping at all. They would sit on either side of the fireplace and chat about a thousand and one trivial things, taking great care never to let the conversation flag. There was a wide space between them in front of the hearth. When they turned their heads they imagined that Camille had brought up a chair and was sitting in this space, warming his feet with a grimly mocking air. The vision they had had on their wedding night now came back every night. This corpse, this silent mocking listener to all their talk, this horribly disfigured body that was always there, weighed them down with ceaseless anxiety. They dared not move, they blinded themselves by staring into the blazing fire, and when something forced them to glance nervously to one side, their eyes, dazzled by the red-hot coals, created the vision and gave it a ruddy glow.

Laurent finally refused to sit down any more, but he did not explain to Thérèse why he had taken this idea into his head. She realized that he must be seeing Camille just as she was, and so she declared that she could not stand the heat and would feel better a few feet away from the fire. She moved her chair to the foot of the bed, and there she sat slumped in a heap while her husband resumed his pacing up and down the room.

Now and again he opened the window and let the cold night air of January fill the room with a freezing draught. It cooled him down.

Thus the newly married pair spent the whole of every night for a week, managing to drowse and get a little rest in the daytime, Thérèse behind her counter and Laurent in his office. But at night they were a prey to anguish and fear. The strangest thing of all was the attitude they maintained towards each other. Not a single affectionate word was said, and they pretended to have forgotten the past, appearing to accept and put up with each other, just as sick people experience a hidden feeling of sympathy for each other's sufferings. Both hoped that their revulsions and fears would remain concealed, and neither appeared to notice anything strange about the nights they went through, nights which should have revealed to them the true state of their natures. When they stayed up until morning, scarcely exchanging a word, blanching at the slightest sound, they appeared to believe that all newly married couples behaved like that for the first few days. It was the clumsy hypocrisy of two crazy people.

But soon they were so utterly weary that one night they made up their minds to lie down on the bed, but without undressing;

they threw themselves fully clothed upon the eiderdown for fear that their bodies might touch. They felt that the slightest contact would give them a sharp pain. Then, having slept fitfully in this way for two nights, they ventured to take off their clothes and slip between the sheets, but keeping well apart and taking great care not to come into contact. Thérèse would get in first and go right across against the wall, Laurent waiting until she was properly settled, when he would pluck up courage to lie on the near side, right on the edge. There was a wide space between them. That was where Camille's corpse lay.

When the two murderers were lying under the same sheet, with eyes closed, they seemed to feel the slimy body of their victim lying in the middle of the bed, and it turned their flesh to ice. It was like a loathsome obstacle separating them. A feverish delusion came over them in which this obstacle turned into solid matter — they could touch the body, see it spread out like a greenish, putrefying lump of meat, breathe the horrible stench of this mass of human decomposition — for all their senses became hallucinated and heightened their sensations beyond endurance. The presence of this disgusting bedfellow kept them motionless, dumb, horror-struck. Sometimes Laurent thought he would seize Thérèse roughly in his arms, but he dared not stir, for he told himself that he could not stretch out his hand without grasping a handful of Camille's soft flesh. It then occurred to him that the drowned man came and lay between them purposely to prevent their embracing, that, in fact, he was jealous.

And yet they did try to exchange an occasional furtive kiss to see what would happen. He would teasingly order her to give him a kiss, but their lips were so cold that it seemed as if death had come between their mouths. They both felt sick. Thérèse shook with horror, and Laurent, who could hear his own teeth chattering, would round on her.

'What are you shaking for?' he would cry. 'Surely you're not afraid of Camille, are you? Get along with you, the poor devil hasn't any feeling left in his bones by now.'

But they both avoided telling each other the real cause of their terrors. When hallucination held the pallid face of the dead man in front of one of them, he or she, with eyes tightly shut, would remain isolated in panic, not daring to mention the vision to the other for fear of precipitating an even more terrible scene. When Laurent, driven to distraction and in a frenzy of despair, accused Thérèse of being afraid of Camille, that name, spoken aloud, made the horror worse than ever and he shouted hysterically:

'Yes, yes, you're afraid of Camille . . . yes, I can see you are. You're a silly little thing, you haven't a ha'p'orth of courage. All right, sleep away in peace. Do you think your first husband's going to come and pull you by the feet just because I'm in bed with you?'

This thought, this supposition that the drowned man might come and pull their feet, made Laurent's hair stand on end. He went on more violently than ever, piling on the self-torture:

'I shall have to take you to the cemetery one night. . . . We'll open Camille's coffin, and then you'll see a nice rotted mess. And then let's hope you'll stop being afraid. Go on! Just as though he knows we threw him in the water!'

Stifled moans came from Thérèse, who had her head under the bedclothes.

'Yes, we chucked him in the water because he got in our way,' he went on. 'And what's more, we'd chuck him in again, wouldn't we? Now don't you be so childish. Be strong. It's silly to upset our happiness. Don't you see, my dear, when we're dead we shan't be a jot happier or unhappier under the daisies because we pitched a silly bugger into the Seine, and we shall have enjoyed each other to the full, and that's something. . . . Come on, give us a kiss.'

She kissed him, but she was ice-cold and desperate, and he was shaking as much as she was.

For over a fortnight Laurent tried to think what he could do to kill Camille over again. He had thrown him into the river, but still he was not dead enough, and came back every night to sleep in Thérèse's bed. Just when the killers thought they had brought off the murder and could give themselves up in peace to the pleasures of their love, their victim rose from the dead and turned their bed to ice. Thérèse was not a widow; Laurent found he was married to a woman who had a husband already — a drowned man.

23

Gradually Laurent went completely crazy. He resolved to drive Camille out of his bed. He had begun by going to bed fully dressed, then he had avoided touching Thérèse's body. Driven on by rage and despair he made up his mind to hold his wife tight to his breast and crush the life out of her rather than give her over to his victim's ghost. It was a superbly brutal gesture of defiance.

For after all, it was only the hope that Thérèse's embraces would cure his insomnia that had ever brought him into her bedroom. When he had found himself installed in that room as master, his body, racked by even more atrocious sufferings, had not even dreamt of trying the cure. And for three weeks he had stayed inert, forgetting that he had done all this in order to possess Thérèse, and now that he had her, unable to touch her without redoubling his agonies.

The very excess of his anguish shook him out of his torpor. In the first stage of stupefaction, that strange inertia of the wedding night, he had managed to forget the reasons that had just led him into marriage. But the repeated assaults of his horrible dreams had filled him with a smouldering vexation which overcame his cowardice and restored his memory. He recalled that he had married in order to drive away his nightmares by clinging closely to his wife. And so one night he suddenly seized Thérèse in his arms at the risk of passing over the dead man's body, and roughly pulled her to him.

She, too, was at the end of her tether and would have hurled herself into the flames if she had thought they would purify her flesh and deliver her from these evils. She returned Laurent's embrace in a determination to be destroyed by his caresses or find relief in them.

They crushed each other in a horrible embrace, pain and fear taking the place of desire. When their limbs touched they felt as though they had fallen into a furnace, but they cried aloud and strained still closer so as not to leave any space between their bodies for the dead man. Yet they could still feel bits of Camille's flesh squashed disgustingly between them, freezing their bodies in places whilst the rest was on fire.

Their kisses were appallingly cruel. Thérèse's lips sought out Camille's bite on

Laurent's stiff and swollen neck, and there she frenziedly kept her mouth, for that was the open wound, and if only it were healed the murderers could sleep in peace. She realized that and was trying to cauterize it with the fire of her kisses. But it was her own lips that were burned, and Laurent pushed her roughly away with a low moan, for it felt like a red-hot iron searing his neck. Thérèse frantically returned to the attack and made to kiss the wound again, for she derived an agonizing thrill from fixing her lips to the very skin into which Camille's teeth had bitten. It crossed her mind to bite her husband on the same place and tear away a great chunk of flesh so as to make a new and deeper wound and obliterate the marks of the old, for she thought she would stop being afraid if she saw simply the marks of her own teeth. But Laurent defended his neck against her kisses; it smarted too painfully, and each time she brought her lips near he pushed her away. And so they struggled, panting and writhing in their horrible caresses.

But they well knew that they were only making their troubles worse. In vain they carried their terrible embraces to breaking point; they shouted with pain, they burned and bruised each other, but they could not calm their terror-stricken nerves. Each embrace merely heightened their loathing, and while they were exchanging these horrible kisses, they were haunted by appalling hallucinations in which the drowned man seemed to be pulling at their feet and violently rocking the bed.

They let each other go for a moment, defeated by irresistible repugnance and uncontrollable nervous reactions. Then they made up their minds not to be beaten, and took each other back in a fresh embrace, only to be forced to release each other again as if red-hot needles were sticking into their limbs. Time after time they tried to overcome their revulsion and find total oblivion by wearing out their nerves. But each time their nervous excitement and tension led to such utter frustration that they might have died of strain if they had stayed in each other's arms. This struggle against their own bodies had worked them up into a fury; still they persisted, they were determined to win. But at length an even more desperate effort finished them, and the unparalleled violence of the shock made them think they were going to have a seizure.

Back at each side of the bed, hot and worn out, they began to cry.

And in their sobs they seemed to be hearing the triumphant laughter of the drowned man, who was once again slipping between the sheets with a sneer. They had been unable to drive him out; they were beaten. Camille calmly lay down between them, whilst Laurent wept over his impotence and Thérèse trembled lest the corpse might have the idea of using its victory to take her into its putrefied arms as her lawful master. They had made a supreme effort, and in the face of their defeat they understood that from then onwards they would never dare to exchange the slightest familiarity again. The orgasm of frantic passion they had tried to bring about in order to kill their terror had plunged them still deeper into it. Feeling the chill touch of the corpse that was now going to keep them apart for ever, they wept tears of blood and wondered in agony what was to become of them.

24

As old Michaud had hoped when he
schemed for the marriage of Thérèse and
Laurent, the Thursday evenings resumed
their former jollity immediately after the
wedding. These evenings had been in deadly
peril when Camille died. It was only with
great diffidence that the guests had ventured
into the house of mourning, and each week
they were terrified of being finally dismissed.
The thought that the shop door might in the
end be shut against them scared Michaud
and Grivet, who clung to their habits with the
instinctive stubbornness of animals. They
told themselves that one fine day the old
mother and young widow would go away and
mourn their dead at Vernon or somewhere,
and that they would find themselves out in
the street on Thursday evenings with nothing
to do; they saw themselves wandering up and
down the Passage, heartbroken, dreaming of
colossal games of dominoes. Pending these
evil days, they enjoyed their last bits of happiness in fear and trembling, coming into the
shop with an anxious but ingratiating

manner, telling themselves each time that they might never come again. For over a year these fears possessed them, and they dared not let themselves go and have a good laugh, in the presence of Madame Raquin's tears and Thérèse's silences. They did not feel at home as they had done in Camille's time; they seemed, as it were, to be stealing each evening they spent round the dining-room table. It was in these desperate circumstances that Michaud's self-interest had led him to the masterstroke of marrying off the dead man's widow.

On the Thursday after the wedding Grivet and Michaud made their triumphal entry. They had won. The dining-room was theirs once again, and gone was the fear that they might be sent packing. They came full of happiness, they spread themselves and ran right through the repertoire of their old jokes. It was clear from their beatific, confident attitude that from their point of view a revolution had been carried through. The memory of Camille had gone; the dead husband, that icy spectre, had been driven away by the living one. The past had come back to life with all its joys, Laurent was in Camille's place, there was no reason for sadness left, and the guests could laugh away without upsetting anybody; nay, it was even their duty to laugh and cheer up this excellent family that had so kindly invited them into its midst. And so from now on Grivet and Michaud, who for nearly eighteen months had been coming on the pretext of consoling Madame Raquin, could cast their little deception aside and come openly to doze opposite each other to the click-click of dominoes.

Each week brought round a Thursday evening and each week once more brought together these grotesque death's heads who formerly had so infuriated Thérèse. She spoke of showing them the door, for they got on her nerves with their silly bursts of laughter and idiotic remarks; but Laurent made her realize that such a dismissal would be a mistake, for the present must resemble the past as closely as possible, and above all they must keep on the right side of the police, that is to say of these fatheads who shielded them from all suspicion. Thérèse gave way, the guests were welcomed and blissfully saw a long vista of cosy evenings stretching away ahead.

It was at about this time that the couple began to live a kind of double life.

In the morning, when daylight dispelled the terrors of the night, Laurent dressed at full speed. He only felt at ease and recovered his self-centred calm in the dining-room, sitting in front of a huge bowl of coffee and milk made for him by Thérèse. Madame Raquin, now so feeble that she could hardly get down to the shop, watched him with motherly smiles as he ate. As he swallowed his toast and filled his stomach he gradually recovered confidence. After coffee he would take a small glass of cognac, and that completed the cure. He said, 'See you this evening,' to Madame Raquin and Thérèse, without ever kissing them, and then strolled off officewards. Spring was in the air, the embankment trees were bursting into leaf, covering themselves with a filmy pale-green lace. The river below flowed on with a caressing murmur and up and above the rays of the early sun shed a gentle warmth. In the keen air Laurent felt himself coming back to life and took great lungfuls of the breath of youth that falls from the skies in April and May. He made for the sun and stood still to look at the patches of silver dappling the Seine, listening to the noises along the embankment, letting the pungent morning smells soak into him, enjoying the bright and happy morning with every sense in his body. And indeed the thought of Camille scarcely troubled him at all — sometimes he happened to glance mechanically at the

Morgue across the water, and then he thought of the dead man, as a brave man might look back at some silly scare he had once had. With stomach replete and face freshly washed he recovered his solid tranquillity, reached the office, and there yawned the day away waiting for its end. He was just an employee like the others, dull, bored, with nothing in his head. The one idea he had was to give in his notice and rent a studio, for he was now dreaming of a new life of idleness, and that was enough to keep him busy until evening. The thought of the shop in the Passage never bothered him at all, but in the evening, having looked forward to closing time all day long, he came out unwillingly and took the road back along the embankment with vague worry and misgiving. However slowly he walked, he had to return to the shop. And there terror lay in wait.

Thérèse went through the same sensations. As long as Laurent was not with her she felt all right. She had got rid of the charwoman on the pretext that there was muddle and dirt everywhere in the shop and the flat upstairs; she was becoming house-proud. But the truth was that she had to keep walking about and doing things in order to tire herself out. She ran round all the morning, sweeping, dusting, turning out rooms, washing up, doing jobs that would have made her sick before. These domestic tasks kept her on her feet until midday, busy and silent but with no time left for thinking of anything but dustwebs on the ceiling or grease on the plates. Then she turned to cookery and got the lunch ready. At table Madame Raquin was distressed to see her constantly jumping up to go and get the next course, concerned and vexed at her niece's ceaseless activity, and she scolded her, but Thérèse answered that they had to save money. After lunch she would get changed and really make up her mind to go down and join her aunt behind the counter. There she was overcome by drowsiness and, worn out by insomnia, she would doze and give in to the delicious sleepiness that took possession of her as soon as she sat down. It was never more than a partial loss of consciousness, and full of vague pleasure, but it calmed her nerves. The thought of Camille left her, and she enjoyed the sense of deep restfulness of a sick person whose pain suddenly stops. Her body felt relaxed and her mind free, and she sank into a kind of warm, refreshing oblivion. Had it not been for these few moments of calm, her organism would have broken down under the nervous strain, and in them she found the strength needed for more suffering and another night of terror. Not that she really fell asleep; she scarcely lowered her lids as she sank into a dream of peace, and if a customer came in she opened her eyes, sold the few penceworth of goods required, and promptly fell back into her floating reverie. Three or four hours went by in this way and she was perfectly happy, answering her aunt in monosyllables, blissfully letting herself slip off into these moments of semiconsciousness that suspended thought and let her sink into herself. Only very occasionally did she glance towards the Passage, and she was most comfortable in dull weather when it was very dark and she could hide her lassitude in the shadows. Then the dingy, wet Passage, with its passing stream of poor devils soaked with rain, their umbrellas dripping on the flagstones, seemed to her like the entrance to some haunt of evil, a kind of dirty, sinister corridor through which nobody would come tracking her down and bothering her. There were moments when she noticed the dingy gloom surrounding her and smelled the sharp smell of damp, and imagined that she had been buried alive, that she was in the ground, deep down in a common grave swarming with dead. It was a consoling and reassuring thought, for she told herself that she was safe now, she was going to die and end her sufferings. At other times she was obliged to keep her eyes open: Suzanne sometimes came in and sat by the counter all the afternoon doing her embroidery. Thérèse now quite liked Olivier's wife, with her flabby face and sluggish movements, for she found a strange relief in watching this poor shapeless creature. She had made a friend of her and liked to see her about, smiling her wan smile, only half alive, giving the shop a sickly, funereal atmosphere. When Suzanne's transparent, glassy blue eyes gazed into hers she felt a grateful coolness in her very bones. And so Thérèse waited for four o'clock. At that hour she went back to cooking and once again tried to tire herself out, preparing Laurent's dinner with feverish haste. When her husband appeared on the doorstep her throat contracted and her whole being was once again racked with anguish.

Every day the couple went through just about the same sensations. In the daytime, when they were not face to face, they enjoyed delightful hours of respite, and in the evening, as soon as they were together again, they were filled with agonizing embarrassment.

Yet the evenings were quiet enough. Trembling at the thought of going to their room, Thérèse and Laurent sat up as late as possible, with Madame Raquin, half recumbent in a big armchair, chattering away between them in her placid voice. She used to talk about Vernon, always thinking of her son but avoiding his name out of a sense of decorum, and she smiled at her dear children and made plans for their future. The lamp cast its pale beams on her white face and her words sounded extraordinarily gentle in the still, dead air. And each side of her the murderers sat silent and motionless, apparently listening attentively, though in reality they made no attempt to follow the old lady's ramblings but were merely grateful for the sound of soft words which prevented their hearing the shouting of their thoughts. They dared not look at each other, but kept their eyes on Madame Raquin so as to have the right expression on their faces. They never mentioned going to bed and would have stayed like that until morning with the soothing chatter of the old lady and the peacefulness she spread around her, had she not herself expressed a desire to go to her own bed. Then and then only did they leave the dining-room and go into their own room, with death in their hearts, as though hurling themselves into an abyss.

Soon they found Thursday evenings very much preferable to these intimate family ones. Alone with Madame Raquin they could not entirely forget about themselves; the thin trickle of their aunt's voice and her affectionate gaiety could not drown their inner cries of anguish. They felt bedtime getting nearer and shuddered when their eyes happened to glance at the bedroom door, and this wait for the moment when they would be alone became more and more painful as the evening wore on. But on Thursdays they could forget themselves in silliness, forget each other's presence, and suffer less. In the end even Thérèse came to long for these guest nights, and if Michaud and Grivet had not come she would have gone and fetched them. With strangers in the room between herself and Laurent she felt calmer, and she would have liked to have visitors and noise all the time, something to drug and isolate her. In public she put on a sort of nervous gaiety. Laurent, on his side, brought out his coarse peasant jokes, smutty laughter, and art-student tricks. Never had the parties been so bright and noisy.

And so, once a week, Laurent and Thérèse could face each other without revulsion.

Soon a fear struck them. Little by little paralysis was coming over Madame Raquin, and they foresaw the day when she would be chair-ridden, powerless in body and mind. The poor old soul was beginning to mutter disconnected phrases, her voice was failing, and her limbs one after another were becoming useless. She was turning into a mere object. Thérèse and Laurent were panic-stricken as they watched the dissolution of this human being who still kept them apart and whose voice dragged them out of their nightmares. When she had finally taken leave of her reason, and stayed dumb and motionless in her chair, they would be alone. In the evenings there would be no other means of avoiding their dreadful dialogue. And then the horrors would set in at six instead of midnight, and that would drive them mad.

So their every effort was concentrated on preserving Madame Raquin in a state of health so vital to them. They called in doctors, waited on her hand and foot, finding the job of sick-nursing a means of forgetting, a rest to the spirit which spurred them on to renewed efforts. They were anxious not to lose the third party who made their evenings bearable, anxious to prevent the dining-room and the whole house from becoming a cruel, sinister place like their bedroom. Madame Raquin was particularly touched by the loving care they lavished on her, and with tears in her eyes congratulated herself upon having brought them together and having made over to them her forty-odd thousand francs. Never, since her son's death, had she expected such affection during her last days, and her old age was warmed by the tenderness of her beloved children. She did not notice the implacable paralysis which in spite of everything was making her stiffer day by day.

Meanwhile Thérèse and Laurent went on with their double life. There were, so to speak, two distinct creatures in each of them: one a nervous and terrified being who shuddered as soon as dusk began to fall, and the other a sluggish and abstracted one who breathed freely as soon as the sun came up. They lived two lives: screaming with anguish when alone together, smiling serenely when there was company. Their public faces never hinted at the agonies that had just been torturing them in private; they looked calm and happy, instinctively concealing their sufferings.

Nobody, seeing them so tranquil in the daytime, would have suspected that every night they were tormented by hallucinations. They would have passed for a couple blessed by heaven and living in perfect felicity. The gallant Grivet called them 'the turtle-doves', and when their eyes had dark rings after sleepless nights he would naughtily ask them when the christening was to be. There was general mirth at this. Laurent and Thérèse scarcely changed colour, and managed to raise a smile, for they were getting used to the old clerk's suggestive jokes. So long as they were in the dining-room they were able to master their terrors, and the appalling change that came over them as soon as they shut the bedroom door behind them was something that defied the imagination. On Thursday nights, especially, this change was so crudely violent that it seemed to owe something to supernatural factors. The weirdness and wildly excessive nature of their nightly dramas was quite incredible and remained hidden deep down in their tortured souls. If they had spoken about it they would have been thought raving mad.

'What a happy pair they are!' old Michaud frequently said. 'They don't say very much, but they think all the more. I bet that when we've gone they just kiss each other to death!'

Everybody was of the same opinion. In fact Thérèse and Laurent were held up as an ideal couple. The whole Passage du Pont-Neuf extolled their affection, quiet happiness, in fact endless honeymoon. But only the two of them knew that Camille's corpse lay between them; they alone could feel, beneath the outward calm of their faces, the nervous twitchings that distorted them horribly at night, turning their placid features into repulsive, aching masks.

25

By the time four months had elapsed, Laurent began to think about reaping the benefits he had counted on from his marriage. Three days after the wedding he would have left his wife and fled from Camille's ghost, if self-interest had not kept him tied to the shop in the Passage. He accepted the nights of terror, and stayed there amid the unbearable agonies, so as not to forgo the profits of his crime. If he left Thérèse he was back in poverty and obliged to go on working; if he stayed with her he could, on the other hand, indulge his love of idleness, pamper himself, and do nothing, on the income Madame Raquin had settled on his wife. He probably would have decamped with the forty thousand if he could have turned it into cash, but on Michaud's advice the old lady had prudently safeguarded her niece's interests in the marriage contract. Thus Laurent was bound to Thérèse by a powerful tie. By way of compensation for his dreadful nights he meant at any rate to be kept in blissful idleness, with plenty of food, warm clothes, and enough pocket money to satisfy his whims. Only on these terms would he agree to sleep with the drowned man's corpse.

One evening he announced to Madame Raquin and his wife that he had given in his notice and was leaving the office at the end of the fortnight. As Thérèse looked upset he hastened to add that he was going to rent a little studio and take up painting again. He held forth at some length on the unpleasantness of his job and the broad horizons opened out before him by art; now that he had a little money and could make a bid for success he meant to see if he was capable of something really big. The speech he delivered along these lines merely concealed a fierce determination to go back to the old studio life. Thérèse kept a tight-lipped silence, it was not her idea at all that Laurent should squander the little fortune that guaranteed her freedom. When her husband pressed her with questions to try to make her consent, she snapped a few curt answers, giving him to understand that if he left the office he would earn nothing and be totally dependent upon her. But while she was speaking he looked at her in a peculiar way which threw her off her balance, and the refusals she was about to make stuck in her throat, for she thought she could read in her accomplice's eyes the threat: 'If you don't agree I shall tell everything.' She began to stammer. At that point Madame Raquin exclaimed that her dear boy's wish was perfectly justified, and that he should be given the means to become a man of talent. The good lady was spoiling Laurent just as she had spoiled Camille; she had been quite softened by the young man's constant attentions, and she was always on his side and of his opinion.

Accordingly it was decided that the artist should rent a studio and receive one hundred francs a month for his out-of-pocket expenses. The family budget was apportioned in the following way: the profits from the haberdashery business would cover the rent of the shop and flat above and almost suffice for the regular housekeeping; Laurent would take the rent of his studio plus his hundred francs per month out of the two-thousand-odd francs income from investment, and the balance of this would be given over to common needs. In this way the capital would remain untouched. Thérèse felt a little less worried. She made her husband swear never to go beyond his allowance. Anyhow, she told herself, Laurent could not get at the forty thousand francs without her signature, and she resolved never to sign any document.

The very next day Laurent took a little studio towards the lower end of the rue Mazarine that he had been looking at with a covetous eye for a month past. He did not intend to leave his job without having a retreat where he could spend his days in peace, far from Thérèse. At the end of the fortnight he bade his farewells to his colleagues. Grivet was stunned at his going. A young fellow, he said, with such a great future before him, a young man who in four years had reached the salary that he, Grivet, had taken twenty years to reach! Laurent amazed him even more when he said he was going to devote himself entirely to painting again.

At length the artist moved into his studio. It was a sort of attic fifteen to eighteen feet square, with a steeply sloping ceiling in which was a big window which shed a glaring white light on the floor and dirty grey walls. No sound from the street came up as high as this, and the silent room, with its crude lighting from the sky above, seemed like a hole or vault hollowed out of grey clay. Laurent furnished this hole after a fashion with two chairs with broken seats, a table he propped against the wall to prevent its falling down, an old kitchen cupboard, his paintbox and old easel. The one luxury was a large divan that he had picked up for thirty francs in a second hand shop.

He let a fortnight go by without even dreaming of touching his brushes. He got there between eight and nine, lay on the divan smoking until noon, happy that it was still morning with long hours of daytime ahead of him. At twelve he went home for lunch, but hurried back so as to be alone and free from having to look at Thérèse's pale face. Then he let his lunch digest, had a sleep, and lolled about until evening. His studio was a haven of peace in which he knew no fear. One day his wife asked if she could visit his beloved refuge. He refused, and as she came and knocked at the door in spite of his refusal, he did not open it. That evening he mentioned that he had spent the day in the Louvre. He was afraid she might bring Camille's ghost in with her.

In the end idleness got on his nerves, and he bought a canvas and some paints and set to work. Not being able to afford models he decided to paint as the spirit moved him, without bothering about nature. He began on a man's head.

Besides, he did not stay indoors so much, but spent two or three hours at work each morning and in the afternoons wandered about Paris and the suburbs. Coming back from one of these long walks, in front of the Institut he ran into an old school-friend who had had a great success, thanks to the loyalty of his friends, at the last Salon.

'What, you!' cried the painter, 'why, poor old Laurent, I wouldn't ever have recognized you. You've got thinner.'

'I've got married,' Laurent answered awkwardly.

'Married! What, you? No wonder you look so funny. . . . And what are you up to these days?'

'I've taken a studio and I do a bit of painting in the mornings.'

Laurent told him about his marriage in a word or two, and then excitedly began developing his plans for the future. The look of astonishment on his friend's face flustered and unnerved him. The truth of the matter was that the painter did not recognize in Thérèse's husband the lumping and commonplace fellow he had known in the old days. Laurent, he thought, was getting quite distinguished-looking; his face was thinner and elegantly pale, and his whole figure was slenderer and more graceful.

'But you are getting quite handsome,' the artist exclaimed in spite of himself, 'as well turned out as an ambassador. All in the latest fashion. Where are you picking all this up?'

Laurent did not at all enjoy being cross-examined in this manner, but had not the nerve to walk off abruptly.

'Won't you come up to my studio for a minute?' he asked eventually, as his friend made no move to go.

'I'd love to.'

Unable to understand the changes he had noticed, the painter was curious to see his old friend's studio. Of course he was not climbing five flights of stairs just to see Laurent's new works, which would certainly make him sick. All he wanted was to satisfy his curiosity.

But when he was up there and had glanced at the canvases on the walls his amazement redoubled. There were five studies, two female heads and three male ones, painted with real energy; the work was rich and solid, and each one stood out in magnificent relief from its pale grey background. The artist rushed over to them, astounded and not even trying to conceal his surprise.

'Did you do those?' he asked.

'Yes, they are sketches for a big picture I'm thinking of doing.'

'Look here, no leg-pulling. Are you really the painter of these things?'

'Yes, of course; why shouldn't I be?'

The painter did not dare to say: 'Because those canvases are the work of an artist and you were never anything but a hopeless bungler.' He stood looking at them for a long time in silence. They were clumsy, of course, but there was such a strange character, such power in them that they showed a highly developed artistic sense. They looked like painting that had been lived. Laurent's friend had never seen sketches so full of the highest promise. After carefully studying the canvases he turned to their creator:

'Well, frankly, I wouldn't have thought you had painting like that in you. Where the devil did you pick up all that talent? It can't usually be learnt.'

On considering Laurent he thought that his voice was gentler and his every movement had a sort of refinement. He could not guess what a shattering upheaval had changed this particular man by developing in him a feminine nervous system with sensitive and delicate reactions. Evidently some strange phenomenon had come about in the organism of Camille's murderer. It is difficult for analysis to plumb such depths.

Laurent had perhaps become an artist in the same way as he had become a coward, as the result of the breakdown that had thrown his mind and body out of gear. Formerly he had been overcome by the sheer weight of his sanguine nature, blinded by the dense fog of his bodily health; but now, thinner, pulsatingly alive, he had the restless animation and keen, acute sensations of nervous temperaments. In the life of terror he was living his mind was delivered from reason and could rise to the ecstasy of genius. The quasi-moral disease or neurosis which had disturbed his whole being had developed in him a strangely lucid artistic sense. Since he had killed a man his flesh was, as it were, appeased, and his distracted mind seemed limitless; and in this sudden broadening of his thought there floated before him exquisite creations and poetic visions. Just as his bodily movements had taken on a sudden elegance, so his paintings were beautiful through having all at once become personal and alive.

His friend gave up any attempt to explain the birth of this artist. He went away, still amazed. But before leaving he glanced once again at the pictures and said:

'I have only one criticism to make, and that is that all your studies have a family

286

likeness. These five heads are all similar. Even the women have got something violent about them that makes them look like men in disguise. You must realize that if you mean to make a picture out of these sketches you must alter a few of the faces. You can't have all of them brothers, people would laugh.'

He went out, but added banteringly on the landing:

'No, but seriously, my dear chap, I have enjoyed seeing you. Now I shall begin to believe in miracles. Gosh, you really are getting somewhere!'

He went down. Laurent returned to the studio feeling very upset. When his friend had pointed out that all these heads had a family likeness he had turned away quickly to hide his change of expression. This unavoidable likeness had already struck him too. Slowly he took up his position again in front of the pictures, and as he looked at them, one after another, a cold sweat broke out on his back.

'He's right,' he murmured, 'they're all the same, like Camille.'

He fell back on to the divan and sat down but never took his eyes off the heads he had sketched. The first was an old man's face with a long white beard, but under the beard the artist could make out Camille's weak chin. The second was of a fair-haired girl, and this girl was gazing at him with his victim's blue eyes. Each of the other three faces had some feature of the drowned man. It was as though Camille were made up as an old man or young girl, taking on whatever disguise the painter liked to give him, but always keeping the general character of his face. And there was another terrible sameness about the faces: they looked agonized and terrified as if they were all overwhelmed by the same feeling of horror. Each had a slight contraction to the left of the mouth which distorted the lips and made them grimace. This twist, which Laurent remembered seeing in the contorted face of the drowning man, showed that they all belonged to the same horrible family.

Laurent realized that he had spent too long gazing at Camille in the Morgue, and that the picture of the corpse was etched deep into his mind. Now, every time, his hand unconsciously drew the features of that dreadful face that followed him everywhere.

Gradually, as he lay there on the divan, he thought the faces came to life. And there were five Camilles in front of him, five Camilles, all powerful creations of his own hand, who through some eerie change were of all ages and either sex. He jumped up, slashed the canvases to pieces, and threw them out. If he himself peopled it with portraits of his victim, he would die of fright in his own studio.

A new fear had come over him, that of never again being able to draw a face without drawing that of the murdered man. He made up his mind to find out at once whether he was master of his own hand. He put a new canvas on the easel, and with a piece of charcoal sketched a face in a few strokes. It was Camille's face. He hastily rubbed it out and tried another. For a whole hour he wrestled with the compulsion that guided his fingers. At each fresh attempt he came back to the drowning man's face. Try as he might to force his will-power and avoid the lines he knew so well, in spite of himself he drew those lines, obeyed his muscles and rebellious nerves. He had begun by dashing off rapid sketches, so next he concentrated upon moving the charcoal slowly. The result was the same: Camille, grimacing and agonized, appeared regularly on the canvas. Then he drew in turn the most varied types of heads: virgins with haloes, Roman warriors with helmets, rosy golden-haired children, old ruffians slashed with scars; but back came the drowned man always and always, whether as angel, virgin, warrior, child, or ruffian. So next he threw himself into caricature and overdid the features, made gigantic profiles, invented grotesque faces, but all he succeeded in doing was to add horror to the striking portraits of his victim. Finally he drew animals, cats and dogs. The cats and dogs were vaguely reminiscent of Camille.

A helpless rage possessed him. He put his fist through the canvas and despaired of his great picture, which was now quite out of the question, for he realized that he would never again draw anything but Camille's head and, as his friend had said, a lot of faces all looking the same would make him a laughingstock. He visualized what his picture would have looked like, with the pallid and staring face of the drowned man on the shoulders of all the figures, men and women alike, and the weird vision he conjured up seemed atrociously silly and filled him with fury.

And so he would never dare work again, for he would be afraid that the slightest stroke of his brush would call his victim back to life. If he wanted to live in peace in his studio he must never paint in it. The thought that his fingers had this inescapable

involuntary power of continuously repro-
ducing Camille's portrait made him look at
his hand in terror. It seemed to be no longer
his.

26

The blow with which Madame Raquin had been threatened suddenly fell. Paralysis, which for months past had been creeping through her limbs, ever on the point of striking, seized her by the throat and pinioned her body. One evening, as she was quietly talking to Thérèse and Laurent, she stopped in the middle of a sentence, open-mouthed, gaping, feeling as if she were being strangled. She tried to shout for help but could only utter raucous sounds. Her tongue had turned to stone. Her hands and feet had stiffened. She was struck dumb and motionless.

Thérèse and Laurent jumped up, appalled by the thunderbolt which in less than five seconds reduced the old woman to a twisted wreck. When she was quite rigid, gazing at them with imploring eyes, they plied her with questions to find out the cause of the trouble, but she could not answer and went on looking at them in deep anguish. Then they realized that there was nothing left facing them but a body, a body half alive who could see and hear them but could not speak. The stroke filled them with dismay; not that they really cared much about the paralysed woman's sufferings, but they wept for themselves, condemned for evermore to live alone with each other.

From that day on their life became unbearable. They spent dreadful evenings with the impotent old woman who could no longer lull their fears with her gentle chatter. There she lay in an armchair like a bundle, a mere thing, and they sat alone, one at each end of the table, embarrassed and apprehensive. This inert body no longer kept them apart; sometimes they forgot it was there and took it for part of the furniture. And then the nocturnal terrors would come over them, and the dining-room became, like the bedroom, a terrible place where Camille's ghost rose up before them. In this way four or five extra hours of suffering were added to each day. As soon as dusk fell they began to tremble, lowering the lampshade so as not to see each other, trying to believe that Madame Raquin was about to say something and so remind them of her presence. The only reason they kept her and did not get rid of her was that her eyes were still alive, and it gave them some occasional relief to watch them move and shine.

They always put the paralysed old woman in the direct light of the lamp so that her face was well lit up and always in front of them. That shapeless, pallid face would have been an unbearable sight for others, but they felt such a strong need for companionship that they let their eyes rest upon her with real joy. It was like the decomposing mask of a dead woman with two living eyes set in it, and the eyes alone moved and turned quickly in their sockets, whilst the cheeks and mouth were petrified and set in a frightening stillness. When Madame Raquin dropped off to sleep and lowered her eyelids her face, quite white and still, was indeed that of a corpse, and at such times Thérèse and Laurent, not conscious of anybody left with them at all, would make a noise until she raised her lids and looked at them again. In this way they forced her to stay awake.

They thought of her as a distraction to drive away their bad dreams. Since her infirmity they had had to look after her like a baby, and the care they lavished upon her compelled them to shake themselves out of their thoughts. Every morning Laurent lifted her out of bed and carried her to her chair, and at night he put her back to bed. She was still heavy, and he needed all his strength to take her carefully in his arms and move her. He also moved her chair about. The other duties fell to Thérèse, who dressed the invalid, fed her, and tried to interpret all her wishes. For a few days Madame Raquin kept the use of her hands and could write on a slate and ask for what she wanted; but then her hands went dead too, and it became impossible for her to raise them or hold the pencil. From then onwards she only had the language of her eyes and her niece had to guess what she wanted. Thérèse devoted herself to the hard task of sick-nurse, which provided an occupation for mind and body that did her a great deal of good.

To avoid being alone together they would bring the poor old woman's chair into the dining-room first thing in the morning. They had her between them like a necessity of life, made her sit at all their meals, listen to all their discussions. When she showed a desire to go to her own room they pretended not to understand. Her only function was to keep them from being alone together, she had no right to any life of her own. Laurent went off to his studio at eight, Thérèse went down into the shop, leaving her alone in the dining-room until noon; then after lunch she was alone again until six. Her niece often came up during the day and hovered round to make sure she had everything she wanted. Friends of the family were at a loss to find praises enough to extol the virtues of Thérèse and Laurent.

The Thursday parties went on, and the powerless woman was there as in the past. Her chair was brought up to the table, and from eight until eleven she kept her eyes open and looked hard at each guest in turn. The first few times old Michaud and Grivet were a little nonplussed in the presence of their old friend's lifeless body, and hardly knew what sort of expression to assume, being only mildly upset and wondering just what amount of grief it would be suitable to display. Should they speak to this death's head, or ought they to take no notice at all? Gradually they took the line of treating Madame Raquin as though nothing had happened to her, and finally pretended to be quite unaware of her condition. They chatted to her, doing both questions and answers themselves, laughing on her behalf and on their own and never letting the rigid, expressionless face throw them off. It was a strange sight; these men appeared to be conversing rationally with a statue, as little girls do with their dolls. There she sat, stiff and silent in front of them, and they talked away, gesticulated freely, and carried on most animated conversations with her. Michaud and Grivet congratulated themselves upon their perfect behaviour. By acting in this way they believed they were showing their politeness and, what was more, they avoided the usual tiresome business of expressing sympathy. Madame Raquin must be gratified to see herself treated as a person in normal health, and that left them free to indulge in frivolity in her presence without any qualms.

Grivet had a fixed idea. He alleged that he and Madame Raquin were in complete sympathy, and that she had only to glance at him and he grasped her meaning instantly. This was yet another delicate attention. Only he was wrong every time. Often he would break off a game of dominoes, look attentively at the paralysed woman whose eyes were quietly following the game, and then declare that she was asking for such and such. The truth proved to be that Madame Raquin was not asking for anything at all, or wanted something quite different. But that did not discourage Grivet, who would utter a triumphant: 'Now what did I tell you?' and start again a few minutes later. It was a very different matter when she really did express a wish: Thérèse, Laurent, and the guests would call out in turn things she might need, and on these occasions Grivet was remarkable for the ineptitude of his suggestions. He named anything that came into his head, quite at random, and it was always the opposite of what Madame Raquin wanted. Which did not prevent his repeating:

'I can read her eyes like a book. There, she is saying I am right. Aren't you, dear lady? ... Yes, yes.'

Not that it was easy to grasp the old lady's wants. Thérèse was the only one who knew how. She could communicate quite easily with that imprisoned mind buried alive in a dead body. What was going on inside this poor creature who was just sufficiently alive to be a witness of life but not to take any part in it? Possibly she could see, hear, and reason in a clear and sensible way, but she had neither movement nor voice left to bring out the thoughts that arose within her. Maybe her thoughts choked her. She could not have raised her hand or opened her mouth even if a movement or a word from her could have decided the fate of the world. Her mind was like one of those people accidentally buried alive who wake up in the darkness of the earth two or three yards below the surface; they shout and struggle, but people walk about above them without hearing their dreadful lamentations. Often, as he looked at her with her tight lips and hands lying on her knees, putting the whole of her life into her keen and darting eyes, Laurent reflected:

'Who knows what she may be thinking to herself? . . . some cruel tragedy must be playing itself out in that dead body.'

He was wrong. Madame Raquin was happy, quite happy in the care and affection of her dear ones. She had always dreamed of ending her life in this way, slowly, in an atmosphere of devoted attention and love. Naturally she would have liked to keep her power of speech so as to thank the kind friends who were helping her to pass peacefully away. But she accepted her lot without resentment; the tranquil, retired life she had always lived, and her placid temperament, prevented her from suffering too acutely from the loss of speech and movement. She had gone back to childhood, living her days without boredom, looking straight in front of her, thinking of the past. She even came to enjoy the delights of just sitting quiet in her chair, like a little girl.

Day by day her eyes took on a more penetrating sweetness and limpidity. She had learned to use her eyes like a hand or mouth, to ask and give thanks, and in a strange and charming way made up for the organs she had lost. Her eyes became lovely with a heavenly loveliness, in a face where the flesh hung loose and grimacing. Since her twisted, inert lips had lost the power to smile, she smiled with her eyes, with expressions of endearing tenderness; gleams of liquid light and rays as of the dawn shone from them. Nothing could be more strange than these eyes laughing like lips in a dead face, the lower part of which remained bleak and colourless while the upper was filled with divine radiance. All the gratitude and affection of her soul were especially reserved for her beloved children. When Laurent took her up in his arms to move her every night and morning, she thanked him with an outpouring of love.

And so she lived for several weeks, waiting for death, believing herself safe from any further misfortune. She had had her share of suffering, she thought. She was mistaken. One evening a frightful blow struck her down.

It was useless for Thérèse and Laurent to put her between them in a strong light; she had not enough life left in her to keep them apart and protect them from their tortures, and when they forgot she was there, seeing and hearing them, they were seized with panic, saw Camille, and tried to drive him away. At such times their speech became confused, and in spite of themselves they let out admissions and phrases which finally revealed everything to Madame Raquin. And then one day Laurent had a sort of hysterical fit and talked as though in a trance. Suddenly she understood.

A terrible spasm passed across her face, and she felt such a shock that Thérèse thought she was about to leap up and scream. Then she relapsed into an iron rigidity. This shock was all the more frightening because it seemed to galvanize a corpse. Sensitivity returned for one moment and then disappeared, leaving the powerless woman even more shattered and pallid. Her eyes, usually so soft, had gone black and hard, like bits of metal.

Never had despair fallen so brutally upon a human being. The awful truth scorched her eyes like a flash of lightning and entered her soul with the shattering crash of a thunderbolt. Had she been able to get up, utter the shriek of horror that rose to her throat, and curse the murderers of her son, she would have suffered less. But after hearing and understanding everything she had to stay motionless and silent, bottling up her grief within herself. She felt as if Thérèse and Laurent had bound and nailed her to her chair to prevent her leaping up and were deriving a fiendish pleasure from telling her over and over again 'We killed Camille,' having first fixed a gag in her mouth to stifle her sobs. Terror and agony coursed madly through her body and could find no way out. In vain she summoned her last bit of strength, she felt her tongue lying cold against her palate, she could not snatch herself from death. She was held rigid by the inertia of a corpse. Her sensations were like those of a man buried while in a trance, who, pinioned by the bonds of his own flesh, hears the thud of the spadefuls of earth above his head.

The ravages of her heart were even more terrible. A sense of total collapse broke her completely. Her whole life was laid waste, for all her tenderness, her kindnesses, her devotion to others had been brutally thrown down and trampled underfoot. She had lived a life of affection and gentleness, and in her last hours, just when she was about to carry to the grave her belief in the calm happiness of life, a voice screamed at her that everything is a lie, everything is a crime. Through the rent veil, beyond the loves and friendships she had thought she could see, appeared a horrifying spectacle of blood and shame. If she had had the voice to blaspheme she would have cursed God. God had deceived her for more than sixty years, treating her like a nice, good little girl, deluding her eyes with false pictures of peaceful happiness. And she had remained a child, foolishly believing in a thousand babyish things, not seeing real life dragging itself through the bloody mire of the passions. God was wicked, he should have told her the truth before, or else let her depart with her innocence and blindness. Now there was nothing left but to die denying love, denying friendship, denying self-sacrifice. Nothing existed but murder and lust.

So Camille had died at the hands of Thérèse and Laurent and they had planned the crime amid the filth of adultery! To Madame Raquin this thought was such an abyss that she could not fathom it with her reason or lay hold of it in any clear and detailed fashion. She only felt a single sensation, that of an awful fall, as though she were going down into a cold, black pit. And she said to herself: 'I shall be smashed to pieces when I hit the bottom.'

After the first shock the monstrousness of the crime seemed unthinkable. Then she was afraid of going mad as the certainty of adultery and murder took root in her and she recalled little incidents that she had not understood at the time. Yes, Thérèse and Laurent really were the murderers of Camille — Thérèse whom she had brought up, Laurent whom she had loved like a devoted and tender mother. It went all round and round in her head like a huge wheel, making a deafening noise. She guessed at such disgusting details, plumbed the depths of such immense duplicity, witnessed in her mind a double spectacle so atrocious in its irony that she would willingly have died so as not to have to think of it any more. One single idea went on grinding round in her brain mechanically and implacably with the weight and relentlessness of a millstone: 'It is my own children who have killed my child.' And that was the only way she could find to express her despair.

In the sudden change that had come over her heart she wildly looked for her former self, but all knowledge of that self had gone, and she remained overwhelmed by a brutal invasion of thoughts of vengeance that drove away all the goodness in her life. When the transformation was complete all went black within her, and she felt a new being springing to life in her dying body, a pitiless and cruel one who would have liked to tear her son's murderers to pieces.

When she had accepted the deadly embrace of paralysis and realized that she could not leap at the throats of Thérèse and Laurent whom she would have liked to strangle, she resigned herself to silence and stillness, and great tears fell slowly from her eyes. Nothing could be more heartbreaking than this mute, motionless despair. These tears running one by one down the dead face, not one wrinkle of which ever moved, this inert, waxen face that could not weep with all its features, in which the eyes alone were sobbing, was agonizing to contemplate.

Thérèse was moved by terrified pity.

'She must be put to bed,' she told Laurent.

He hastened to wheel the stricken woman into her room. Then he bent down to lift her up in his arms. At this moment Madame Raquin hoped that some mighty spring would put her on her feet, and she made one supreme effort. God could not let Laurent hold her close to his breast; she expected lightning to strike him dead if he had such unspeakable impudence. But no spring animated her and Heaven withheld its thunder. She stayed limp and passive like a bundle of rags, was grasped, lifted up, and carried by the murderer, and had the agony of feeling herself soft and helpless in the arms of Camille's killer. Her head rolled over on to Laurent's shoulder and she looked at him with eyes dilated with horror.

'All right, go on, have a good look,' he muttered, 'your eyes won't eat me.'

He flung her roughly on to the bed. The paralysed old woman lost consciousness. Her last thought had been one of terror and loathing. From now on, morning and night, she would have to submit to the abomination of Laurent's embrace.

27

Nothing but a fit of panic could have brought the pair to the point of talking and making admissions in front of Madame Raquin. Neither of them was cruel by nature, and they would have avoided such a revelation out of humanity, even if their security had not already imposed a law of silence.

On the following Thursday they were peculiarly anxious. In the morning Thérèse asked Laurent if he thought it wise to allow the paralysed woman to be in the dining-room that evening. She knew everything, she might give the alarm.

'Rubbish!' answered Laurent, 'she can't move her little finger. How do you expect her to talk?'

'She may find some way. Ever since the other night I have seen an implacable determination in her eyes.'

'No, you know the doctor told me there's no hope for her. If she ever speaks again it will be in her last expiring gasp. She can't last long anyway. It would be silly to have still more on our consciences by preventing her from being there tonight.'

Thérèse shuddered.

'You've misunderstood. Oh, you are right, there's enough blood about already. . . . I only meant that we could shut my aunt in her room and make out that she is not so well, or asleep.'

'Very clever! And that fool of a Michaud would go straight in to see his old friend just the same. It would be a perfect way of finishing ourselves off.'

He hesitated, trying to appear unconcerned, but anxiety made him stammer.

'Better let things take their course,' he went on. 'These people are as stupid as a lot of geese, and they certainly won't see any meaning in the old girl's silent miseries. They'll never suspect the real thing, they're miles away from the truth. Once it has been tried out we shall be easy in our minds about any consequences of being so imprudent. You'll see, it'll be all right.'

That evening, when the guests arrived, Madame Raquin was in her usual place between the stove and the table. Laurent and Thérèse put on a jovial manner, concealing their misgivings and nervously waiting for the incident that was bound to occur. They had lowered the lampshade so that light fell only on the oilcloth table-cover.

As usual the first game of dominoes was preceded by a bit of noisy small talk. Grivet and Michaud duly asked the paralysed woman the regular questions about her health, which they themselves answered beautifully as was their custom. After that, without bothering any more about the poor old soul, the company plunged joyfully into the game.

Since she had known the horrible secret Madame Raquin had been feverishly waiting for this evening. She had mustered all her remaining strength in order to denounce the culprits. Up to the last moment she was afraid she would not be at the party, thinking that Laurent would spirit her away, possibly kill her, or at least lock her up in her room. When she saw that she was being allowed to stay and was actually in the presence of the guests, she felt a thrill of joy at the thought that she was about to try to avenge her son. Knowing that her tongue was quite dead she tried a new language. With an amazing effort of will she managed to force a little life back into her right hand and raise it slightly from her knee, where it had always lain inert, then she made it creep slowly up one of the legs of the table in front of her and succeeded in laying it on the oilcloth. Having reached there she feebly moved her fingers as if to attract attention.

Seeing this white, soft, dead hand in the midst of them, the players were most surprised. Grivet paused with his hand in the air just as he was about to put down a winning double-six. Since her stroke the invalid had never moved her hands.

'Oh look, Thérèse,' cried Michaud, 'look at Madame Raquin moving her fingers. She must want something.'

Thérèse could not answer; she had watched, and so had Laurent, the struggles of the sick woman, and she regarded her aunt's hand, white in the lamplight, as an avenging hand about to speak. The pair of murderers waited, catching their breath.

'Yes, of course!' said Grivet, 'she wants something. Oh yes, we two understand each other. . . . She wants to play dominoes. That's so, isn't it dear lady?'

Madame Raquin gave a violent look of denial and then with infinite difficulty she straightened one finger and bent up the others, and then began painfully tracing letters on the table. But she had not made many strokes before Grivet once again exclaimed in triumph:

'I understand. She says I am quite right to put down the double-six.'

The stricken woman gave him a terrible look and went on with the word she wanted to write. But every moment Grivet kept interrupting her, declaring that there was no need to bother, for he understood, and then bringing out some idiotic idea. Michaud finally shut him up.

'Damn it, let Madame Raquin say it,' he said. 'Now, what is it, my dear?'

And he watched the table-top as though cocking an ear. But the paralysed fingers were getting tired, having begun the same word more than ten times, and now they could not do it without slipping from side to side. Michaud and Olivier leaned over, unable to make it out, and forcing the helpless creature to begin the first letters over and over again.

'I've got it!' Olivier suddenly exclaimed. 'I've read it this time. She has written your name, Thérèse. Look: *Thérèse and* . . . Go on, dear lady, finish it.'

Thérèse nearly screamed in terror. She watched her aunt's fingers moving over the table, and these fingers, she felt, were spelling out her name and denouncing her crime in letters of fire. Laurent had jumped up, wondering whether he had better fling himself upon the old woman and break her arm. All seemed lost and he felt the chill of punishment weighing down upon him as he watched that hand come back to life to reveal the murder of Camille.

Madame Raquin was still writing, but with more and more hesitation.

'That's right, I can read it perfectly,' Olivier went on a moment later, looking at the couple. 'Your aunt is writing both your names: *Thérèse and Laurent . . .*'

The old lady made repeated signs of agreement, while looking at the murderers with eyes that blasted them. Then she tried to finish, but her fingers had stiffened, the supreme effort of will that had animated them was dying, and she could feel the paralysis creeping down her arm and once more gaining her wrist. She hastened to spell out one more word.

Old Michaud read out:

'Thérèse and Laurent have . . .'

And Olivier asked:

'And what have they got, these beloved children of yours?'

Mad with panic, the murderers were on the point of shouting out the end of the sentence. They were staring at the avenging hand with fixed and terrified eyes when suddenly it gave a jerk, went flat on the table, and then slipped off and fell on to the impotent woman's lap like a mass of lifeless flesh. Paralysis had returned and suspended their punishment. Michaud and Olivier sat down again, disappointed, while Thérèse and Laurent felt such keen relief that they nearly collapsed, owing to the sudden rush of blood pulsing through their hearts.

Grivet was piqued at not having been believed, and considered that the time had come for him to re-establish his infallibility by completing Madame Raquin's unfinished sentence, the meaning of which they were all trying to guess.

'It's quite clear,' he said. 'I can gather the whole sentence from Madame's eyes. There's no need for her to write on a table as far as I am concerned; one look from her is enough for me. She wanted to say: "Thérèse and Laurent have been very good to me." '

Grivet had reason to congratulate himself on the power of his imagination, for the whole company agreed with him. The guests began singing the praises of the young couple, who were so kind to the poor lady.

'It is obvious,' old Michaud said pompously, 'that Madame Raquin desired to show due appreciation of the loving care her children are lavishing upon her. It does honour to the whole family.'

And picking up his dominoes he went on:
'Well, now, let's go on. Where did we get to? Grivet was just going to put down the double-six, I believe.'

Grivet put down the double-six. The game went on, stupid and monotonous.

In the depths of her terrible despair the old woman looked at her hand. It had betrayed her. Now it felt as heavy as lead, and never again would she be able to lift it. God did not want Camille to be avenged, but deprived his mother of her only means of publishing his murder among men. And the wretched woman told herself that now she was only fit to go and join her child under the earth. She lowered her eyelids, feeling that her usefulness was over, wanting to believe that she was already in the darkness of the tomb.

28

For two months Thérèse and Laurent had struggled on in the miseries of their union, in which each was a cause of suffering to the other. Hatred steadily developed within them until in the end they looked at each other with furious eyes full of vague threats.

Hatred was bound to come. They had loved each other on a purely animal level, with hot passion wholly physical, and then in the nervous upheaval caused by the crime their love had turned to fear and their embraces had given them a sort of physical revulsion. Now, in the unhappiness of marriage and life in common, they rebelled and flew into rages.

It was a bitter hatred with terrible scenes. They were well aware that they got on each other's nerves, and felt that they would have a peaceful life if only they were not always face to face. When they were together they seemed to be labouring under a great burden which they would have liked to throw off and do away with; their mouths set in a hard line, thoughts of violence flashed in their eyes, and they had moments when they wanted to tear each other to pieces.

In reality they were tortured by a single thought: resentment at their crime itself, useless regret at having upset their lives for ever. Hence all their anger and hatred, for they felt that the ill was incurable and that they would go on suffering until death for the murder of Camille; and it was this prospect of suffering in perpetuity that exasperated them. Not knowing whom to blame, they turned upon each other with execration.

They would not admit openly that their marriage itself was the inevitable punishment for the murder; they refused to listen to the inner voice crying out the truth and setting out before their eyes the story of their lives. And yet, in the midst of their shattering bursts of rage, each of them could clearly look down into the depths of their anger and make out the passionate egoism of their natures that, having forced them to commit a murder to satisfy their appetites, was now getting nothing out of the murder but a desolate, intolerable existence. Remembering the past, they knew full well that the only thing that had brought them to remorse was frustrated hope of sexual pleasure and peaceful well-being. Had they been able to embrace in peace and live for lust they would never have shed a tear for Camille, but would have prospered on their crime. But their bodies had recoiled from the married state and they wondered with dread where the terror and disgust were going to lead them. They could see only a horrible future of pain with a sinister and violent end. So now, like two enemies fettered together and struggling in vain to escape from their enforced embrace, they strained and tautened every nerve but could not get free. Then, understanding that they would never free themselves, irked by the cords cutting into their flesh, sickened by contact with each other, feeling their discomfort growing hour by hour, forgetting that they themselves had forged their own bonds, they flung bitter reproaches at each other, and unable to bear their shackles an instant longer, they tried to alleviate their sufferings and heal their mutually inflicted wounds by cursing each other and deafening themselves with their ravings and accusations.

Every night there was a scene. It was as though they sought out pretexts for maddening each other in the hope of relieving their nervous tension. They watched each other, mentally felt each other all over, probing their wounds right to the quick and taking the keenest pleasure in making each other scream with pain. And so they existed in a continual state of irritation, sick of themselves, unable to bear a single word, gesture, or glance without being hurt and flying off into a rage. Their whole being was ready and waiting for violence, and the slightest impatience, the most ordinary vexation was magnified in the strangest way in their unbalanced organism and in a moment became charged with brutality. The merest nothing raised a storm that lasted until the next day. A dish too hot, a window left open, contradiction, even a simple observation, would suffice to throw them into outbursts of real lunacy. And inevitably at some stage in the quarrel they threw the drowned man up at each other. One word led to another until they blamed each other for the drowning at Saint-Ouen, and then they saw red and flew into paroxysms of fury. There were appalling scenes in which they choked with rage, hit each other, shouted disgusting words, and committed shameful brutalities. It was usually after meals that Thérèse and Laurent lost control in this way, and they would shut themselves up in the dining-room so that the noise of their desperation could not be heard outside. There they could fight undisturbed, hidden away in this damp, cavernous room lit by the fitful yellow gleams of the lamp. In that quiet, still air their voices sounded harsh and shrill. And they never stopped until they were exhausted, for only then could they go and enjoy an hour or two of rest. These quarrels became a need, a means of finding sleep by stupefying their nerves.

Madame Raquin listened. She was always there in her chair, with her hands lying useless on her knees, her head straight, her face mute. She heard it all and not a tremor ran through her dead body. Her eyes stared at the murderers hard and unflinching. It must have been an atrocious torture for her; she learned, detail by detail, the facts that had preceded and followed the killing of Camille, and thus slowly sank deeper and deeper into the filth and crimes of those she had called her dear children.

The quarrels between the two cast light on the minutest circumstances of the horrible story and set out all its episodes one by one. And as she waded further and further into this bloody mire she prayed for mercy, for when she thought she had plumbed the depths of infamy she found she had still further to go. Every night she learned some new detail, and still the dreadful tale stretched out before her; she seemed to be caught up in a nightmare of horror without end. The original admission had been brutal and shattering, but she was still more hurt by these repeated blows, these small facts which the couple let slip during their outbursts, and which threw sinister light upon the crime. Once a day the mother listened to the recital of her son's murder, and each day the story was more terrible and more circumstantial, and was shouted into her ears with more crudity and violence.

Sometimes Thérèse was overcome by remorse at the sight of that waxen mask down which big tears silently ran. Pointing at her aunt she would implore Laurent with her eyes to be quiet.

'Well, what of it?' he bawled, 'you know she can't give us in charge. . . . Anyway, am I any happier than she is? We've got her money, so why should I worry?'

And on went the quarrel, bitter, noisy, killing Camille all over again. Neither of them dared give in to the compassionate thought that came to them at times, to shut the paralysed woman in her room when they had an argument and so spare her the tale of the crime, for they were afraid of striking each other down unless this half-living corpse was there between them. Thus their pity yielded to their cowardice, and they subjected Madame Raquin to unspeakable suffering because they needed her presence as a protection against their hallucinations.

All their disputes were alike and they all led to the same accusations. As soon as Camille's name was mentioned and one of them accused the other of killing him, there was a frightful scene.

One dinner-time Laurent, looking for an excuse for losing his temper, found that the water in the carafe was tepid. He declared that warm water made him feel sick and demanded some cold.

'I couldn't get any ice,' she answered curtly.

'All right, I shan't drink any.'

'That water is perfectly all right.'

'It's warm, and it tastes muddy. It might just as well be river water.'

'River water!' echoed Thérèse.

She burst into tears. One idea had suggested another.

'What are you crying about?' asked Laurent, seeing the answer coming and already changing colour.

'Because . . . I am crying because . . . you know why. Oh God, oh God! It was you who killed him.'

'You liar!' he shouted. 'You're lying, you

know you are. I may have thrown him into the Seine but it was you who egged me on.'

'Me? me?'

'Yes, you! Don't make out you know nothing about it, don't make me have to get the truth out of you by force. I need you to own up to the crime and accept your share in it. It calms me down and relieves me.'

'But I didn't drown Camille.'

'Yes, you did, a thousand times yes. It was you. Oh, you can pretend you are surprised and have forgotten. Wait a minute. I'll refresh your memory.'

He stood up, leaned over her, and, purple with rage, shouted in her face:

'You were on the bank, you remember, and I said under my breath, "I'm going to chuck him in." And you agreed, and you got into the boat. So you see you killed him just as much as I did.'

'It isn't true. I was out of my mind, and I've no recollection now what I did, but I never meant to kill him. You did that, and you alone.'

These denials infuriated Laurent. As he said, he found relief in the thought that he had an accomplice, and had he dared he would have attempted to prove to himself that the full horror of the murder lay at Thérèse's door. At times he felt like hitting her to make her own up that she was the more guilty.

He began striding up and down the room, shouting and raving, followed by the fixed stare of Madame Raquin.

'The bitch! the bitch!' he choked, 'she's trying to drive me off my head. Look here, didn't you come up to my room one night just like a whore and drive me crazy with your caresses so as to bring me to the point of doing away with your husband? You didn't like him, he smelt like a sick child, you used to say, when I came to you here. Three years ago did I know about any of this? Was I a criminal? No, I lived in peace like a respectable man, doing no harm to a soul. I wouldn't have hurt a fly.'

'You killed Camille,' Thérèse went on saying, with a desperate obstinacy that drove Laurent out of his mind.

'No, you did. I tell you it was you,' he answered in a terrible voice. 'Now look here, don't you go too far with me or something will happen. You bitch, so you don't remember anything! You gave yourself to me like a tart in there, in your husband's bedroom, and you taught me sensations that drove me crazy. Own up that you had worked it all out. You hated Camille and had meant to kill him for a long time. Of course that's why you took me for a lover, so as to throw me at him and smash him.'

'It isn't true. What you are saying is outrageous. You've no right to criticize my weakness either. I can say just as much as you that before I met you I was a respectable woman who had never done any harm to anybody. If I drove you crazy, you drove me crazier still. Don't let us start arguing, Laurent, do you hear? There are too many things I could bring against you.'

'Oh, and what could you bring up?'

'Nothing. . . . Instead of saving me from myself you took advantage of my unguarded moments and amused yourself by wrecking my life. I forgive you all that. . . . But for pity's sake don't accuse me of killing Camille. Keep your crime to yourself, and don't try to make things still more awful for me.'

Laurent raised his hand to strike her in the face.

'Hit me, I'd rather have that. I shan't suffer so much.'

And she offered her face. He desisted, took a chair, and sat down by her side.

'Now listen,' he said in a voice he struggled to keep calm, 'it's a coward's trick to refuse to take your share of the blame. You know perfectly well that we did it together, you know you are just as guilty as I am. Why do you want to make my burden heavier by making out you are innocent? If you had been innocent you wouldn't have consented to marry me. Think of the two years that followed the murder. Do you want to put it to the test? I shall go and tell the whole story to the Public Prosecutor, and then you'll see whether we shan't both be condemned.'

A shudder ran through them both. Thérèse answered:

'Men might condemn me, but Camille knows it was you who did it all. He doesn't torment me in the night as he does you.'

'Camille doesn't bother me,' said Laurent, but he was pale and trembling. 'It's you who see him in your nightmares. I've heard you shouting out.'

'Don't you say that!' she cried angrily. 'I've never shouted out, I don't want his ghost to come. Oh, I understand, you are trying to head him off from yourself. I'm innocent! I'm innocent!'

They stared at each other, terrified and exhausted, afraid they had called up the dead man's ghost. Their quarrels always ended in this way; they protested their innocence and tried to deceive themselves so as to dispel their evil dreams. Each one in turn strained every nerve unceasingly to decline responsibility for the crime; they defended themselves as in a court of law by levelling the most serious accusations against the other. The strangest thing about it was that they never succeeded in being taken in by their own sworn statements, for both of them remembered every circumstance of the murder perfectly clearly. They could read admissions in each other's eyes at the very moment when their lips were contradicting each other's charges. There were childish lies, ridiculous statements, merely verbal distinctions, for the miserable creatures were lying for the sake of lying and unable to hide the fact. Each in turn played the part of prosecutor, and although the trial to which they subjected each other never reached a verdict, yet they started it afresh every evening with fierce obstinacy. They knew they would never prove anything, never succeed in blotting out the past, and yet they were always trying to do so, always returning to the charge, goaded on by pain and fear, defeated in advance by the overwhelming reality of things. The most obvious advantage they gained from their disputes was a storm of words and cries that by its very din numbed their sensations for a spell.

And all through their scenes, throughout

their accusations, the paralysed woman never took her eyes off them. When Laurent raised his big hand to strike Thérèse, her eyes blazed with joy.

29

A new phase set in. Panic-stricken and not knowing where to turn for a consoling thought, Thérèse started to bemoan her drowned husband in Laurent's presence.

Her vitality suddenly collapsed. Her over-strained nerves snapped, her hard and violent nature softened. Even in the first days of her marriage she had been subject to moments of emotionalism, and now these outbreaks came back like a logical and inevitable reaction. Having fought against Camille's ghost with all her nervous strength and lived for months in a state of pent-up irritation and revolt against her sufferings, trying to cure them by sheer will-power, she now suddenly felt so utterly weary that she gave in and was beaten. And so, having become just a woman again, a little girl even, with no more strength left to brace herself and stand up desperately to her terrors, she threw herself into self-pity, tears, and regrets in the hope of finding some relief. She tried to utilize the weaknesses of body and mind now overtaking her; possibly the drowned man, who had not yielded to her anger, would be touched by her tears. Thus there was calculation in her remorse, for she told herself that that might be the best way to placate and satisfy Camille. Like certain church-going females who think they can deceive God and get a pardon out of Him by praying with their lips and putting on a humble attitude of penitence, Thérèse humiliated herself, beat her breast, found words of repentance, but had nothing in her heart but fear and cowardice. Moreover she derived a sort of physical pleasure from letting herself go, feeling unresisting and crushed, passively giving herself up to grief.

She overwhelmed Madame Raquin with her tearful misery. The paralysed woman became a daily need, to be used as a sort of prayer-stool, a piece of furniture in front of which she could confess her sins without fear and beg forgiveness. Whenever she felt the need to have a good cry and relieve herself in tears she would kneel down in front of the impotent old woman and there she would shout and choke with passion, acting a one-woman drama of remorse which comforted her by tiring her out.

'I am a vile creature,' she would say in a faltering voice, 'and don't deserve forgiveness. I deceived you, I sent your son to his death. You can never forgive me. . . . And yet if you could only see inside me and understand my stabbing remorse, if you knew what torments I am going through, you might have some pity. But no, there can be no pity for me. I wish I could die like this, at your feet, overcome by shame and grief.'

She would talk like this for hours on end, passing from despair to hope, self-condemnation to self-forgiveness, speaking in the voice of an invalid child, sometimes pettish, sometimes doleful. She would lie flat on the floor and then rise up, actuated by every whim of humility and pride, repentance and defiance that passed through her head. Sometimes she even forgot she was on her knees in front of Madame Raquin and went on with her monologue as in a dream. When she was quite stupefied with her own words she would get up, staggering and dazed, and go down to the shop, feeling calmer and no longer afraid of bursting into nervous sobbing in front of her customers. But when a fresh need for remorse came over her, she hurried upstairs again and once again knelt down at the old woman's feet. And the same scene was enacted ten times a day.

It never occurred to Thérèse that her tears

and displays of remorse must subject her aunt to unspeakable suffering. And indeed, if anybody had tried to devise a form of torture for Madame Raquin, he could certainly not have found one more horrible than this farce of remorse played out by her niece. She saw through to the selfishness underlying these outpourings of grief. These long monologues she was forced to undergo at every moment, which constantly re-enacted Camille's murder in front of her, caused her untold pain. She could not forgive, but entrenched herself in an implacable desire for vengeance made all the more implacable by her impotence, and yet all day long she had to listen to prayers for forgiveness and humble abject entreaties. She would have liked to answer back; certain of her niece's phrases brought crushing retorts to her mouth, but she had to stay silent, letting Thérèse plead her cause and never interrupting. Her inability to shout out and stuff up her ears filled her with indescribable torment. And one by one the younger woman's words sank into her mind, slow and plaintive, like an annoying tune. It crossed her mind that the murderers were inflicting this kind of torture upon her with diabolically cruel intention. Her only means of self-defence was to shut her eyes as soon as her niece knelt down: even if she heard her she did not look at her.

Finally Thérèse had the effrontery to kiss her aunt. One day, in a fit of repentance, she pretended to see a look of mercifulness in the paralysed woman's eyes, and crawled along on her knees and raised herself, crying wildly: 'You forgive me! you forgive me!' and then kissed the forehead and cheeks of the poor old woman, who was unable to move back her head out of the way. The cold flesh against her lips made her feel sick, but she thought that the revulsion, like the tears and remorse, would be an excellent sedative for her nerves, and so she went on kissing her daily, by way of a penance and relief.

'Oh, how good you are!' she sometimes exclaimed. 'I see my tears have touched your heart. . . . Your eyes are full of pity. . . . I am saved!'

And she smothered her with caresses, laid her head on her knees, kissed her hands, smiled happily at her, and lavished upon her the most extravagant marks of affection. As time went on she believed in this farce herself, imagined that she had really obtained Madame Raquin's forgiveness, and talked to her of nothing else but the happiness this forgiveness had brought her.

This was too much for Madame Raquin.

She nearly died. When her niece kissed her she felt the same acute sense of repugnance and rage that filled her night and morning when Laurent lifted her in his arms to get her up or put her to bed. She was forced to submit to the vile endearments of the creature who had deceived and killed her son, and she could not even use her hand to wipe off the imprint of the kisses the woman left on her cheeks. For long hours she felt those kisses burning her. So she had become the plaything of Camille's murderers, a doll they dressed, turned right and left, and used according to their whims and needs. She was inert in their hands as though she were merely stuffed with sawdust, and yet inside her there were living organs, to be disgusted or lacerated at the slightest contact with Thérèse or Laurent. What exasperated her above all was the wicked mockery of the younger woman's pretending to read thoughts of mercy in her eyes when those eyes would have liked to blast her dead. Often she made frantic efforts to utter some cry of protest, and put all her hatred into her eyes. But Thérèse, whom it suited to keep telling herself twenty times a day that she was pardoned, redoubled her caresses, refusing to notice anything. So the paralysed woman had to accept gushing thanks that her heart repudiated, and she lived in a state of bitter, powerless irritation, shut in with a chastened niece always trying to think of some beautiful token of affection with which to repay her for what she called her heavenly loving-kindness.

But if Laurent was there when his wife knelt down in front of Madame Raquin, he pulled her up again roughly.

'Stop that play-acting,' he said. 'Do I cry and throw myself on the floor? You are doing all this just to annoy me.'

Thérèse's remorse affected him strangely. He had been finding life more difficult since his accomplice had taken to moping round him with reddened eyes and entreaties on her lips. The sight of this living self-reproach redoubled his own fears and increased his feeling of insecurity. It was as if a perpetual reproach were stalking about the house. Moreover, he feared that remorse might drive his wife to reveal everything one day. He would have preferred her to remain cold and threatening, obstinately defending herself against his accusations. But she had changed her tactics and now freely accepted her share in the crime, accused herself, went passive and fearful, which led to pleadings for redemption made with fervent humility. This attitude got on Laurent's nerves, and each evening their quarrels grew more fierce and more sinister.

'Listen,' Thérèse said to her husband, 'we are guilty of a great crime, and we must repent if we want to enjoy any peace of mind. Since I have been crying I have felt calmer, don't you see? Do the same as me. Let us admit together that we are being justly punished for a horrible crime.'

'Rubbish!' he snapped, 'you can say what you like. I know you are devilishly clever and hypocritical. Cry away if it amuses you. But for God's sake don't drive me dotty with your tears.'

'Oh, you are wicked, you turn away from repentance. And yet you are a coward, you took Camille unawares.'

'Do you mean I'm the only guilty party?'

'No, I don't say that. I'm guilty, more so than you, for I should have saved my husband from your hands. Oh, I realize the full horror of my sin, but I am trying to earn forgiveness, and I shall succeed, Laurent, but you will go on living a life of misery. . . . You haven't even the decency to spare my poor aunt the sight of your disgusting exhibitions of temper. You have never addressed a single word of sorrow to her.'

Thereupon she kissed Madame Raquin, who shut her eyes. She fussed round her, lifting the pillow supporting her head, lavishing countless little attentions upon her. Laurent was infuriated.

'Oh, do leave her alone!' he shouted. 'Can't you see she hates the very sight of you and your attentions? If she could raise her hand she would hit you.'

His wife's slow, doleful talk and her attitudes of resignation gradually filled him with blind fury. He could easily see through her tactics: she wanted to stop making common cause with him and isolate herself amid her regrets, so as to elude the drowned man's embraces. At times he thought that she had perhaps taken the right course and that her tears would cure her of her terrors, and this made him shudder at the idea of being the only one to suffer, the only one afraid. He would have liked to repent too, or at any rate act the part of remorse just to try, but the necessary sobs and words would not come, and so he fell back upon violence, gave Thérèse a shaking in order to anger her and make her join him again in outbursts of rage. On her side she made a special point of remaining passive, countering his angry shouting by tearful shows of submissiveness, and making herself all the more humble and penitent as he became more blustering. All this lashed Laurent into madness. To put the finishing touch to his rage, Thérèse invariably ended up by singing Camille's praises and setting forth his virtues.

'He was so good,' she said, 'and we must have been cruel indeed to turn against such a kind heart who never had an evil thought.'

'Oh, yes, he was good, I know,' sneered Laurent, 'and by that you mean he was daft, don't you? Have you forgotten, then? You used to make out that the least little thing he said got on your nerves, and that he couldn't open his mouth without saying something silly.'

'It's nothing to laugh at. . . . So far that's the only thing you haven't done, insult the man you murdered. You don't know anything about a woman's heart, Laurent; Camille loved me, and I loved him.'

'You loved him! Oh, really, that's a good one! I suppose it was because you loved him that you took me to bed with you? . . . I remember one day when you were crawling over my chest and saying that Camille made you sick as your fingers sank into his flesh like clay. Oh, I know why you took me. You wanted some much stronger arms than that poor devil's.'

'I loved him like a sister. He was my benefactress's son, he had all the refinement of a delicate nature, he was noble and generous, kindly and affectionate. . . . And we killed him, oh God, oh God!'

And more weeping and swooning. Madame Raquin threw her a piercing look, outraged at hearing Camille's praises sung by such a mouth. Laurent was powerless against this flood of tears, and rushed up and down looking for some means of stifling her remorse once and for all. All the good he kept hearing about his victim ended by making him painfully uneasy, for he sometimes let himself be carried away by his wife's heartrending cries and really believed in Camille's virtues, and this redoubled his terror. But what sent him clean out of his mind and made him actively violent was the comparison the drowned man's widow never failed to draw between her first husband and her second, wholly to the advantage of the first.

'Yes, indeed,' she would cry, 'he was a better man than you. I wish he were alive now and you were lying in the earth instead.'

At first Laurent merely shrugged his shoulders.

'I don't care what you say,' she went on, working herself up; 'perhaps I didn't love him when he was alive, but now I remember, and I love him . . . I love him and hate you, do you see? You are the murderer. . . .'

'Will you shut up?' shouted Laurent.

'. . . and he is the victim, a decent man killed by a blackguard. Oh, I'm not afraid of you. . . . You know perfectly well you are a brutal, heartless, soulless wretch. How do you expect me to love you, now you are covered with Camille's blood? Camille was all tenderness to me, and I would kill you, do you understand, if that would bring him back to life and give me his love again.'

'Will you shut up, you bitch?'

'Why should I shut up? I'm telling the truth. I would willingly buy my pardon with your life. Oh, the tears and agonies I am going through! It's my fault that that wretch killed my husband. . . . I must go one night and kiss the ground where he lies at rest. That will be my final joy.'

Driven crazy like a drunken man by the appalling pictures Thérèse kept displaying before his eyes, Laurent flung himself at her, threw her down, and knelt on her body, raising his fist.

'That's right, hit me, kill me! . . . Camille never once raised a finger against me, but you are a monster!'

Lashed by her words, Laurent shook her violently, beat her, and bruised her body with his fists. Twice he nearly strangled her. Thérèse went limp beneath his blows, deriving a keen pleasure from being hit; she yielded, offered herself, and provoked her husband to make him hit her more. This was another remedy for the sufferings of her life; she slept better at night if she had had a good beating during the evening. Madame Raquin felt the most exquisite delight when Laurent was dragging her niece round the floor and belabouring her body with kicks.

From the day when Thérèse had conceived the infernal idea of expressing aloud her remorse and her grief for Camille, the murderer's existence became dreadful. From then onwards the wretched creature lived continually with his victim, and at every moment he was obliged to hear his wife praising and bewailing her first husband. The slightest thing was an excuse: Camille used to do this, Camille used to do that, Camille had such and such a quality, Camille used to show his love this way. Always Camille, always some touching phrase to mourn his death. Thérèse drew upon all her vindictiveness to make still crueller the torture she inflicted upon Laurent in order to safeguard herself. She went into the most intimate details, narrated the thousand trifling events of her childhood with sighs of regret, and thus mingled the memory of the drowned man with every act of daily life. The corpse that already haunted the house was now openly brought in. He sat on the chairs, sat at table, lay on the bed, used the furniture and things lying about. Laurent could not touch a fork, a brush, or anything, without Thérèse making him feel that Camille had touched it first. By constantly being brought up against the man he had killed he came to experience a sensation that nearly drove him insane: through being compared with Camille, using things he had used, he imagined he was Camille, and identified himself with his victim. Then his mind snapped and he rushed at his wife to silence her, so as not to hear any more of the words that goaded him into frenzy. All their quarrels ended in blows.

30

There came a time when Madame Raquin had the idea of letting herself starve to death so as to escape the sufferings she was enduring. Her courage was at an end, she could no longer bear the martyrdom of continual proximity to the murderers, and she dreamed of finding the final deliverance of death. Each day the torture of being kissed by Thérèse or taken up in Laurent's arms and carried about like a child became more excruciating, and she made up her mind to escape from caresses and embraces that filled her with horrible disgust. Since she already was too dead to avenge her son, she preferred to be quite dead and leave nothing in the murderers' hands but a body without feeling, which they could do what they liked with.

For two days she refused all food, putting all her remaining strength into clenching her teeth and spitting out anything they managed to force into her mouth. Thérèse desperately wondered whether there would be anything for her to kneel in front of in tears and repentance when her aunt had gone. She talked to her incessantly to prove that she must go on living, she wept, lost her temper even, and went back to her old rages, opening the old woman's jaws as one opens those of an obstinate animal. Madame Raquin held firm. It was a hateful battle.

Laurent stayed quite neutral and indifferent. He was surprised at Thérèse's frenzied efforts to prevent the old woman's suicide. Now that her presence was useless, he wished she would die. He would not have gone so far as to kill her, but since she wanted to die he did not see any necessity to deny her the means.

'Oh, do leave her alone,' he shouted. 'Good riddance! Perhaps we shall be better off when she's gone.'

Frequent repetition of such sentiments in front of her produced a strange emotional state in Madame Raquin. She became afraid that Laurent's hope might be realized and that after her death the couple might enjoy peaceful and happy lives, and she persuaded herself that it would be cowardly of her to die and that she had no right to depart before witnessing the climax of the sinister adventure. Then and only then could she go down into the underworld and say to Camille: 'You are avenged, my son.' The idea of suicide became distasteful when it occurred to her that she would carry her ignorance to the grave, and that there, in the cold silence of the earth, her sleep would be disturbed for ever by her uncertainty whether his killers had been punished. To sleep the good sleep of death she must sink into unconsciousness feeling the keen enjoyment of revenge, she had to take with her a dream of hatred satisfied, a dream to go on dreaming throughout eternity. So she accepted the food her niece gave her, and agreed to go on living.

Moreover, it was clear to her that the climax could not be long delayed. Day by day the situation between husband and wife became more strained and untenable. At any moment a single spark would blow everything up. Hour by hour Thérèse and Laurent faced each other more menacingly. It was now not only at night that they suffered from being close together; the whole of the daytime was filled with anxieties and painful scenes. For them everything led to panic and suffering. They lived in an inferno, hurting each other, turning everything they said and did into bitterness and cruelty, each trying to push the other into the abyss yawning at their feet, and at the same time falling in.

Of course each of them had thought

about separation. Each had entertained the dream of flight, of going off and finding some kind of peace far away from the Passage du Pont-Neuf with its murk and damp which seemed specially made for the emptiness of their existence. But they neither dared run away nor could. It seemed impossible not to go on rending each other to pieces, not to stay there suffering and inflicting suffering. They were possessed by a lust for hatred and cruelty. A sort of repulsion and attraction at one and the same time drove them apart and held them together; they were going through that strange experience of two people who want to get away from each other after a dispute, but keep on turning back to shout insults at each other. And also there were material difficulties in the way, for they did not know what to do with the impotent old woman or what to say to the Thursday guests. If they ran away it might give rise to suspicions, and then they imagined they would be tracked down and guillotined. So they stayed where they were out of cowardice, they stayed and dragged their horrible existence miserably on and on.

When Laurent was out in the morning and afternoon, Thérèse wandered aimlessly between dining-room and shop, uneasy, unsettled, not knowing how to fill the emptiness she felt more each day. When she was not weeping at Madame Raquin's feet or being beaten and sworn at by her husband, she seemed at a loose end. As soon as she was alone in the shop she felt weighed down with depression and gazed unseeing at the people going along the dirty black arcade, falling into mortal dejection down in this dark hole that smelt like a burial ground. She took to inviting Suzanne to come and spend whole days with her, in the hope that the presence of this poor, gentle, colourless creature would soothe her.

Suzanne accepted the invitation with joy, for she still always regarded Thérèse with a kind of hero-worshipping affection, and had long wanted to come and do her work with her while Olivier was at the office. She brought her embroidery and took Madame Raquin's place behind the counter.

From then on Thérèse was less attentive to her aunt, not going upstairs so often to weep on her knee or kiss her dead face. Now she had something else to do. She tried to listen with interest to Suzanne's long-winded chatter about her household cares and the dull little things of her monotonous life. It took her out of herself, and sometimes she was surprised to catch herself taking an interest in such nonsense, and later smiled bitterly at the memory.

She gradually lost all her regular customers. Since her aunt had been tied to her chair upstairs, she had let the shop go and abandoned the stock to dust and damp. There was a mouldy smell about the place, spiders dropped down from the ceiling, and the floor was hardly ever swept. But what really drove the customers away was the strange way Thérèse sometimes treated them. If she was upstairs, being beaten by Laurent or racked by one of her attacks of panic, and the shop bell rang insistently, she had to go down almost without time to tidy her hair or dab her tears away, and on these occasions she served the waiting customer resentfully, or sometimes did not even take the trouble to serve her at all, but called down from the top of the stairs that she had run out of whatever it was. Such discouraging ways were not calculated to keep customers, and the local work-girls, used to Madame Raquin's honeyed civilities, ran away from Thérèse's surliness and wild looks. By the time she had taken Suzanne to sit with her the desertion was complete, for the two young women managed to drive away the last customers so as not to be disturbed in their chatter. And so the haberdashery business stopped bringing in a single penny towards housekeeping expenses, and the capital of forty-odd thousand francs had to be broken into.

Sometimes Thérèse went out for whole afternoons, nobody knew where. Possibly that was why she had taken Suzanne in with her, not only for her company, but also to mind the shop when she went out. On her return in the evening, dead beat and with black rings of exhaustion round her eyes, she found Olivier's little wife still behind the counter, sitting unobtrusively there and smiling her vague smile, in exactly the same position as when she had left her five hours earlier.

About five months after her marriage Thérèse had a fright. She found out for certain that she was pregnant. The thought of having a child of Laurent's seemed revolting, though she did not know why. She dimly feared that she might give birth to a drowned body, and it seemed as though she could feel inside her the cold sensation of a soft, decomposing corpse. At all costs she was determined to rid her womb of the child, which froze her and which she would not carry any longer. She did not tell her husband, but one day, having cruelly provoked him, she turned her belly towards him as he gave her a kick, and let him go on kicking her there until she felt she would die. Next day she had a miscarriage.

Laurent was leading a dreadful life, too. The days seemed intolerably long and each one brought back the same agonies, the same leaden emptiness which overcame him at the same times with crushing monotony and regularity. He was dragging himself through life, horror-struck every night by the recollection of the day just over and the expectation of the morrow. He knew that henceforth all his days would be the same and all bring the same suffering, and he could see weeks, months, and years ahead, waiting for him, sombre and implacable, one after the other, falling upon him and gradually smothering him. When the future holds no hope, the present takes on a vile and bitter flavour. There was no fight left in him, he let himself go, gave himself up to the void already compassing him about. Idleness was killing him. He left home in the morning with no idea where he was going, nauseated at the prospect of doing what he had done the day before, but forced in spite of himself to do it all over again. He would make for his studio through force of habit, or driven by some obsession. This room, with its grey walls and no view except an empty square of sky, filled him with gloomy depression. He lolled about on his divan with hands unoccupied and mind in a daze. Of course he no longer dared to touch a brush. He had made one or two fresh attempts, but inevitably Camille's face had grinned back at him from the canvas. To prevent himself from going mad, he had finally thrown his paintbox into a corner and deliberately elected to do absolutely nothing. But this enforced idleness was unbelievably tedious.

In the afternoons he desperately asked himself what he should do. He would stand for half an hour on the pavement of the rue Mazarine working it out, hesitating over the pastimes he could go in for. He turned down the idea of going up to his studio again, and always decided to go down the rue Guénégaud and then along by the river. And so until nightfall he followed his nose, half dazed but a prey to sudden shuddering fits when he looked at the Seine. But whether in the studio or in the streets, his dejection was the same. The next day he would begin all over again, spending the morning on his divan and wandering about along the embankments in the afternoon. This had been going on for months and might well go on for years.

Sometimes Laurent reflected that he had killed Camille simply so as to have nothing to do any more, and he was quite astonished, now that he was doing nothing, to have to endure such sufferings. He would have liked to force himself to be happy, and indeed he proved to himself that he was wrong to be unhappy, that he had achieved that supreme felicity which consists of just folding one's arms, and that he was a fool not to enjoy this felicity in peace. But his arguments collapsed in the face of the facts, and he had to admit that his idleness made his torments still more cruel, by leaving all the hours of his life free for musing on his despair and delving into its incurable intensity. Idleness, this animal existence he had dreamed of, was his punishment. At times he longed for some occupation that would take him away from his own thoughts. But then he let himself drift again, and succumbed beneath the weight of the inexorable fatality that fettered his limbs the better to crush him.

In fact, he felt some slight relief only when he was beating Thérèse in the evenings. That took him out of his numbing pain.

His most acute suffering, both physical and moral, came from the bite in his neck made by Camille. There were times when he imagined that this scar covered the whole of his body. If he did happen to forget the past, the stinging pain he seemed to feel brought the murder back to his body and mind. He could not stand in front of a mirror without seeing the phenomenon he had so often noticed before but which frightened him still: under the stress of his emotion the blood rose to his neck and inflamed the wound, which began to itch. This wound living on him, so to speak, waking up, reddening, and biting him at the slightest upset, was a cause of dread and torture to him. He came to fancy that the drowning man's teeth had implanted some creature there which was gnawing at him. The part of his neck where the scar was seemed to have ceased to belong to his own body, but was like some stranger's flesh grafted on, a piece of poisoned meat rotting his own muscles. Wherever he went he carried with him a living and devouring reminder of his crime. Whenever he hit Thérèse she tried to scratch him on the place, and sometimes she dug her nails in and made him scream with pain. Usually she pretended to cry when she caught sight of the bite, so as to make it still more unbearable for him. Her whole revenge for his ill-treatment of her consisted in torturing him by means of this bite.

Many times while shaving he had been tempted to cut his neck and obliterate the tooth-marks. When he raised his chin and saw in the glass the red mark showing through the lather, he flew into sudden tempers and jabbed with the razor as if to cut right into the flesh. But the cold steel on his skin always brought him back to himself, and then he felt faint and had to sit down and wait for his cowardliness to settle down and let him finish shaving.

He only shook off his lethargy in the evenings when he flew into blind and childish rages. When he had had enough of nagging at Thérèse and beating her, he would start kicking the walls, just like a child, and looking for something to break. It relieved him. He had a particular hatred for François, the tabby cat, who fled for safety to Madame Raquin's lap as soon as he came in. Indeed, the only reason why Laurent had not killed him already was that he was afraid to catch hold of him. The cat's big round eyes gazed at him with fiendish steadiness. These eyes constantly fixed upon him drove Laurent to desperation, for he wondered what they wanted of him, and came to have real nightmares, imagining absurd things. When, in the middle of a meal, at some odd moment, in the course of a quarrel or during a long silence, he happened to turn his head suddenly and see François's eyes scrutinizing him, dour and implacable, he paled, lost his head and almost shouted at the cat: 'Go on, say it then, tell me what you want me to do.' If he had the chance to tread on one of his paws or his tail he did it with a scared joy, and the miaowing of the poor creature filled him with a vague terror, as if he had heard a human being crying in pain. Laurent was literally afraid of François. Since the latter had taken to living on Madame Raquin's lap as in an impregnable fortress from which he could safely direct his green eyes at the foe, Camille's murderer had begun to notice a certain similarity between the angry animal and the paralysed woman. He persuaded himself that, like Madame Raquin, the cat knew all about the crime and would denounce him if ever a day came when he could speak.

Eventually one evening François stared so hard at him that Laurent, infuriated beyond measure, decided that an end must be put to all this. He opened the dining-room window wide and seized the cat by the scruff of the neck. Madame Raquin understood, and two big tears ran down her cheeks. The cat swore and stiffened, trying to turn round and bite Laurent's hand, but he held on, swung the cat round two or three times and then flung him with all the strength of his arm against the high, black wall opposite. The cat was flattened against the wall, his back was broken, and he fell on to the glass roofing of the passage. All night long the wretched creature dragged himself along the guttering, miaowing raucously, and that night Madame Raquin wept for François almost as bitterly as she had for Camille. Thérèse had a terrible attack of hysterics. The moaning of the cat in the dark beneath the windows was sinister.

Soon Laurent had fresh cause for worry. He was frightened by certain changes of attitude he noticed in his wife.

She became sombre and taciturn. No more outpourings of repentance or grateful kisses were lavished upon Madame Raquin, but she went back to her former attitude of cold cruelty and self-centred indifference. It was as if she had tried remorse, and remorse not having succeeded in bringing relief, had turned to another remedy. No doubt her depression came from her failure to make her life calmer. She now regarded the impotent old woman with a kind of scorn, as a useless object that could no longer even serve as a consolation. She only gave her the attention necessary to prevent her from dying of starvation. From then on she moved about the house silent and dreary, and went out more and more often, being away as many as four or five times a week.

These changes surprised and alarmed Laurent, who thought that a new kind of remorse was showing itself in Thérèse in the form of this dismal apathy he noticed in her. This apathy seemed much more disquieting than the talkative despair she had formerly inflicted upon him. Now she said nothing at all, stopped quarrelling and appeared to keep everything locked in the depths of her being. He would rather have heard her giving vent to her suffering than see her so withdrawn into herself. He was afraid that one day her agony would choke her and she would seek relief by going and telling the whole story to a priest or a magistrate.

Thérèse's numerous outings then took on an alarming significance in his eyes. He thought she was looking for somebody outside to confide in, that she was getting ready to denounce him. Twice he attempted to follow her but lost her in the streets. He began spying on her again. One obsessive thought had taken hold of him: Thérèse, reduced to desperation, was about to give something away, and he must gag her and stop the confession in her throat.

31

One morning, instead of going to his studio, Laurent took up his position in a wine-shop on one of the corners of the rue Guénégaud opposite the Passage. From there he proceeded to examine the people who emerged on to the pavement of the rue Mazarine. He was on the look-out for Thérèse. On the previous day she had said she was going out early and would probably not be back until the evening.

He waited a good half-hour. He knew his wife always went along the rue Mazarine, but for a moment he feared she might have given him the slip and taken the rue de Seine. He did think of going back into the arcade and hiding in the side passage of the house itself, but just as he was getting tired of waiting he saw her hurry out of the arcade. She was dressed in bright colours, and for the first time it occurred to him that she was wearing a long train like a street-walker; and indeed she was now swaying along the pavement provocatively, looking at men and gathering up the front of her skirt so high that you could see her laced boots and white stockings and right up her legs. She went up the rue Mazarine. Laurent followed.

It was a mild day, and she walked slowly along with her head held well up and her hair down her back. Men who looked at her as she approached turned round to look again after she had gone past. She went along the rue de l'École de Médecine, and Laurent was terrified at this, knowing that somewhere in that direction there was a police-station, and he told himself that there could be no more doubt about it, his wife was certainly going to give him in charge. He decided to rush at her if she crossed the threshold of the station and implore, attack, force her to keep quiet. At a corner she looked at a passing policeman, and he trembled lest she might go up to him; he hid in a doorway, overcome by a sudden fear that he would be arrested there and then if he were seen. The walk was a veritable agony for him: while his wife swaggered along the pavement in the sunlight, dragging her train, shameless and unconcerned, he followed behind pale and trembling, telling himself over and over again that it was finished, there was no escape and he would be guillotined. Her every step seemed one step nearer retribution. Fear gave him a kind of blind conviction in which his wife's slightest movements all added up to certainty. He followed her, went where she went, just as one walks to the place of execution.

But suddenly, as she came out into the former Place Saint-Michel, Thérèse made for a café which at that time was on the corner of the rue Monsieur-le-Prince. She sat down in the middle of a group of women and students at one of the tables on the pavement, giving a friendly handshake all round. She then ordered an absinthe.

She seemed quite at home, talking to a fair young man who had probably been waiting for her. Two tarts came and leaned over her table, calling her 'dear' in their husky voices. All round there were women smoking cigarettes, men kissing women in the open street, in full view of passers-by who did not even turn round to look. Obscene words and coarse laughter reached Laurent as he stood motionless in an entry across the square.

When she had finished her absinthe, Thérèse rose, took the fair young man's arm, and went down the rue de La Harpe, Laurent following them until they reached the rue Saint-André-des-Arts, where he saw them go into a lodging-house. He stood in the middle of the road looking up at the front of the house. His wife appeared for a moment at an open window on the second floor. Then he thought he saw the hands of the fair young man slipping round Thérèse's waist. The window shut with a bang.

Laurent understood. He went calmly off at once, reassured and happy.

'Well, why not?' he asked himself as he made for the river. 'It's better that way, it gives her something to do and keeps her out of mischief. She's bloody well cleverer than I am.'

He was surprised that he had not been the first to think of going in for vice. It might provide a remedy for his terrors. He had no thought of it, because his flesh was dead and he had not the slightest desire for debauchery left. His wife's unfaithfulness left him quite cold, without any stirring of the blood or nerves at the thought of her being in some other man's arms. On the contrary, it struck him as amusing, as though he had been spying on the wife of a friend, and he laughed at the nice trick this woman was playing on her husband. He had become so indifferent to Thérèse that she was no longer alive in his heart at all, and he would have sold her and given her up a hundred times, to buy himself one hour's peace.

He began wandering about, enjoying the

sudden happy reaction that had taken him out of terror into serenity. He almost thanked his wife for going to a lover when he thought she was making for the police. The adventure had a quite unforeseen outcome that pleasantly surprised him. The most obvious thing that struck him was that he had been wrong to be afraid and that he, too, should try vice to see whether it might not help him by stupefying his mind.

That evening, on coming back to the shop, Laurent decided to ask his wife for a few thousand francs, and to stop at nothing in order to get them. Vice, he reflected, was expensive for a man, and he was by way of envying women who can sell themselves. He impatiently waited for Thérèse, who was not yet back. When she came in he put on a pleasant manner and made no mention of his morning's spying. She was slightly tipsy, and her clothes, not properly done up, gave off that pungent smell of tobacco and spirits that hangs about in bars. Thoroughly washed-out, with livid patches on her face, she walked unsteadily and was worn out by the shameful fatigues of the day.

Dinner was had in silence. Thérèse ate nothing. Over dessert Laurent put his elbows on the table and bluntly asked her for five thousand francs.

'No!' she snapped. 'If I let you do as you liked you would bring us to a bad end. Don't you know how we stand? We are heading straight for starvation.'

'That's as may be,' he blandly replied. 'I don't mind. I want some money.'

'No, a thousand times no! You have thrown up your job, the drapery business has gone to pot, and we can't live on the income from my dowry. Every day as it is I am eating into the capital to keep you and give you the hundred a month you have got out of me. You aren't going to get any more, see? Nothing doing.'

'Think it over, and don't refuse like that. I tell you I want five thousand and I'm going to get it, and you are going to give it me, say what you like.'

This quiet determination annoyed Thérèse and put the finishing touch to her fuddled condition.

'Oh yes, I know,' she yelled, 'you want to end up as you started. We've been keeping you for four years now. You only came here to get food and drink and you have been on our hands ever since. His lordship does nothing at all, his lordship has arranged things so as to live at my expense, with his arms folded. No, you won't get anything, not a penny! . . . Do you want me to tell you? All right, I will, you're a . . .'

She said the word. Laurent began laughing, shrugging his shoulders. His only answer was:

'You're picking up some nice words in the company you're keeping now.'

This was the only reference he allowed himself to her goings-on. She glanced up quickly and said in a hard voice:

'Anyhow, I don't go with murderers.'

Laurent went very white. For a moment he stared at her in silence, then in a shaky voice:

'Listen my girl, don't let us lose our tempers, it wouldn't be any use to either of us. I am at the end of my tether. It would be wiser to come to an understanding, if we don't want something nasty to happen. I have asked for five thousand francs because I need them. I can even say that I mean to use them to make sure of our peace of mind.'

He went on with a peculiar smile:

'Come on, think it over, give me your last word.'

'It's all been thought over already,' she answered. 'I've told you, you won't get a penny.'

He jumped to his feet. She was afraid of

being beaten, and ducked, but was determined not to give in to violence. Laurent did not even come in her direction, however; he simply stated coolly that he was sick of life and was going to the nearest police-station to tell them the whole story.

'You're pushing me too far,' he said, 'and making life unbearable. I'd rather have done with it. . . . We'll both be tried and condemned together, that's all.'

'Do you think you can frighten me?' she cried. 'I'm just as sick of it as you are. I shall go to the police myself if you don't. Right-oh, I'm quite prepared to follow you to execution, not being such a coward as you are. Come on, come with me now.'

She was on her feet already, and making for the stairs.

'Er . . . All right,' stammered Laurent. 'Let's go together.'

But once they were down in the shop they stood staring at each other, hesitant and afraid. They felt as if they had been riveted to the ground. The few seconds it had taken to come down the stairs had sufficed to show them in a flash the results of such a confession. At one and the same time, clearly and rapidly, they saw police, prison, trial, and guillotine, and deep within them each was weakening and tempted to fall at the other's feet with supplications to stay and not give anything away. Fear and embarrassment kept them motionless and silent for two or three minutes. It was Thérèse who decided to break the silence and give in.

'After all,' she said, 'it's pretty silly of me to argue with you about the money. In any case you will get through it one of these days, so I might as well give it you straightaway.'

She gave up even trying to hide her defeat, but sat down at the counter and signed an order for five thousand that Laurent could cash at the bank. There was no further reference to the police that evening.

As soon as he had some money in his pocket, Laurent drank, picked up women, and gave himself up to a noisy and rackety life. He stayed out all night, slept all day, spent the nights on the prowl hunting for violent emotions, trying to escape from reality. But he only succeeded in sinking deeper still into his lethargy. In the midst of the tumult all round him he could hear the terrible, deep silence within; even when he was in a woman's arms or when he was draining his glass, all he could find behind his satiety was an oppressive gloom. He was no longer cut out for lust and gluttony, and his whole being, as it were frozen and numbed within, merely chafed at embracing and feasting. Nauseated before he started, he could not work up his imagination and excite his passions or appetite. By forcing himself to go through with debauches he felt a little worse, that was all. Afterwards, when he came home and saw Madame Raquin and Thérèse again, his weariness laid him open to dreadful fits of panic, and he swore he would never go out again, but stay with his suffering, get used to it, and so conquer it.

For her part, Thérèse went out less and less. For a month, like Laurent, she lived in the streets and in cafés, coming home for a moment in the evening to give Madame Raquin some food and put her to bed, and then going off again until the next day. Once she and her husband went four days without seeing each other. Then she felt an overwhelming disgust, and realized that vice was no more use to her than play-acting at remorse. In vain had she trailed through all the lodging-houses in the Latin Quarter and lived a life of filth and rowdiness. Her nerves had snapped, and debauchery and physical pleasure no longer provided sufficiently violent sensations to tire her into forgetfulness. She was like one of those drunkards whose burnt-out palate remains insensitive even to the most fiery of spirits. In the midst of sexual excitement she remained limp and passive, and all she now found with her lovers was boredom and weariness. And so she gave them up, realizing that they were useless. The slothfulness of despair came over her and kept her at home in soiled clothes, unkempt, with dirty hands and face. She found oblivion in squalor.

When at length the pair found themselves face to face again, worn out, and with every means of escape from each other used up, it became clear to them that they would never have the strength to go on with the struggle. Debauchery had refused them and spewed them back into their agonies. So there they were once again in the dark, dank house in the Passage, but henceforth they were to be imprisoned there, for they had made frequent bids for salvation, but had never been able to break the bloody bonds uniting them. They gave up even the thought of attempting the impossible; so conscious were they of being pursued, ground down, bound together by the facts, that they realized that any resistance would be ridiculous. Life in common was resumed, but their hatred turned into raging fury.

The evening scenes began again, though

as a matter of fact blows and shouts went on all day. Suspicion came as well as hatred, and suspicion put the finishing touch to their madness.

Each became frightened of the other. The scene that had followed the demand for the five thousand francs now recurred morning and night. They were obsessed with the idea that each wanted to hand the other over to justice, and nothing could shake them from it. If one said a word or made any movement, the other imagined it was a preliminary to going to the police, and that led to fights or supplications. In their fury they declared they were going off to reveal everything, and frightened each other to death, but then they trembled with fear, grovelled, and promised with bitter tears to remain silent. They suffered horribly, but could not muster enough courage to cure themselves by cauterizing the wound with a red-hot iron. Their sole reason for threatening to confess was to terrify each other and drive such an idea out of their minds. They would never have been strong enough to speak out and seek peace in punishment.

More than a score of times one followed the other right to the door of the police-station. Sometimes it was Laurent who was for confessing to the murder, sometimes it was

Thérèse who was rushing to give herself up. But they always overtook each other in the street, and after exchanging insults and desperate pleas always decided to wait a little longer.

Each new crisis left them more suspicious and more on edge.

From morn till night they spied on each other. Laurent never left the house now, for Thérèse never let him go out alone. Their mutual mistrust and their fear of confession brought them together in a frightful intimacy. Never, since they were married, had they lived so closely tied to each other, and never had they suffered so acutely. Yet, despite the tortures they forced each other to go through, they never took their eyes off each other, preferring to endure the most excruciating pain so long as they were not apart for a single hour. If Thérèse went down into the shop, Laurent would follow her for fear that she might blab to some customer; if Laurent stood in the doorway watching the people going up and down the Passage, Thérèse took up her stand beside him in case he spoke to anybody. On Thursday evenings, when their guests were there, they would look at each other with supplicating eyes and listen to each other in terror, each expecting to hear some admission from the other, each reading compromising meanings into sentences the other had begun.

Such a state of war could not last much longer.

Independently of each other, Thérèse and Laurent came to the point of envisaging a second crime as a way of escape from the consequences of their first. One of them simply had to disappear so that the other could find some sort of peace. The thought came to them simultaneously: they both felt the urgent necessity of a separation, and an eternal separation at that. Murder, which came to their minds, seemed natural and inevitable, the logical outcome of the murder of Camille. They did not even weigh the pros and cons, but accepted the idea as the only means of salvation. Laurent decided to kill Thérèse because she was in the way, could ruin him by a single word, and was inflicting intolerable sufferings upon him; Thérèse decided to kill Laurent for the same reasons.

The clear decision to kill calmed them down somewhat. They laid their plans. But they went to work hastily, with few precautions, only dimly taking into account the probable consequences of a murder committed without adequate measures to ensure escape and avoid punishment. They were possessed by an irresistible urge to kill each other, and obeyed it like wild beasts. They would not have given themselves up for their first crime, which they had concealed with so much skill, but now they were courting the guillotine by committing a second that they were not even thinking about hiding. It was a contradiction in behaviour that they did not even notice. They merely supposed that if they succeeded in getting away they would go abroad, taking all the money with them. For Thérèse had taken out the remaining few thousand francs of her dowry and for two or three weeks now had kept them in a drawer that Laurent knew all about. Not for one moment did they wonder what would become of Madame Raquin.

A few weeks previously Laurent had met an old school-friend who was working as laboratory assistant to a famous scientist whose special interest was toxicology. This friend had taken him round the laboratory where he worked, shown him the apparatus, and pointed out the drugs by name. One evening, after he had made up his mind to kill her, Thérèse was drinking a glass of sugar and water in his presence, and this reminded him that he had noticed in the laboratory a little earthenware phial containing prussic acid. Recollecting what the young laboratory assistant had told him about the deadly effects of this poison, which kills instantly, leaving scarcely a trace, he made up his mind that that was the poison he wanted. He managed to get away next day, went to see his friend, and, while his back was turned, stole the little phial.

On the same day Thérèse took advantage of Laurent's absence and had a big kitchen knife sharpened, one which was used for breaking up sugar and was all jagged. This she hid in a corner of the sideboard.

32

On the following Thursday the evening party at the Raquins' (as the guests still called their hosts) was quite unusually gay. It went on until half past eleven. Grivet, as he was leaving, declared that he had never spent happier hours.

Suzanne, now pregnant, talked all the time to Thérèse about her pains and joys. Thérèse appeared to be listening with great interest, eyes intent, lips pursed, and nodding now and again; her lowered eyelids shadowed all her face. For his part, Laurent was listening attentively to the stories of old Michaud and Olivier. These two gentlemen were inexhaustible, and it was only with the utmost difficulty that Grivet could get a word in edgeways between two sentences of father and son. In any case he held them in a certain awe, for in his opinion they were good speakers. As on this occasion talk had taken the place of a game, he naïvely declared that he enjoyed the ex-superintendent's conversation almost as much as playing dominoes.

For nearly four years the Michauds and Grivet had spent Thursday evenings at the Raquins', and they had never once wearied of these monotonous functions, which came round with maddening regularity. Never for one moment had they had any suspicion of the drama that was being played out in this home, so peaceful and quiet as they entered it. Olivier regularly maintained, by way of a policeman's little joke, that the dining-room reeked of respectability, and Grivet, not to be outdone, had named it the Temple of Peace. More than once in recent weeks Thérèse had explained away the bruises on her face by telling the guests that she had had a fall. Not that any of them would have recognized the marks of Laurent's fist, for they were convinced that their hosts were a model couple, all sweetness and love.

The paralysed woman had made no further attempt to reveal the infamies that lay hidden behind the dreary tranquillity of those Thursday evenings. In the presence of the rending torments of the murderers, and sensing the crisis that must burst upon them any day now as the outcome of the fatal sequence of events, she came to realize that the facts had no need of her help. And so she effaced herself and let the logical consequences of Camille's murder run their course, which was to end with the killing of the killers themselves. All she prayed for was to be vouchsafed life enough to witness the violent climax she could foresee; her last wish was to feast her eyes on the spectacle of the final agonies that would destroy Thérèse and Laurent.

That evening Grivet came over to her side and chatted away at great length, doing both questions and answers himself, as was his wont. But not a single glance could he get out of her. When it struck eleven-thirty the guests jumped to their feet.

'We are so happy here,' declared Grivet, 'that we never dream of going.'

'The fact is,' Michaud added by way of corroboration, 'that I never feel sleepy here, and I usually go to bed at nine.'

Olivier thought that this was the moment to bring in his little joke.

'Well, you see,' he grinned, showing his yellow teeth, 'this room reeks of respectability; that's why we are so comfortable.'

Grivet, vexed at having been cut out, began declaiming with a dramatic gesture:

'This room is the Temple of Peace.'

Meanwhile Suzanne was tying the ribbons of her bonnet and saying to Thérèse:

'I'll be round in the morning, at nine.'

'No, don't,' Thérèse hastily replied; 'don't

come until the afternoon. . . . I may go out in the morning.'

Her voice sounded strange and emotional. She went down to the Passage with the guests. Laurent went down, too, holding a lamp. When they were alone each breathed a sigh of relief; they must have been devoured by impatience all the evening. Since the previous day they had been more dour and more ill at ease in front of each other. Now they went upstairs in silence, not looking at each other. Their hands were shaking with convulsive tremors, and Laurent had to put the lamp down on the table for fear of dropping it.

Usually before putting Madame Raquin to bed they tidied the dining-room, prepared a glass of sugar and water for the night, and generally busied themselves round the old woman until everything was ready.

But on this night, when they went upstairs again, they sat down a moment, a puzzled look in their eyes, and their lips bloodless. After a period of silence Laurent seemed to jump up out of a dream and said:

'Well, aren't we going to bed?'

'Yes, yes of course, let's go to bed,' answered Thérèse, shivering as though she were very cold.

She stood up and took the carafe.

'All right,' said her husband in a voice he tried to make sound natural. 'I'll do the glass of sugar and water. You see to your aunt.'

He took the carafe out of her hands and filled a glass with water. Then, half turning away, he emptied the little phial into it and put in a lump of sugar. At the same moment Thérèse had bent down in front of the sideboard and taken out the kitchen knife which she tried to slip into one of the big pockets that hung from her waist.

Just then that strange sensation that warns of approaching danger made both of them instinctively turn round. They stood looking at each other. Thérèse saw the phial in Laurent's hand and he saw the white gleam of the knife between the folds of her skirt. For several seconds they remained gazing at each other, silent and frozen, the husband by the table and the wife bending down at the sideboard. They understood. Each was rooted to the spot, seeing his own thought in his accomplice. Each read the secret purpose in the other's stricken face, each regarded the other with contempt and horror.

Feeling that the end was near, Madame Raquin stared at them with a fierce, unblinking gaze.

Suddenly Thérèse and Laurent burst into tears, and in a final breakdown fell into each other's arms, as weak as children. Something gentle and tender seemed to awaken in their breasts. They wept and said nothing, thinking of the sink of filth in which they had been living and would go on living if they were cowardly enough to remain alive. And then, as they remembered the past, they felt so weary and sick of themselves that an immense longing for rest and oblivion came over them. They exchanged one last look, a look of gratitude in the presence of the knife and the glass of poison. Thérèse took the glass, drank half of it, and gave it to Laurent, who finished it in one gulp. It was as quick as lightning. They fell on each other, struck down instantly, and at last found consolation in death. Her mouth hit her husband's neck on the scar left by Camille's teeth.

The bodies lay all night twisted and sprawling on the dining-room floor in the yellowish light cast down on them by the shaded lamp. And for nearly twelve hours, until about noon next day, Madame Raquin, stiff and silent, contemplated them at her feet, unable to feast her eyes enough, eyes that crushed them with brooding hate.

We hope you have enjoyed this Large Print book. Other Thorndike, Wheeler or Chivers Press Large Print books are available at your library or directly from the publishers.

For more information about current and upcoming titles, please call or write, without obligation, to:

Publisher
Thorndike Press
295 Kennedy Memorial Drive
Waterville, ME 04901
Tel. (800) 223-1244

Or visit our Web site at:
www.gale.com/thorndike
www.gale.com/wheeler

OR

Chivers Large Print
published by BBC Audiobooks Ltd
St James House, The Square
Lower Bristol Road
Bath BA2 3SB
England
Tel. +44(0) 800 136919
email: bbcaudiobooks@bbc.co.uk
www.bbcaudiobooks.co.uk

All our Large Print titles are designed for easy reading, and all our books are made to last.